THE PACT

BOOK 4

KATZ' CAT ~ TWINKLE, TEXAS

DAWN GREENFIELD IRELAND

ARTISTIC
ORIGINS

The characters you love in Twinkle, Texas are alive and well.

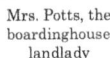

Jimmy Katz, the main
character

Mrs. Potts, the
boardinghouse
landlady

Chief Price

Brian, Jimmy's best
friend from the Big
City

Maddy, Jimmy's cat

Guppy, Jimmy's Amazon
parrot

The Pact, Book #4 in the Katz' Cat/Twinkle, Texas cozy mystery series by Dawn Greenfield Ireland

Published by Artistic Origins

Copyright © 2025 by Dawn Greenfield Ireland

All rights reserved.

Caricatures by @sami1155 Ashba Maryiam on Fiverr.com

Cover by Bella R(@bella_rose007) on Fiverr.com

Interior layout by Yours Truly (me)

ISBNs:

Paperback 9781940385938

eBook: 9781940385921

BISAC FIC022000 (fiction), PET000000, PET002000, PET003000 (pets), LCO019000 (women authors)

Dawn Greenfield Ireland

Artistic Origins

www.degreenfield.com

Get in touch, but don't spam me.

Be kind = leave a review!

HINT: don't regurgitate the synopsis for your review. Just tell people what you liked, didn't like – that's what people want – your opinion.

❀ Formatted with Vellum

Nonfiction	
The Puppy Baby Book	Mastering Your Money (2022)
Puppy Adoption and Beyond	Writers Preparation Handbook
Mastering Your Money (2008)	What's Breaking Your Budget
Online Classes	
Writers Preparation Handbook	How to Format Word Docs Like A Pro
Cozy Mysteries	**Sci-Fi-Fantasy**
The Alcott Family Adventures	**The Thol Series**
Hot Chocolate	Prophecy of Thol
Bitter Chocolate	Gifts From Thol
Spicy Chocolate	Love of Thol
Nutty Chocolate	King of Thol
Katz' Cat Series	Earth Calling Thol
Katz' Cat	**Sci-Fi Romance Adventure**
Bill Hill's Pills	Forced Dreams
The Detectives	**Dystopian**
The Pact	The Last Dog
	Texmexzona
Books by my Alter Ego ~ DG Ireland	
Bonded Shapeshifter Billionaire Series	
Bonded	
Tothars	
Tilted	
Unforeseen	
Connected	
Need A Notebook?	
See my 54 themed notebooks on my website www.degreenfield.com/notebooks	
Screenplays formatted as books	
Plan B (Dark Comedy)	Where's Ralphie? (Family Comedy)
The God Child (Action Adventure)	Standing Dead (Drama/Tragedy)
The Far Corner (Sci-Fi/Psychological/Creatures)	
Screenplays as TV Episodes	
Hot Chocolate ~ Episode 1	Prophecy of Thol ~ Episode 1
Bonded ~ Episode 1	
See my screenplays and awards on my website: degreenfield.com Filmfreeway, ISA Network	

ACKNOWLEDGMENTS

I wanted my main characters on the cover to show who started The Pact in the Katz' Cat / Twinkle, Texas cozy mystery series books.

Fiverr.com is my resource for artists. I discovered a talented caricature artist whose work speaks for itself. Many thanks to @sami1155 Ashba Maryiam on Fiverr.com for the outstanding caricatures of Mrs. Potts, Jimmy, Chief Price, and Brian.

More thanks to Bella R(@bella_rose007) on Fiverr for creating the paperback cover.

Many thanks for my two writers critique group peeps who whack me every month when they catch boo-boos in my work. I could not do it without Dickie Stone and Joe Thompson. One of us is typically in the woodshed at one time or another.

For everyone on FB, X, and LI, thanks for your follows, your encouragement and all the rest of it. Writing can be a lonely occupation.

CHAPTER ONE

Jimmy Katz and his great Aunt, Betty Diaz, sat at the small conference table in her home office in the largest house in Twinkle, Texas. They examined photos they found in a box from Jimmy's storage unit. There were hundreds of loose pictures dating back to before Jimmy was born that he could not identify.

Twinkle, Texas, in Starlight County, was 385 miles from the nearest mall. Betty Diaz, the oil baroness and philanthropist, found her great nephew through an article he wrote for the Twinkle Independent News (TIN). Betty immediately called Sylvan Stonerich, the publisher of the TIN demanding he round up his reporter and present him to her.

When Betty called, people jumped into action. Sylvan and Bill Trance, the managing editor, rushed Jimmy to the matriarch's home on Diaz Circle, where Betty eyeballed Jimmy. She declared he looked just like his father, her nephew, Errol Katz.

In marched the DDS attorneys, Pete Daigle, Judson Diaz, and Godfrey (Stoney) Stonerich. The DDS were the attorneys for the Katz-Diaz multi-billion-dollar empire. Out popped a

DNA swab test kit, a fingerprint kit, and documents equaling half a ream of paper.

Jimmy received an envelope of pocket money that surpassed what he made in six months as a reporter. Then Pete Daigle marched him over to the Twinkle Bank and Trust where Jimmy met the bank president, FeBe Morales, who would personally handle his account.

Mrs. Bertha Potts, Jimmy's landlady at the boarding house where he and Guppy, his Amazon parrot lived, calmed him from the mind-altering experience. Three months later, Jimmy discovered a tiny kitten on the bottom stair at the back door of the boarding house. Jimmy adopted Maddy. She and Guppy became best friends, and things got interesting.

"Aunt Betty, who's this?" Jimmy turned the photo so she could see the people.

Betty took the photo and eyeballed it. "That's your maternal grandfather, Robert Schlumbacher, and your mother when she was a young girl. Your grandmother must have taken the picture." She handed it back to Jimmy.

"Wow. I've never seen this picture before." He stared at the picture, trying to determine what his mother's life was like at that age. He didn't know that much about the Schlumbacher's, which was a mystery all on its own. Jimmy turned the photo over and wrote on the back to identify his grandfather and mother.

He pulled another picture out of the box. He was at the beach. "Look how skinny I was as a kid!" Jimmy was all knobby knees with braces on his teeth. "I hated those braces, but I'm glad my teeth are nice and straight now. They were all bunched up when I was a kid. I hated to smile."

Aunt Betty pulled a handful of photos out of the box. She spread them before her on the table. "Oh, look, Jimmy! This shows Twinkle before we developed it. And here's Clem's Corner."

Jimmy slid the photos over so he could see them. "Wow. Twinkle was a tiny place before you and Clem made your fortunes." He tried identifying what the picture of Twinkle showed, but couldn't figure it out. "Is this the main street?"

Betty slid her chair closer to Jimmy. "Yes. That's Stonerich Boulevard. They developed Diaz Circle here and built Mrs. Potts' boarding house way over there.

Jimmy identified the places on the reverse side of the picture. He set the photo aside to show Mrs. Potts later.

They heard sirens in the distance, then the volunteer fire trucks hauling down the street. Jimmy stood. "I'll let you know where the fire is!" And then he was out of the mansion and jumping into his Honda CRV. As the heir to the vast Katz-Diaz fortune, the DDS forbid him to volunteer for anything remotely dangerous, so he stayed on the sidelines.

JIMMY SPED DOWN THE STREET, FOLLOWING THE SIRENS. He recognized his friends and fellow reporters' cars behind the fire trucks. Danny Stonerich was in the lead, followed by Brian McKinley, who also lived at the boarding house.

Jimmy's fiancé, Detective Celebrity Masters, zoomed past all three cars in the facing lane with lights flashing and sirens screaming. The police chief, Kenton Price, was on her tail with Detective Benito Ramirez bringing up the rear.

The three cops left the reporters in their dust. They all raced down Stonerich Boulevard heading toward, then passing Mrs. Potts boarding house. Jimmy let out a sigh of relief when he saw his landlady standing outside at the edge of the road. The fire trucks turned down Mulberry St.

Jimmy had a moment. He hoped it wasn't Dorothea Ochea's place where Vince Babelton and his Main Coon cat, Expresso, lived while Dorothea was over in Europe, interning with a famous baker.

By the time the reporters arrived at the scene, the firefighters were hosing down a house, and Detective Ramirez was handcuffing a boy, who looked to be a pre-teen. Jimmy saw Vince standing outside of his house watching the fire come under control. They waved at each other.

Vince headed their way, and Jimmy met him halfway. "I saw that kid poking around that house where he had no business being, then called the cops when I saw smoke. Little firebug was just getting started."

Chief Price joined them. "You called it in?" he asked Vince.

"Yes. It's a good thing I was checking the mailbox for mail! That house would have burned to the ground if no one was around to notice the smoke." Vince shook his head.

"Come down to the station sometime today to give your statement," Chief Price stated.

"Will do," Vince agreed.

Celebrity and Ramirez joined them after Ramirez secured the kid in the back of his police car.

"That's Pete Bolenz' kid," Ramirez stated. "He's been in trouble at school, and in his neighborhood. This is going to be tough on Pete and his wife."

Celebrity squinted. "Theo. I remember him from when he got in trouble for throwing rocks at his neighbor's dog. Broke the dog's leg and Pete had to pay for the surgery."

The reporters were scribbling notes as fast as they could.

Meaty, the Foo security guy and a crack computer hacker who sometimes worked with the police and the Feds, sauntered over to the group. His bright yellow volunteer fire department jacket hung open while he tried to cool down from the heat. The temperature of the day had amped up from ninety-eight degrees, according to the Weather Channel's forecast, to the high heat from the flames the fire volunteers doused out.

"Saved that one," Meaty stated. "Only minor damage. If we had received the call ten minutes later, that house would have burnt to the ground from this dry spell." He turned to look at all the dried vegetation surrounding the place. "They really should water their shrubs or remove them."

"I'll bet they take that into consideration from now on... if they're smart, that is," Brian commented.

Jimmy smooched Celebrity, then said goodbye to his pals. He drove back to let Mrs. Potts know the scoop. Brian pulled up in back of him as he parked in front of the boarding house.

Mrs. Potts was on the porch waiting at the front door. "Want some tea and cake?"

"You bet!" Brian called out as he walked up the walkway.

Jimmy and Brian took turns telling the story about the firebug and everything they heard the others saying about the kid.

"Poor Pete! Theo was such a good little boy. I wonder what happened?" Mrs. Potts busied herself with plates for the cake.

"Probably hanging around with the wrong crowd," Brian stated.

Jimmy got glasses down from the cabinet while Brian grabbed the tea pitcher from the refrigerator. Mrs. Potts brought plates of her checkerboard cake to the table.

"Oh, I love this cake, Mrs. Potts," Brian exclaimed. "I don't know how you do this, though."

Their landlady stood, walked over to the dish drainer and pulled the special cake pans out of the drainer where they were air drying. "Whoever invented these pans was a genius." She returned to the table and dug into her chocolate and vanilla cake slice.

Jimmy had a thoughtful look on his face. "What if that was our house? Guppy and Maddy would either burn to death or die of smoke inhalation!"

Everyone stopped eating and stared at Jimmy. The thought never occurred to them, and it was frightening.

"I'm going to have to talk to them and explain the circumstances and what they should do." Horrible scenarios raced through Jimmy's head as he was lost in thought.

After their snack, Brian headed back to the TIN, Mrs. Potts retired to her favorite chair in the living room and continued reading her spicy book, and Jimmy went upstairs to talk to his pets.

WHEN JIMMY ENTERED HIS APARTMENT, HE SAW MADDY watching a children's program on TV, and Guppy was looking out for squirrels that threatened to attack the house. He didn't believe it for a second. His two pets were little detectives who figured things out, sometimes quicker than the police.

Jimmy's hidden cameras caught unbelievable footage of his animals activity. If he hadn't watched the videos with his own two eyes, he never would have believed what he saw these two animals were doing.

Mrs. Potts, Brian, Chief Price, and he swore a pact to keep the deep secrets they discovered these two critters were capable of. The fear of the government discovering Maddy and Guppy and dissecting their brains drove the secrecy.

All those children's programs on TV that Maddy began watching at six weeks old had taught her how to not only spell, but read and how to use the computer. If anyone else had watched the videos, they would have accused Jimmy of doctoring them.

Jimmy kept a supply of yellow number two pencils in his desk drawer. Maddy most likely had the strongest jaws of all house cats from gripping the pencil between her teeth and whacking the keys on the keyboard. Jimmy always kept the laptop open. He didn't have to worry if it was on or off, because that smart little cat knew how to push the on/off button. Guppy was her partner in crime and supplied beak power when Maddy had to cut and paste, or copy something. It took both critters working together to accomplish what fingers on one hand of a human did.

He sat on the sofa and cleared his throat to get their attention, then Jimmy carefully thought about how he would approach the subject of safety. Guppy and Maddy already knew how to work together. When there had been break-ins in his apartment last year, they had worked as a team. Guppy alerted Jimmy and Mrs. Potts to the danger, and Maddy turned into the attack cat with claws and teeth.

When Jimmy had their attention, he delved into the problem and some solutions.

"Maddy, Guppy, there was a house fire over on Mulberry Street where Vince and Expresso live. You most likely heard the sirens from the fire trucks and the police cars. It wasn't their house. Vince witnessed this kid poking around someone's house, then he saw smoke and called 9-1-1." Jimmy checked out his two pets. They had their eyes on him, so he assumed they were listening, but he didn't know if they understood what he was telling them.

"The reason I'm telling you is that if there was ever an emergency, and Daddy, Brian, and Mrs. Potts were not home, you would have to take action to save yourselves. Do you understand?" It was frustrating not getting any sign that his pets understood.

7

"The two of you work together all the time, and you're both strong. Here's what you will have to do. Guppy, get the basket from the pantry. Maddy, jump into the basket. Guppy, grab the basket in your beak or your claws, and go through a window. If there's smoke coming from downstairs, do not fly down there. You could die."

"Gotcha!" Guppy squawked out.

Jimmy eyeballed Guppy. "You understand what to do?"

"Gotcha!" Guppy repeated.

"You don't have to worry about anything in this apartment. It's more important that you save each other." Jimmy eyeballed them, then gave up. He did all he could think of to keep them safe. If ever there was an emergency and no one was home to rescue them, they were on their own.

The heir let out a frustrated sigh. He settled back on the sofa and picked up a notebook he found in a box in the storage unit. It thrilled Jimmy to discover one of his mother's diaries. He opened the diary to the page he had bookmarked with an index card and read silently.

A text message alert dinged on Jimmy's phone. He pulled it out of his pocket and swiped the screen open. "Oops! Forgot about a meeting at the DDS. I'll see you two later."

Maddy and Guppy listened to their human clomp down the stairs and open the front door. Guppy flew to another window and looked out. He watched as Jimmy got into his Honda CRV and slammed the door closed, and took off.

"Daddy's gone."

Maddy jumped onto the sofa and rested her body on the armrest while she pawed the diary open. "I think we left off on page twenty." She read out loud what she called their *grandma's* exploits. Sometimes she had to look things up on the computer, such as the playpen. She and Guppy couldn't believe someone kept their Daddy in a cage when he was a tiny human.

After seeing the picture and reading the description and

explanations from other places on Google, they understood the function of the playpen, and they didn't think someone was tormenting children.

"When Daddy and Celebrity get married and have children, they'll buy a cage," Guppy stated.

"Playpen, not cage." Maddy scowled at her friend. She closed the diary and snuggled down for a nap on the sofa.

CHAPTER TWO

Jimmy rushed into the DDS office and headed directly to the conference room where they met for the mind-numbing meetings. "Sorry I'm late."

"You're here now and that's all that matters," Stoney said, by way of a greeting. He knew Jimmy was struggling with all the information he needed to know about the Katz-Diaz empire he would inherit one day.

"Today, we're going over the tax structures so you can understand how the IRS determines these various taxable and nontaxable projects and organizations. We'll also examine the philanthropic projects Betty established and how they're managed quarterly. Pete was sure Jimmy's eyes were already drooping, and he was barely in his chair.

Another fun session with the DDS. I wish I were getting a root canal, Jimmy thought. He knew everything the DDS tried to teach him was important because he was Aunt Betty's heir. He needed to understand how Betty set things up and guided the DDS to oversee the vast organization.

"Give me a minute," Jimmy begged as he opened the multiple paged document on the table in front of him. He used his finger to scroll slowly down each page to get the gist of what was there. The subject seemed deeply structured, and he would do his best to follow along with Pete, Stoney, and Judson. Junior was not in the room this morning.

"These things and others will be our focus this week, Jimmy. Don't think we're going through all of this today. You'd be totally fried," Judson sympathetically stated.

"Hopefully, I'll have a decade to learn everything Aunt Betty set up and how it works," Jimmy said optimistically.

After two and a half hours, Jimmy stumbled through the front doors of the law firm and collapsed into the front seat of his trusty Honda. He rested his head against the headrest and closed his eyes. *You can do this,* he thought, as facts and figures and tax code ran through his brain.

A tap on the driver's window made him jump. Celebrity stood beside the car, looking through the window with a concerned expression. Jimmy turned the key and lowered the window.

"Hey," he barely got out.

"You okay? Must have been another exciting session with DDS." Celebrity smirked. She knew how Jimmy struggled, trying to learn about his aunt's businesses.

He sat up straighter. "There's just too much for one brain to hold."

Celebrity snorted out a huff. "Think about what's in Betty's head. She knows this stuff by heart."

Jimmy wore the deer in the headlight expression again. "In all fairness, she's the one who built this empire and knows it backwards and forwards. I'm always amazed when someone calls from somewhere in the world and she doesn't even have to open a file or folder. The information is just there in her head and she talks to the person about details and figures. I don't know how she does it."

Celebrity patted his arm. "Let's go to lunch. You need suste-nance to recover."

"K. I'll meet you there."

Celebrity walked back to her police car, and Jimmy drove behind her. They arrived at the Biggem Diner and parked. Jimmy spotted his friend's vehicles. As he emerged from his CRV, Ramirez pulled up beside his car and parked.

"I'm so hungry I could eat a whole pig and a cow," Ramirez stated as they walked to the door of the establishment.

"Do you want fries or a salad with that?" Celebrity smirked at her partner.

They went inside and found Brian and Danny seated at a table for six, slurping iced tea. Danny kicked a chair out for Jimmy.

"You look like you're going to fall over, dude," Danny said as he look Jimmy over. "Must have just come from the DDS office."

Ramirez smirked. "Must be tough being the richest man walking the planet."

Jimmy kicked Ramirez' chair. "I'm not, really. I'm the heir who will one day inherit the title, but right now, I'm just me."

Duanna Oatmeal, aka Oatie, and Danny's girlfriend, who was a server at the dinner, hurried over with her order pad and pen ready. "What's this wild bunch having today?"

Ramirez started. "Double burger with the works, an order of fries and onion rings, and a coffee milkshake."

Celebrity ordered the Caesar salad with shrimp. She knew it was enough for two meals.

Danny, Brian, and Jimmy ordered the double burger with fries.

Oatie gave her boyfriend the evil eye. She mentally sent him a thought to change his fries to a salad, to no avail. "Coming right up."

MARTIN MALDONADO, FONDLY KNOWN AS MARTY THE Mortician at the Twinkle Funeral Parlor, which was established in the 1950s, prepared a file for Gene Jingle. The eighty-four-year-old apparently passed away in his sleep. Mrs. Jingle tried to revive her husband, and after a tearful goodbye on the day after their sixtieth wedding anniversary, she called 9-1-1, and they took him away.

Marty filled in all the details for the death certificate before disrobing and embalming Mr. Jingle, who rested on a table in the mortuary. Marty approached the table to prepare the deceased.

Suddenly, Mr. Jingle sprung upright and gasped. "Wha... Where am I?"

Marty recovered from his surprise and gripped Gene's shoulder so he wouldn't spring off the table. "Welcome back, Mr. Jingle. You almost got yourself embalmed."

"Wha... what happened?" He poked his chest with a finger. "I'm positive I'm not dead yet," Gene stammered as he swayed on the table.

"Evidently, neither your wife nor the EMT could revive you, so you were brought here to the Twinkle Funeral Parlor. I was just typing up your death certificate," Marty explained to the confused man.

Marty helped Gene to swing his legs to the side of the table to get down. "We'd better get you to a chair. Did you use a walker to get around? Don't try to walk just yet."

"Yeah. Do ya think my wife tossed the walker?" Gene asked, not really *with it* yet.

"I doubt if she'd be quick to do anything that harsh, unless you had a contentious relationship, then all bets are off." Marty was a straight forward man.

Marty helped Gene over to his desk chair. "You sit here while I call your wife and break the news to her. We don't want her to have a heart attack if you were to make the call."

He pulled up the phone number and placed the call. The phone rang four times before a weeping woman answered it. "Mrs. Jingle? It's Marty Maldonado with the Twinkle Funeral Parlor." He listened to the distraught woman. "Mrs. Jingle, you can postpone the funeral arrangements. Your husband is alive and well."

Gene heard the shriek from the chair. He held his hand out for the phone. "Mildred, why'd you think I was dead?" They had a back-and-forth conversation for a few minutes. "Better call the TIN and cancel the obit before they go to print. Can you pick me up?" After the conversation ended, Gene handed the phone receiver back to Marty. "She'll be here after she calls the TIN. When we get home, she'll have to call everyone to cancel their plans to attend the funeral. Our kids and grandkids are probably distraught over this false death."

The next day, the headline of the TIN was a shocker. MAN COMES BACK FROM THE DEAD, with a follow-up story with all the details provided by Marty the Mortician. Gene and Mildred Jingle eventually took their landline phone off the hook to stop the calls from ringing one after the other. Brian knocked on their door, but they wouldn't answer it, so he shouted through the door.

"Mr. and Mrs. Jingle, it's Brian McKinley from the TIN. I'm sorry for what you're going through, but we didn't receive your call to cancel the obit in time." Brian didn't even want to go near how the headline affected them. *Oh well*, he thought. *They're not likely to run out of conversation material anytime soon.*

VINCE BABELTON WAS JUST LEAVING THE POLICE DEPARTMENT building as Jimmy was arriving.

"Hey, did you give your testimony about that kid starting the fire?" Jimmy asked.

"Sure did. I hope they get him into some kind of therapy. Not sure if there's a cure for a firebug, though." Vince was thoughtful for a moment.

"I'll have to look up pyromania and see what they suggest." Jimmy had never come across anyone with that affliction. He wasn't sure if pyromania was an affliction or what.

"See ya." Vince continued on to his car, and Jimmy grabbed hold of the front doorknob for the police station.

"Hey, Butch," Jimmy greeted.

Sgt. Butch Gonzales was furiously typing as Jimmy walked inside. "Hey, Jimmy." He never looked up from the monitor. A new visitor would have thought nothing about Butch being so busy. For the rest of the people who stopped by the police station, it was a sight to see. The sergeant, facing a choice of computer training or resignation, became surprisingly productive.

Jimmy walked back to the chief's office and tapped on the open doorframe. "Hey, chief."

"Jimmy. What are you up to today?" Chief Kenton Price's chair creaked as he turned from the computer to greet the heir.

"What's going to happen to that kid you arrested yesterday?" Jimmy wasn't sure if they would hold him at the jail or if there was a special facility for kids.

"He's over at the Youth Detention Center in Derrick," Chief Price said. "The judge will hold a hearing to decide whether to release him or keep him in custody until they set a court date."

"That's all we need, a kid running around unsupervised, setting fires while his parents are at work." Jimmy shook his head, disturbed at the thoughts running through his head. He lowered his voice. "I had a talk with the kids about what they should do in case of an emergency if no one was home."

Chief Price drilled his eyes into Jimmy's. "Are you going to let Celebrity in on this secret? I don't see how you could keep something like this from your fiancé."

Jimmy squirmed in his chair. "I'm going to tell her this week, for sure."

"You'd better."

Jimmy left the chief to his paperwork and headed over to the Wham-A-Rama discount store, then caught himself before he entered the parking lot. He made a U-turn and headed downtown to Hector's Men's Store. Hector and Jorge banned him from ever setting foot in the Wham-A-Rama for any clothing. A gentleman of his ilk did not wear undergarments, or body coverings of any type from the scourge of lowly department stores. Other products were acceptable to purchase at discounts, just not clothing.

When Jimmy first met the clothiers, he was shocked at the prices of everything that he purchased. He recalled how he reeled when presented with the bill for shirts, slacks, a belt, and dress socks.

$15 for a pair of socks?

Really?

His hand trembled as he slid the credit card across the counter to pay for the items. Since then, he depended on Hector and Jorge to dress him properly for the events his Aunt Betty attended, both in person and on Zoom.

As he entered the establishment, he fully expected them to tut-tut his request. Jorge rushed over to his favorite client.

"Jimmy! What can we help you with today? Do you require a new suit?"

"Hey, Jorge. Do you have any purple ties?"

Jorge stared at Jimmy, wondering if he was joking.

Hector finished with a customer and joined his employee and their client. "What can we help you with, Jimmy?"

Jorge's wide eyes worried Hector. Jorge spit it out. "He wants a purple tie!"

Hector practically gave himself whiplash, turning to Jimmy so quickly. "A purple tie? Are you going to a carnival?"

Jimmy huffed out his exasperation at the two snobs. "One of Aunt Betty's clients loves the color purple. He wears something purple every time I see him online. I'd like a purple tie to show my support for when we Zoom next. What's the big deal?"

"Is this man..." Hector looked to Jorge for help with the correct description, but didn't see anything forthcoming from his employee. "Does he have some type of affliction?"

Jimmy balked. "He likes the color purple. How do I know what drove him to that color? Should I just go over to the Wham-A-Rama and see if they have one?"

That's all it took. Jorge took off to the tie section of the store as if there were thievery taking place. He sifted through dozens of ties and held one up for critical inspection. He shoved it back onto the rack and continued his search. Jorge finally found a tie that was the true color of purple. He approached Jimmy and Hector, and held the tie up for inspection.

"Yeah, that's perfect!" Jimmy retrieved the tie from Jorge and felt the delicious silk. They all moved over to the cash register where Jorge rung up the sale. Jimmy presented his black American Express Centurion credit card with the hundred-thousand-dollar credit limit, of which he had only ever used at Hector's Men Store.

Jorge wrapped the silk tie in delicate paper, then placed it in a small custom paper sack with the store logo and handed it to Jimmy.

MRS. POTTS SHELLED PEAS AT HER KITCHEN TABLE. GUPPY SAT perched on his favorite chair-back, and Maddy batted a plastic bottle cap on the floor. The landlady rolled a pea across the table and Guppy snatched it up.

The front door opened, and Brian entered. He took in a deep breath. "Pot roast, Mrs. Potts?"

"You have an excellent sniffer, Brian. Pot roast, mashed potatoes, and peas—if Guppy will share with us."

Brian approached the table and eyeballed the colander. There was enough for one serving. He pulled out a chair and grabbed a handful of pea pods. "Looks like help is required."

They shelled peas in companionable silence for a few minutes, then Mrs. Potts delved into a delicate subject. "Brian, have the Jingles recovered from that headline in the TIN?"

Brian lowered his head and shook it gently. "I don't know why Bill or Sylvan didn't change that headline. I feel so bad for Mr. and Mrs. Jingle."

Mrs. Potts patted his hand. "People will move on to the next headline. Hopefully, the Jingles can plug their phone back in."

"They have one of those old landlines?" Brian asked. "I thought those were long gone since practically everyone has a cellphone."

"The thing about landlines is that if a cell tower has a problem and you don't have a signal, the landline will still work. You'll discover that most people of a certain age prefer a landline." Mrs. Potts nodded knowingly.

"Do they also have a cellphone?" Brian seemed stuck on the issue.

"I don't know. Maybe you should conduct a survey for the paper. That would make an interesting article."

"*MORE!*" Guppy squawked, wanting the humans to get on board with the peas.

"Guppy, you've had more than enough peas," Mrs. Potts declared as she grabbed the colander and headed to the sink. She rinsed off the peas and dumped them in a pot of water on the stove. "I've got to run to the Foo. I'll start the peas just before dinnertime. They only take five minutes."

"Want me to drive?" Brian asked.

"I'll take you up on that!" Mrs. Potts grabbed her purse. She addressed the animals. "We'll be back in a jiffy. Go upstairs and take a nap."

Guppy let out an indignant squawk as the landlady and her boarder left the house.

I'm going upstairs to take a nap, Maddy announced.

Guppy focused on the pot of peas on the stove. The burner wasn't lit, so he knew he wouldn't get hurt. The Amazon parrot flew over to the stove. His claws gripped the knob as he landed. He steadied himself on the knob as he scooped peas out of the pot of cold water. When he had his fill, he lifted off the knob and flew upstairs to his tree perch. The gas flame lit under the pot of peas.

CHAPTER THREE

M rs. Potts and Brian roamed the aisles of the Foo. They couldn't find everything on the landlady's list, so they went over to the Wham-A-Rama.

THE WATER BOILED OUT OF THE PAN, SCORCHING THE BOTTOM. The peas burned to a crisp, and the overheated Teflon pot became so hot that it burst into flames. After several more minutes, the pan disintegrated, parts falling onto the floor spreading the fire.

MADDY LAY ON THE SOFA, FAST ASLEEP. GUPPY SNOOZED ON HIS fake tree. Smoke drifted up the stairs. Maddy's whiskers twitched in her sleep, alerting her to danger. She blinked, sat, and sniffed. She ran to the top of the stairs and saw flames. Maddy rushed over to her friend's fake tree and jumped against the trunk.

"FIRE! GUPPY WAKE UP!"

Guppy squawked as he became alert. He saw the smoke billowing into the apartment.

"BASKET!"

The parrot flew into the kitchen and through the open door of the pantry. He landed on an open shelf on the left side and searched for the gazebo basket. Guppy found the basket, grabbed it with his strong beak, and flew to the kitchen table.

Maddy was frantic as she looked at all of Jimmy's possessions. She spotted grandma's journal on the end table where their daddy read. The smart cat raced over to the end table and snatched up the journal in her mouth, then sprinted over to the table. She leapt up and dropped the journal into the basket.

"GET IN THE BASKET!" Guppy hollered.

The flames reached the upstairs. The fire blocked their escape. Maddy jumped into the basket and hunkered down. Guppy grabbed the basket with his beak and pumped his wings. The big, strong Imperial Amazon parrot, also known as the Sisserou, was the largest of the species and the national bird of Dominica. Their life span in captivity was seventy years.

The grungy sea captain who taught Guppy vulgar language used to taunt him he was a sissy. Guppy flew toward his tree and favorite window. He landed on the windowsill, claws grasping the wooden edge, and tilted his head down. He bashed the screen with all his might, sending it flying. Guppy leapt out of the open window, spread his enormous wings that spanned thirty inches, and flew them to safety.

Guppy flew over to the gazebo and set the basket down on the grass. He and Maddy took turns trying to open the heavy door. The fire engulfed the house in flames.

"Find Daddy!" Maddy yelled. She hopped back into the basket.

Guppy grabbed the basket in his powerful beak and lifted off the ground. He flew over the trees, away from the fire. Maddy sneezed from the smoke. Guppy flew down Stonerich Boulevard to the downtown area screeching at the top of his parrot lungs.

"FIRE! FIRE!"

People pulled out their phones and took pictures of the parrot hauling the basket.

Maddy read store names as Guppy flew them to safety. "Look, Gup, there's the police station! Go there! The chief will find Daddy!"

Guppy flapped his wings for all they were worth, while screaming out, FIRE. He flew into the door, his claws scratching the glass, his loud voice trying to get attention. Maddy meowed loudly as she pawed the glass trying to get attention.

Butch looked up from his monitor. "What the heck? There's a crazy bird with a basket and a cat..."

The chief recognized Guppy's voice and ran out of his office. He turned to Stephanie, the dispatcher. "Alert the fire department! Mrs. Potts' house is on fire!"

Chief Price opened the door, grabbed the basket, and held his arm out for the frantic bird. "Guppy, land here on my arm. Everything's okay. Good job rescuing Maddy and yourself."

The fire truck with siren screaming and horn blowing raced down the street.

MEATY SLURPED A MILKSHAKE AND CRUNCHED DOWN ON A TACO which exploded over his keyboard when he heard the fire alarm sounding outside from the huge speakers.

He shot off his chair, thundered down the stairs

"FIRE! Be back later," he hollered out to his uncle, then he was out the door.

Meaty jumped into his souped-up Camaro while manning his phone to get details. He arrived at the fire station in time to jump on the second firetruck. They screeched down the street, horn blowing and siren screaming to get people out of the way.

"YOU'RE GOING TO HAVE TO COME WITH ME," CHIEF PRICE TOLD the animals. He raced outside to his police vehicle and set the basket in the back seat and encouraged Guppy to get into the car. The chief ran to the driver's door and jumped in. Luckily, the animals were in the back and could go nowhere else because of the wire caging that separated the front and back seats. The new separation configuration hadn't been installed in the chief's car yet.

"Hold on, I'm going to be driving fast!"

Ask him about Daddy! Where's Daddy? Maddy urged Guppy.

"DADDY!" Guppy let out.

Chief Price called Jimmy's cellphone. He knew the heir was with his aunt, the DDS, or he was out interviewing someone for the TIN. After three rings, Jimmy finally answered the call. The chief didn't give him the chance to speak. "MRS. POTTS' HOUSE IS ON FIRE!"

"WHAT? GUPPY! MADDY!" Jimmy was frantic.

"They're here with me. Guppy rescued them with the basket!" the chief reported.

BRIAN AND MRS. POTTS WERE PLACING PLASTIC SHOPPING SACKS in the trunk of his car at the Wham-A-Rama when Brian pointed to the blackened sky. "Oh, no. Another fire. I hope that kid isn't starting more fires!"

Mrs. Potts stopped and shielded her eyes with her hand as she looked in the direction Brian had pointed. "That's a big one!"

Brian closed the trunk of his vehicle and grabbed the shopping cart. He returned the cart to the parking lot cart storage rack while Mrs. Potts got into the front passenger seat.

"Want to go see where the fire is?" Brian asked.

"We need to get the freezer items into the fridge first," Mrs. Potts suggested. "Then we can go ride around."

They were in no hurry, so Brian stuck to the speed limit of 35 MPH. As they turned onto Pine Street and rode down to Stonerich Blvd, the smoke was heavy.

"That fire looks like it's in our neighborhood. I hope Vince's house is not going up in smoke!" Mrs. Potts exclaimed.

When they turned onto Stonerich, Brian and Mrs. Potts witnessed the worst. The fire trucks were along Durbridge Street at the boarding house.

"MY HOUSE!" Mrs. Potts screamed while totally freaked out.

Brian parked as close as he could get to where the emergency response team member waved at them. They scrambled out of the car and stared at their house just as the roof caved in.

"MADDY! GUPPY! OH MY GOD! THE ANIMALS!" Mrs. Potts screeched.

Chief Price spotted Mrs. Potts and Brian and rushed over to them. "Guppy and Maddy are in my car. That parrot flew Maddy in the basket down Stonerich, screeching out Fire. Butch liked to have thought he was hallucinating when Guppy clawed at the front door window."

Mrs. Potts broke down. "It's all gone. Every memory I've carefully stored—all gone."

Jimmy braked to a hard stop, tearing up grass and dirt across the street from his former home. He was out of the car and running over to his landlady and his friend. He hugged Mrs. Potts. "It will be okay."

Mrs. Potts' phone rang. She noticed it was Betty and

answered with tears and hiccupping. "Betty, it's burnt to the ground."

Bertha, all of you are to come over to the mansion as soon as you leave there. I'll take care of everything. Elnora and Toombs are shopping for all of you, including the animals.

Mrs. Potts controlled her crying to squeak out a thank you, then disconnected the call.

Danny jogged over to where they were. "What happened?"

"We have no idea." Brian shook his head.

"I had a roast in the oven at a low temperature. No burners on the stovetop were on. I don't have any idea how this could have happened!" Mrs. Potts wailed.

"There's no point in watching the fire until the last embers are extinguished," Jimmy stated. "Let's head over to Aunt Betty's." He took one last glance. The gazebo was not in any danger. He wondered if they would all congregate there again one day.

Jimmy's car led the way, followed by Brian and Chief Price.

Jenkins and Betty stood on the edge of the driveway, waiting for everyone to disembark from the vehicles. Betty drew Bertha Potts into an embrace, feeling she needed comfort more than her nephew or Brian.

"Oh, Betty," Mrs. Potts sobbed. "It's burnt to the ground. All gone. Everything lost."

"It will be okay, Bertha. Insurance will cover your personal items, and we'll get your place rebuilt better than what you enjoyed for so many years." Betty patted Mrs. Potts on the back and drew her into the house.

Jimmy went over to Chief Price's car. He opened the door behind the caging. "Remember how much fun you had at Aunt Betty's? We're going to be living here for a while. Maddy, hop into the basket. Guppy, get on my shoulder because I don't have your towel."

Maddy hopped into the basket. Guppy waited until Jimmy

was standing up outside the car. He waddled to the edge of the seat, then fluttered up to Jimmy's shoulder.

"Hang on. We'll go upstairs to our old room." He went inside the mansion and up the stairs to his suite. "Toombs is getting your supplies. I hope no one has to go potty. Let me get a bowl of water for you two. You'll have to share for now."

Maddy hopped out of the basket. Jimmy glanced at the conveyance that carried his cat out to the gazebo. He reached inside, grabbed up his mother's diary and clutched it to his chest, his eyes watering. "Oh, Maddy. You rescued grandma's journal!" He placed the journal on the table and picked up Maddy. "Thank you for thinking of this."

When he set Maddy down on the floor, he turned to Guppy, perched on top of a chair-back. He gently hugged his parrot. "Guppy, you rescued Maddy in the basket. What a smart bird!"

Jimmy had a moment. He looked all about, panic sizzling near the surface. He wondered if anyone realized that Maddy was the one who placed the diary in the basket. Their little secret would be in danger of being discovered.

"I'll be back in a little while. Toombs should be here soon with supplies. I want to go downstairs and talk to the chief and Aunt Betty."

Brian remembered the groceries. "Jenkins, Mrs. Potts and I have groceries in the trunk of my car." Brian felt dismayed about what to do with the groceries now.

Jenkins took charge. "Everyone, grab a bag of groceries and follow me to the kitchen."

Duncan Carver, Betty's fabulous cook, carried a tray of teacups, a box of tea bags, and cups while Annie Mays, a kitchen helper, followed with a tray with plates of finger foods and napkins.

"Someone will show you where to put the groceries." Duncan waved Jenkins, Chief Price, and Brian to the kitchen while he placed the large tray on the coffee table in the reading room.

After placing the groceries in the kitchen, Brian joined everyone in the reading room and collapsed into a chair. They were all shell-shocked at the complete loss of the house and all of their possessions.

The chief followed Jenkins and stood where everyone could see him. He announced what would happen. "There will be an investigation to rule out arson. There could have been a faulty appliance, water heater, toaster – anything could be the cause of this catastrophic fire. I'm sure you all had fingers pointing to Theo, but he is still in the Derrick facility."

"What happens next?" Mrs. Potts asked.

"Once the rubble has cooled sufficiently, the Texas Fire Marshal's Office will send a fire investigation officer to determine the cause and origin of the fire. They often work with forensic engineers to examine electrical appliances and wiring." The chief figured all he could do was explain the process to give them information. No one liked to be left in the dark of any investigation.

Toombs and Elnora returned loaded down with shopping bags. Toombs called out to the room.

"Jimmy, Brian, Jenkins, Duncan, Chief—lend a hand with bringing in replacement items. Jimmy, I found Guppy a tree and I have Maddy's litter box and supplies. I've marked the bags with a B for Brian, P for Mrs. Potts, and J for Jimmy, so you can make sure they get to the right rooms."

All the men sprang out of chairs, followed by the others who had been standing.

Betty patted Bertha's hand. "These are preliminary items to get you through two days. Then we can go shopping for a couple of weeks' worth of items. Don't forget, we have two and a half seasons to think about. Cool weather, roasting, and mild."

Bertha dabbed at her watery eyes with a rumpled tissue. "Oh, Betty. You're an angel. Thank you so much for doing this for all of us."

Toombs and Jimmy carried the huge box with Guppy's fake tree. Brian followed with the critical cat supplies.

Celebrity and Ramirez showed up and joined the troops hauling shopping bags and packages. Jenkins took his place by the front door and guided people where to go until they knew the locations where people would be living.

Toombs hurried down the stairs to gather tools for the tree.

The chief had a thought and pulled Jimmy aside. "What about the cameras? You should get some installed for our special project."

Jimmy's mouth opened in an O. "I'll have to buy a laptop and download everything from the cloud."

"I wonder if Mrs. Potts used the cloud for backup? She had a laptop and an iPad, and Brian had a laptop." Jimmy thought about their electronics. Everyone had their phones, so those didn't need to be replaced, but the chargers were required. Maybe he and Brian could go out first thing in the morning and replace those items.

"Chief, you don't think anyone realizes Maddy is the one who put my mother's journal in the basket, do you?" Jimmy was close to hyperventilating.

Chief Price thought it through. He was the first to the basket, which went into the back of his police car along with Guppy and Maddy. "No one saw anything other than Guppy holding the basket with Maddy hunkered down at the door of the police station. Don't spaz out for no reason. Only you and I know what was in the basket."

Jimmy felt relieved. He sprinted up the stairs to get his animals situated.

CHAPTER FOUR

Jimmy and Brian stared at the front page of the TIN. A picture of Guppy flying with the basket with Maddy's head sticking up was on the front page of the paper. The headline read, PARROTT RESCUES CAT. An article by Danny Stonerich followed.

"A bunch of people sent photos to the TIN. Danny and Eddie chose the best one," Brian said.

JIMMY AND BRIAN WENT TO THE COMPUTER STORE IN DIME Water which rivaled the big computer store in the Big City. They perused the computer equipment, followed by an employee looking to score the sale. Once they had three MacBook Pro's, printers, two external monitors, chargers for the cell phones, and three iPads, Jimmy had a thought. He pulled Brian aside and whispered.

"Should I get a, uh, spare iPad?" He winked at Brian several times.

The need for a spare iPad momentarily puzzled Brian. Then

he had a sudden realization. "OH! Yes. That's a good idea. Do they have pencils here? You'll have to get a package of those yellow pencils."

After adding that to the list their associate was managing, they wandered over to the cameras section. Jimmy looked in his phone for where he ordered those items online the year before. He and Brian searched the shelves and found similar products. Jimmy hemmed and hawed, trying to determine where they would need to be installed. He ended up with six of the tiny cameras, figuring spares were a good thing.

Billy, their associate, grabbed an employee and had her snag a shopping cart. They piled all the boxes and bags inside, and Billy even escorted them out to their car and unloaded everything into the trunk. He recognized that this was the highest sale his department ever had for individuals in one day.

They waved as they drove off, and Billy waved in return.

"We can ask Meaty if he can set up Mrs. Potts' equipment, and give us a hand with our external monitors. I don't know about you, but it took me a while to figure out how to configure my old one." Jimmy recalled the head-scratching trying to choose the settings for his big monitor.

"I think I need a desk," Brian thought out loud. "I'm trying to remember if there was a desk in my room when we had to stay here before."

"Ask Jenkins. He keeps track of everything," Jimmy suggested. He thought for a while. "I planned to tell Celebrity about the pact, and I'm wondering if I should include Meaty?"

"Wait until we set up all the equipment. Then we should have all pact members here for the telling and showing." Brian figured that would be the best way to go about things. This secret was too dangerous to get out into the world.

MEATY WAS HAPPY TO HELP SET THINGS UP. HE TACKLED MRS. Potts' equipment first, then gave her lessons and made her take notes on how to use her new equipment. He found her iCloud storage account and connected the new laptop and tablet. After verifying the connection between Mrs. Potts' phone and the online storage, Meaty started downloading her files and folders to the laptop. He printed out her password list, then climbed the stairs to see what help Jimmy and Brian required.

He gave Jimmy lessons about the external monitor and explained all the crazy settings. Since the heir knew how to download his files and folders to his Mac, Meaty left him to it and went down the hall to where Brian now lived. The reporter needed a little more help than Jimmy, so Meaty jumped in and guided him. He believed hands-on experience was the quicker way to learn these things instead of someone doing it while you watched.

Just as the security and hacker expert finished up, Jimmy joined them. "Meaty, can you come by tomorrow for a meeting? I don't have the time yet, but will let you know when I set it up."

"Sure, no problem. I have things set up at the Foo for those times when I have to be away. Just give me at least a twenty-minute leeway so I can check my scanners and let my uncle know."

"Is Mrs. Potts all set up with her equipment?" Jimmy asked.

"She's still rattled, but I made her take notes. I'm sure if she gets stuck and you two are gone, your Aunt Betty can help her. Betty's practically an expert and has taught me a thing or two," Meaty explained.

JIMMY CALLED THE CHIEF AND TALKED TO HIM ABOUT THE PLAN. Next, he went downstairs to Mrs. Potts' room.

"If we meet after breakfast, then we can go shopping for

clothes and other things that need replacing," Mrs. Potts suggested. "You really should include Betty in this meeting. After all, you'll be installing cameras on the ceiling."

Jimmy thought it over, then placed a call to the chief to get his opinion. They decided adding Betty was a good idea.

At nine o'clock the next morning, Jimmy commandeered a meeting room in the mansion that had sufficient seating, a table, and a large screen mounted on the wall. He set up his brand-new laptop, plugged in the cord to keep a charge, then greeted Mrs. Potts and Brian. Jenkins led the chief, Meaty, and Celebrity into the room, while Jimmy ran to fetch his great aunt.

Nerves were ratcheted up, but Celebrity and Betty blamed the fire for the tension. The chief closed the door, then took a seat. Jimmy began.

"Mrs. Potts, Chief Price, Brian, and I have a secret pact that we are going to share with you. You see," Jimmy wiped his sweaty hands down his jeans while trying to form words that would make sense to his aunt, his fiancé, and especially Meaty. "I discovered my pets are very special animals. So special that if their secret got out, the government would confiscate them and dissect their brains. And we'll all be branded as crackpots or animal experimenters or something."

Chief Price jumped in. "You cannot ever divulge what you hear and see in this room. Do you understand?" With a voice and expression that threatened arrest and serious trouble, he addressed the three people about to hear the pact secret.

"Maddy knows how to use my laptop. She has communicated via the text function with a yellow pencil." Jimmy held up a pencil.

Mrs. Potts interrupted. "The animals watch children's programs on TV. There had been times when I thought Jimmy left the TV on, but we discovered Maddy would grip the pencil in her jaws and whack the on-off button. She also controls the sound. She and Guppy are very sneaky."

Celebrity had been quiet. "Oh, come on." She snickered thinking this was a good joke.

Betty studied Chief Price. She trusted the man explicitly. "Kenton, you have seen this with your own two eyes?"

Chief Price nodded. "Jimmy, start at the beginning, then bring up specific videos."

Jimmy manned the new laptop. It had taken all night for his files to download. He clicked on a video and it appeared on the big screen on the wall. Everyone saw Maddy jump onto the chair. She grabbed the pencil Jimmy had left on the desk with her powerful jaws. Everyone watched as Maddy whacked the letters C, A, and T.

She raced to the other side of the laptop and whacked the Return key. Next, she returned to the other side of the laptop and whacked the tab key. Once she seemed to be satisfied with the cursor placement, she whacked the B, R, and D keys. Jimmy had explained that *bird* needed the letter I. "She obviously understood and made the correction."

The newcomers were on the edges of their seats. Jimmy brought up another video file. This one was when he received a text from home that said HELP. They watched a couple of dozen videos, then Jimmy figured that was enough.

"Does anyone have any thoughts or questions? Do you believe your own eyes?"

"Well, I certainly would have been calling Doctor Canada to have your head examined if I had not seen these videos with my own two eyes," Betty exclaimed.

"So, that's why I saw a shopping bag filled with camera boxes upstairs," Meaty deducted.

Brian snorted a laugh.

"Yup. Have to get them installed immediately." Jimmy shook his head. "The trick is to make sure Maddy and Guppy think they're motion sensors to catch anyone trying to break in through the windows. It would be a challenge trying to outsmart their thinking."

Celebrity pondered deeply. "I'm never ever going to see ordinary animals after this. Who knows what they're thinking when I visit you?"

Mrs. Potts stood. She held her hand out toward the center of the table. "This is the pact. You have to do everything in your power to protect these animals. Never ignore a call for help or question what they watch on YouTube." She stared Meaty down.

The security man shook his head. "I can't get over how they figured things out." He stared down the chief. "So, that day in your office. You led me down the road of the bank problems from Maddy and Guppy discovering that Reggie Armbruster was the person who hacked accounts?"

The chief nodded. "Had to take what they discovered and have it solved by a human."

Meaty stared at the table's surface. "Wow. Just plain wow."

He added his hand to the others across the table, which now included Betty and Celebrity's hands. Jimmy, Chief Price and Brian added their hands.

"We are sealing the pact by adding the three of you. Never let Maddy and Guppy know you are aware of what they do because I'm afraid they will not communicate like they have been," Mrs. Potts said.

"I've bought Maddy an iPad. I don't know how this is going to go over, because I'm telling her I know what she and Guppy are up to." Jimmy shook his head. "How do I keep one step ahead of them? I realize they must know I know because of her texts and typing."

Meaty was lost in a thoughtful moment. "Can they go downstairs? I think they should not be in the apartment when we install the cameras."

"Of course they can. Guppy would enjoy the conservatory, and Maddy would most likely want to sit on my desk to see what I do all day," Betty announced. "Have Jenkins show you where the ladder and tools are after you bring the animals downstairs."

Everyone went about their business. Jimmy took the stairs two at a time. He opened the door and found Guppy monitoring the trees for danger, and Maddy watched a cheesy romance movie on the big TV.

"Everyone want to go downstairs? Aunt Betty thinks you'd love the conservatory, Guppy. Maddy, she invited you to sit on her desk to watch her work."

"LET'S GO!" Guppy belted out.

Maddy pranced to the door and waited. She didn't need to ride in the basket for this outing.

Jimmy grabbed a dishtowel and draped it over his arm. "Come on, Guppy. All aboard!"

The Amazon parrot climbed onto Jimmy's arm. He opened the apartment door and Maddy dashed out. Meaty was sitting in a chair in a reading room near the bottom of the stairs, pretending to read a magazine.

"Don't go too far, Maddy. I'll show you where Aunt Betty's office is in a moment. Let's go to the conservatory first." Jimmy hurried to keep up with his cat.

Guppy squawked excitedly when he saw the room filled with trees and plants.

"Want to sit in this tree, Gup?" Jimmy asked.

"YES!" The parrot was so excited, he didn't make sentences —a first for him.

"Okay, you stay here while I bring Maddy to Aunt Betty's office," Jimmy said, then walked away. Maddy darted all over. He tapped on the open doorframe of his aunt's office. Then he reached down and picked Maddy up and showed her the setup of Aunt Betty's desk. He walked around the desk to stand beside his aunt.

"Hello Maddy!" Aunt Betty was much more interested in his

cat than Maddy being just a pet. "This is where I work and take care of the Katz-Diaz estate. Why don't you sit here?" Betty tapped a place to her side. "You can watch everything that goes on. Just don't touch the keyboard if I'm in a Zoom meeting or on the phone with someone. People from all across the world meet with me online."

Maddy observed. She meowed as if saying *okay*.

"I'll be upstairs with Meaty, then Mrs. Potts, Brian, and I are going shopping," Jimmy explained.

"Maddy and I will get to know each other. I'll have Jenkins keep an eye out for Guppy to make sure he's happy in the conservatory."

Maddy reached out and touched Betty's notepad.

"Maddy, I don't think writing is within your capabilities with those big paws, honey," Aunt Betty told her. "But you can read my notes when I write them."

JIMMY TOOK THE STAIRS TWO AT A TIME. HE FOUND MEATY ON the ladder that Jenkins provided. Jimmy closed the door so the animals would not catch them installing the cameras if they came back for a nap.

Meaty suggested where they should install the cameras. One pointed at the TV. Jimmy showed him where he planned to place Maddy's iPad. He and Meaty checked to make sure this placement would capture what was on the TV screen. Another camera would be off to the side so they could see what Maddy was doing on the iPad.

"They read the newspaper," Jimmy informed Meaty.

The security expert stopped turning a screw and stared at Jimmy. He shook his head. "Of course they do. If I hadn't seen things with my own two eyes from those videos, I would laugh you out of town. But, I'm not surprised. They probably know more about what's going on in this town than we do."

Jimmy busied himself with unboxing the cameras and making them ready for Meaty to install. When they were all installed and tested to make sure they worked properly, they downloaded the software to their phones. Jimmy also downloaded the app to his laptop.

Then he dragged out the vacuum and made sure there were no telltale signs of ceiling matter on the floor. He didn't want them looking up if he could help it. While the cameras were tiny, and hard to detect, animal eyes were sharper than human eyes.

Meaty configured Maddy's iPad. He created an email address for her through Yahoo.com. He also used Jimmy's contacts to load up the contacts on the animal's iPad.

"Do they need a credit card?" Meaty's questioning eyes pegged Jimmy with a stare.

Jimmy stared back. "Hhmm. I guess I could get a VISA gift card." He felt unsure about it.

Meaty figured it out. "Why don't I program a set of questions to be asked when the card is used?" Something like, would Jimmy approve of this purchase? Is this really important?"

Jimmy nodded. "Use Daddy, not Jimmy. Good idea. I want to make sure they use discretion and not order something expensive or stupid."

Meaty clacked away on the iPad, creating accounts and setting things up. "All set."

Jimmy had a thought. "I want to mark the floor with something to show the exact alignment of the iPad. That would make it easier to keep it where the cameras can record things."

"Good idea, use clear tape," Meaty expressed.

After Jimmy and Meaty checked that everything was in place, Meaty opened the door wide enough to stick his head outside. No animals.

"Grab the tool bag and the shopping bag with the empty camera boxes," he called out to Jimmy.

They snuck down the stairs and returned the items where Jenkins directed Meaty to put them, then Meaty carried the bag of empty boxes out to his vehicle. It was a challenge to hide things from curious, smart pets.

After Meaty returned to the Foo and his security job, Jimmy checked on Guppy. The parrot seemed in love with the conservatory. Jimmy hoped Guppy didn't do any harm to the trees or plants his aunt cherished.

Next up, Jimmy stopped by his aunt's office to check on Maddy. His cat watched the keyboard or the monitor. "Is Maddy behaving?"

"We had a good time Zooming with Myoshia in Japan. Maddy introduced herself and gave her opinion several times," Aunt Betty explained with a smirk.

"As long as she doesn't try to type." Jimmy chuckled. He turned to his cat. "You remember where we live upstairs? That's where your potty box, food, and water are."

Maddy rubbed against Jimmy, which he interpreted to mean she understood and remembered.

"I'm going to head over to the police station and talk with the Chief, and see if Celebrity is there. I want to determine how she really feels about the pact, and if she said anything to the chief. Meaty seems okay with everything." Jimmy was concerned about his fiancé and hoped this new revelation didn't damage their future together.

CHAPTER FIVE

When Jimmy entered the police station, Butch stopped him. "I saw the videos on the TINs website! I'm so sorry to see what happened to Mrs. Potts' boarding house! Where are you all staying?"

Jimmy stopped to talk to Butch, a rare event. "We're staying with my aunt and trying to adjust to our new living arrangements." He started to step away when he realized something Butch had mentioned. "I'll have to look at those videos. Brian and Danny were there, so they must have filmed the house fire."

"Well, good luck, Jimmy. I'm really glad your animals saved themselves. That was something to see, let me tell you!"

"Thanks, Butch. I can't tell you how freaked out I was when the chief called me about the fire. I thought for sure Maddy and Guppy were dead. They're like my children." Jimmy explained. He tapped the counter and walked to the chief's office.

Jimmy looked through the open door and saw the chief staring into space. "Hey, you okay?"

Chief Price started, then moved his head to the right, then left, which made a cracking noise. "Yeah, just thinking. Come on in and have a seat."

Jimmy slumped into a chair. "Moving out for a couple of weeks is one thing, but living at my aunt's permanently is another story."

"I can't imagine losing everything. The mansion is spacious, so the three of you, plus Maddy and Guppy, should be okay until the investigation is complete and Mrs. Potts knows how the insurance company will handle things."

"We're going shopping after I leave here. There's a lot of personal items the three of us have to replace. Toombs lucked out and found Guppy a tree. We assembled it last night. I have to buy his sleep cage and a few other items." Jimmy was still in the shell-shocked phase. "Has Celebrity said anything to you? I'm worried that this may change things between us."

Chief Price shook his head. "She's on board. I think she's looking forward to somehow communicating with Maddy. Maybe she'll write down her email address and leave it some place where Maddy will see it."

"Meaty installed Contacts on her new iPad. I'd better get going. So much to do. I'm pretty sure things will slip through the cracks. Everything used to be automated, so I don't remember everything." Jimmy stood. "See you later."

Jimmy left the police station after not seeing Celebrity at her desk. He drove over to Hector and Jorge's store. The door flew open and the two clothiers came outside and swamped their favorite client in a bear hug.

"Oh, Jimmy! We saw the fire on the news. I'm so sorry for your loss," Hector said.

"You were so lucky that no one died!" Jorge said.

They untangled themselves from the hug.

"I need to replace EVERYTHING. Head to toe," Jimmy said. "All I have is the suit I wore that day, and some emergency clothes Toombs picked up, which were most likely from the Wham-A-Rama."

"We'll take care of everything. Come inside. There are a few suits, shirts, slacks, ties and socks we have in stock you can take with you today." Hector announced.

"Don't forget shoes!" Jorge practically flipped out that they would forget Jimmy's shoes. "I ordered another purple tie for your meetings."

"Oh, thanks, Jorge!" Jimmy hadn't even thought about the tie. They went inside and Jorge was like a whirling dervish going through the racks. He made several trips to the front and hung offerings. Hector perused the shoes and socks and brought them to the front counter.

Jimmy went through the hanging clothes Jorge had hung up, and could not find fault with the choices. With everything loaded onto the front counter or the hanging bar, Hector snipped the price tags while Jorge manned the register. Jimmy slid his trusty Stratus Rewards Visa credit card across the counter. The final amount was staggering, but he knew there was more to come. Hector had to order new high-end suits and a tux.

"Take Mrs. Potts to Marivelle Twinster's store, Bottoms Top. There's also a new ladies' clothing store that opened last month. It's Amanda Jane's Fashionable Clothing. Amanda Jane Thompson is a fashion diva. She lives above her store." Hector announced.

"Good to know. I plan on bringing Mrs. Potts shopping as soon as I go back to the mansion," Jimmy replied.

Hector and Jorge helped him haul the purchases out to his car, hugged him again, and Jimmy took off to his new home.

JIMMY PARKED THE HONDA CRV AS CLOSE TO THE FRONT DOOR of the mansion as the driveway allowed. He popped the trunk, got out of the car and grabbed a suit bag from the hook in the back seat. He grabbed one shopping bag from the trunk and went to the front door. Jimmy was about to ring the doorbell with an elbow since his hands were full, but Jenkins beat him to it by opening the door.

"Need help?" Jenkins asked.

"Hector and Jorge loaded me up with what they call their *low-end* clothing until they order *appropriate* replacements. Which, to me, it's top of the line bespoke fare." Jimmy explained.

Jenkins chuckled. "They're snobs, but they know how to dress us. I'm sure they told you they've banned you from setting one toe inside Wham-A-Rama for anything that goes on your body, clothing wise?"

Jimmy joined Jenkins, laughing about the clothiers. They brought the purchases into the house and climbed the stairs to Jimmy's apartment. Maddy was curled up on the sofa and Guppy was dozing on his fake tree.

"I have to buy Guppy a sleeping cage. I'm not sure if there's anything else I'm overlooking."

They emptied the car of all Jimmy's new clothing, then the TIN reporter went in search of Mrs. Potts. He found Brian along the way and asked him if he wanted to go to Hector and Jorge's.

"That's a little over the top for me," Brian suggested.

"Okay, just suggesting. I'm going to take Mrs. Potts to a couple of places in town to get her some clothes," Jimmy said.

They fist-bumped and went on their separate ways. Jimmy made a sneaky phone call to Hector. He knew Brian would head over to Wham-A-Rama, or order things online, but he needed quality clothing, so Jimmy stepped in.

The heir found Mrs. Potts in her suite, sitting in a chair with a book on her lap, but not reading. She looked depressed, and he couldn't blame her. Not even her nephews, George and Jerry, could cheer her up when they visited.

"Hey, Mrs. Potts. Let's go to these two places Hector and

Jorge told me about so you can find some new clothes," Jimmy urged.

She snapped out of her funk. "Oh, where's that?"

"Amanda Jane's Fashionable Clothing and Bottom's Top." Jimmy announced. "Maybe you'll discover your new favorite store."

Mrs. Potts sat thinking for a moment, sighed, then set her book aside and stood. "Okay. Let me grab my purse and we can go. I really appreciate Betty opening her house to us, but knowing I can never go home again is beyond upsetting."

Jimmy pulled her into a hug. "When the fire investigators determine the cause of the fire, they'll report to the chief, and most likely the insurance company. Then it will be time to plan a new boarding house. There are probably things you would want to include in the plans that were not in the original house. Larger rooms, more storage, butler's pantry—things like that. At least the gazebo is still standing."

They parted, and Mrs. Potts grabbed her purse, and they left the house. Jimmy spotted a shoe warehouse and turned his Honda into the parking lot. "I don't remember seeing this store before. I'll bet you can find every shoe type you want here."

"Oh, I hope they have my favorite slippers." Mrs. Potts made a mental list of what she could get at this store. Forty-five minutes later, she had new slippers, tennis shoes, regular flats in four colors; blue, black, brown, and white. She found socks and nylon ankle wear. "That definitely lifted my spirits."

"Let's go to those two ladies' stores." Jimmy started the car. They stopped at Bottoms Top first. It was the closest thing to Victoria's Secret that Twinkle could get. Mrs. Potts bought all manner of underclothing, pajamas, two robes, one for cool weather and a light one for the Texas heat. There was nothing sexy about her purchases, just comfortable functional items.

The trunk of the Honda was filling up with shopping bags. They stopped at the last place, Amanda Jane's Fashionable

Clothing, and Mrs. Potts was in heaven. "This store is practically like walking into one of my favorite catalogs. We may be here a while, Jimmy. If you want to go somewhere and come back, that's okay by me."

"Tell you what. I'll stop by the TIN and see what's going on. Why don't you text me when you get to the register. I'm picking up the tab, no arguments. We don't know how long it will be before you get anything from your homeowner's policy, and you can't go through what money you have in your checking account." Jimmy gave her a stern look.

"Oh, okay. You run to the TIN, and I'll wander around here," Mrs. Potts said, distracted by the racks of clothing drawing her attention.

Jimmy stopped at the check-out counter and spoke with the woman, pointing to Mrs. Potts. He wanted to make sure his landlady didn't try to pull a fast one and use her credit card.

THE TIN WAS A WHIRLWIND OF ACTIVITY WHEN JIMMY STEPPED through the employee entrance at the back door. Eddie Garcia, the production, tech support, and website developer, was the first to spot Jimmy.

"Hey! Look who's here!" Eddie called out. He whacked Jimmy on the back and pumped his hand. "You doing okay? So sorry about what happened!"

Gert Pruptek, who was in charge of classifieds, circulation, and sales, stuck her head out of her office. "Hey, Jimmy. Glad to see you are okay." She popped back into her office when the phone rang.

Milly Montoya, the TIN receptionist and all-around admin, turned in her chair and waved at the heir. "Hey, Jimmy! I've got a gazillion messages for you!"

Deuce Bainbridge, whose first name was actually Kingston,

stood and shook Jimmy's hand. As was typical for Deuce, the sports writer wore one of his team shirts. "Hey, man, that fire was taking one for the team." Jimmy wasn't sure what that meant, but he smiled anyway and gave a little wave.

Bill Trance, the managing editor of the TIN, and Sylvan Stonerich, the publisher, came out of their offices to greet their on-hold writer. Danny and Brian waved from their desks.

"How are you holding up?" Bill asked.

Jimmy glanced over at Brian. "We're struggling, but surviving. I dropped Mrs. Potts off over at that new store, Amanda Jane's Fashionable Clothing. She's really depressed, and I don't blame her. It's one thing to lose some things, but when everything you ever owned goes up in flames, it's hard to recover."

"No word from the fire inspectors yet?" Sylvan asked.

Jimmy and Brian both shook their heads.

A FIRE ENGINE RED COMMAND VEHICLE PARKED IN FRONT OF THE police department. Onlookers thought it seemed to be a specialized big SUV from an out-of-town fire department. The Twinkle fire department and the volunteers sure didn't have anything close to what this vehicle looked like.

A rather large man stepped out of the vehicle holding a notebook and headed to the front door of the police station. Butch, being Butch, puffed up his chest to look important when he spied the badge the man wore. Bureau of Alcohol, Tobacco, Firearms and Explosives (ATF) meant this guy was here to investigate Mrs. Potts' boarding house fire.

"May I help you?' Butch inquired.

"I'm here to see Chief Price." No pleasantries, just to the point.

Butch stammered a moment. "Sure. Let me call the chief." He actually texted Chief Price.

Chief Price stood and walked to the front. He offered his hand to the stranger. "Chief Kenton Price. How may I help you?"

"Rodney White, Certified ATF Fire Investigator. I'm here to determine what happened to the house that burned to the ground."

Chief Price nodded. "Come on back." He led Rodney White back to his office, invited him inside, offered him a chair, then closed the door. The chief took his seat behind his desk. "This was a terrible event. Mrs. Potts' boarding house was beloved by everyone who ever stayed there or visited. We're devastated."

"I'll find out what happened. Do you suspect arson?" Rodney asked.

"Well, we do have a little firebug, but he was in the Youth Detention Center over in Derrick at that time, so we can't blame this fire on him," Chief Price explained.

Rodney opened his notebook and pulled a pen out of his pocket. He jotted down information. "Who was living at the boarding house at the time of the fire?"

"Mrs. Bertha Potts, the proprietor. Jimmy Katz, the heir of the Katz-Diaz conglomerate, with his Amazon Parrot named Guppy, and his cat named Maddy. And Brian McKinley, Jimmy's friend, who moved here from the Big City and is a reporter for the TIN, our local newspaper."

Rodney jotted notes.

"Where are they staying now?" Rodney asked.

"They're over at the mansion with Jimmy's great aunt, Betty Katz-Diaz. She's the matriarch of Twinkle and Starlight County, and the richest person in the United States," the chief explained.

Rodney nodded as he scratched notes. "Would you be able to introduce me? I'd like to interview people to find out what they know."

"Sure. Let me text Jimmy to find out where they are. If I remember correctly, they were going shopping to replace clothes and necessities today." Chief Price sent a text to the heir. His phone dinged back a reply text.

I'm over at the TIN with Brian. Mrs. Potts is over at Amanda Jane's picking out clothes. Want us to come to the station?

The chief texted back a *yes.* He turned to the fire investigator. "They'll be here shortly. Would you like some coffee?"

Jimmy paid for Mrs. Potts' haul, set the bags into the back of the SUV, and they took off to the police station. When they arrived, Brian was getting out of his car. They all stared from the sidewalk at the command vehicle parked out front.

"Wow. I've never seen one of those vehicles before," Brian said. He snapped several photos with his phone.

"Me neither, but I've never written any stories about fires back in the Big City," Jimmy stated.

"Let's go meet this person," Mrs. Potts urged.

They went inside, greeted Butch as they bypassed his desk and headed to the chief's office.

"Let's go to the conference room," the chief said, before making introductions. They all followed the chief to the room with the big table. They stood in back of their chairs as the chief made the introductions.

"This is Rodney White. He's a Certified ATF Fire Investigator. This is Mrs. Potts, Jimmy Katz, and Brian McKinley." They all shook hands with the investigator, then took their seats.

Investigator White explained what he did, which was organized and systematic. "This investigation may take a while because of the complete destruction of the building. I start by evaluating the scene, looking for fire patterns and heat indicators to figure out the fire's origin before I take any photographs. You'll see me collecting evidence samples for analysis. If there were any eyewitnesses, I'll interview them, and neighbors."

Mrs. Potts sobbed when he finished.

Rodney reached across the table and patted her hand. "I'll find out what happened, Mrs. Potts. I promise."

All she could do was nod.

The notebook opened. The fire investigator asked who was where when they had left the house. He asked Mrs. Potts about the history of the building. Everything went neatly into the notebook.

CHAPTER SIX

Maddy climbed down several stairs, sat, and took in the rooms below. Guppy fluttered down and landed on the newel post.

Front door where everybody comes inside or goes out, Maddy observed. *There's those small rooms where people can read or visit with strangers.*

Guppy took off and headed toward the conservatory. *I'll be on this tree if you need me!*

Maddy descended the rest of the stairs and strolled through the large rooms. She jumped up on a surface here and there to study what was in the room. She was about to swat a dangling crystal from a lamp when Jenkins appeared.

"Careful of that, Maddy. That lamp costs more than anything else in the room," he informed her. "It's made with rare crystals, and the lamp is very old."

Maddy studied the lamp, crystal, and Jenkins. She chirped. *I'll be careful.*

"I know you'll be careful," Jenkins said with a twitch. The priceless lamp was from the late 1700s.

Maddy jumped to the floor and strolled out of the room, tail held high, looking to the right, then left at all the different things she had never seen before. She joined Guppy in the conservatory and wandered through the plants. They smelled good. She missed going outside to the round house, where she watched squirrels and birds.

Hey, Gup. I'm going to see Aunt Betty.

K. I'm going to take a nap.

Maddy entered the office and jumped onto the desk.

Betty was typing away on her computer. "Well, hello Maddy. Are you going to be my spellchecker?"

You've got that editing program, Aunt Betty. It checks your spelling and grammar as you type. I like watching it.

Betty's phone rang. She glanced at Caller ID and didn't recognize the number. She hit the speakerphone button. "Hello?"

"Mrs. Diaz? It's Walter Drumbrol. I had to get a new phone, and this is my new number."

"Typically, they replace the phone and you keep your phone number," Betty quantified.

"I was getting so many calls and texts from these political people, then the insurance people, that I wanted a new start. So, I'm calling everyone on my list to let them know the new number," Walter stated.

Betty thought about it. "Good idea, Walter. "How are things going?"

Walter Drumbrol was the mayor of Clem's Corner. He revered the time when he was a teenager when he had met Clemento Diaz, Betty's late husband. More than a decade later, Walter never imagined he would win every mayoral election in his town unopposed.

"People have been asking if we were ever going to do anything with the original little houses Clem built. They've been sitting there as tourist exhibits since the town grew, and we think they would be the ideal size for small shops or offices." Walter sounded a little nervous.

"That's a good idea, Walter. Maybe save one or two for the tourists so they can see what life looked like back then?" Betty suggested. "What type of shops came up in the discussions?"

"Well, you know there's not much here in Clem's Corner. Most people work out of their homes, and instead of building spaces, they like the idea of moving their businesses into one of Clem's shacks. So far, these are the businesses that would like to lease a shack. There's a realtor, a nail shop, a hairdressing salon, a lawyer, barbershop, candy store, and office supplies. The Wellness Center would like to open up a shop here."

"Clem's Corner would bring in people from Dime Water, Bridge, and all the way from Derrick." Betty took a moment. "Yes, let's set this in motion, Walter. The lease amount will be fifty dollars a month, and those businesses will be required to have insurance."

"Fifty dollars a month, Betty? We figured the businesses would pay at least four or five hundred in rent. This will encourage more businesses moving out of their homes and getting the attention they deserve." Walter's excitement was hard to contain.

"Maybe have one for the office of the Mayor and town business?" Betty knew Walter had conducted all the town's business out of his house, and it was only a thousand square feet to begin with. He and the wife were empty nesters now, but his home office took up what would have been the dining room.

"Oh, excellent idea! I can't wait to let everyone know this good news!" Walter's enthusiasm was gung ho.

Betty thought about the construction of the buildings her husband had built. "Those shacks might require plumbing and electrical updates. Let me send George and Jerry Potts to see what, if anything, should be upgraded. Might as well have cabling installed for internet and Wi-Fi while they're at it." Betty made notes in her daily To Do book.

"We never thought about that, but I wouldn't be surprised what needs to be done with the electrical and plumbing." Walter nodded to himself.

"I'll give George and Jerry your phone number," Betty said, then ended the call with a goodbye.

She turned to Maddy. "See, Maddy. There's no telling what comes through the phone and email."

Betty slid the desk drawer across the front open and perused the list of names and phone numbers taped to the drawer, then dialed the number.

"George? Oh, hi Jerry. The shacks in Clem's Corner are going to be turned into shops for the townspeople who have been operating their businesses out of their own houses. I'd like you to go up there, meet with Walter Drumbrol, the mayor, who's in charge of this initiative, and look these shacks over. They're old and will most likely require plumbing and electrical updates, as well as the internet."

Sounds like Clem's Corner will see some growth. I like this idea, Betty, Jerry exclaimed. *Who are we billing?*

"I'll set up purchase orders for each shack. Walter can tell you which shack is for what business, and the purchase orders will include the updates. You invoice me with the purchase order and address so I can keep track of the work to be done."

Okay. We'll detail the invoices as we always do on your projects.

"We have a plan. Let Walter know when you can be there."

That call ended. Betty decided against calling Jimmy, as he was likely consumed with the fire and its aftermath. She hit the number seven on the speed dial button on her phone.

"Sylvan?" Betty gave the publisher of the TIN the details of what was happening up in the town named for Clemento Diaz. "Wait for a couple of weeks before you send someone to talk with Walter. George and Jerry will need time to go

through twenty-five shacks and determine what the require-
ments are."

*Betty, this is wonderful news. I wonder why it took them so long to
come up with this idea?*

"They probably thought I'd want to keep those shacks as a
shrine to Clem. I told Walter to keep two shacks for the tourists
so that history wouldn't be lost. Walter will tell me the exact
number of businesses and which shack each one will be
assigned to, then I'll create the list of purchase orders for each
one."

I'll call Walter and get things rolling for an article.

"Excellent!" Betty ended that call. She hit the number for the
kitchen. "Annie, could you bring me an iced tea?" Betty glanced
over to Maddy. "And a smidgen of milk in a small dish for
Maddy?"

Mrrfft. Maddy rubbed against Betty's arm.

DANNY, BRIAN, CELEBRITY, AND RAMIREZ JOINED JIMMY AND
Mrs. Potts at the edge of the road where the boarding house
used to stand. They watched Rodney White walk the perimeter
while geared up in his personal protective outfit, taking
nonstop pictures.

"He must be roasting in that outfit," Celebrity announced.
The investigator wore protective turnout coveralls, gloves,
safety boots, safety goggles, a bright yellow helmet, and a
respirator.

"No worse than our fire department volunteers," Ramirez
stated.

Mrs. Potts sniffed back tears. "I want to see if anything
survived."

"You'll have to wait until the fire investigator finishes,"
Jimmy said as gently as he could. He, too, wanted to sift through

55

the debris. Brian just watched, not commenting on the tragedy in front of them.

They hung around for another ten minutes, then left the scene.

Rodney walked through the site to see the extent of the damage and to determine if any intact evidence remained. He recalled the picture of the house Jimmy drew that showed the layout. He made his way back to where the kitchen was located. The water heater had been in a closet and he needed to see if there were any electrical components left of it and the kitchen appliances.

A lot of fires started in the kitchen. The liquid could have boiled away in the roasting pan, causing the pan to smoke and ignite, despite Mrs. Potts setting the oven to 250 degrees while she went shopping.

As he went through the debris, Rodney looked for burn patterns and heat indicators. Because the building had burnt to the ground, there were no walls or ceilings to examine areas where charring would help identify where the fire began. There were a few partial 2 x 4 studs still standing, some only inches high, a couple two or three feet high.

Rodney examined the charred lumber closely, taking extensive photographs of all sides of the studs to determine burn patterns and heat indicators. He would later upload the evidence to create a computer modeling to simulate the fire and analyze how it may have spread.

Every once in a while, the fire investigator bent to study something from the ashes. He inspected the object, photographed its location, placed it in an evidence bag, and labeled the bag with a water-proof Sharpie.

TEN DAYS LATER, RODNEY WALKED INTO THE POLICE DEPARTMENT to speak to Chief Price. Butch called the chief, then waved the fire inspector back. Kenton stood and greeted the investigator. "Rodney, have you come to a conclusion about the fire?" Chief Price asked.

Rodney sat and jumped right into his findings. "Everything points to the stove. A pan on the stove ran out of water, which caused it to catch fire. I found evidence of the pan, which I believe contained peas. Believe it or not, I discovered charred peas among the rubble."

The chief kept his mouth shut while he processed what the fire investigator said. "Was this an accident, so we can sort out insurance and keep track of everything?"

The fire investigator nodded. "No doubt in my mind. What bothers me is Mrs. Potts only mentioned the roast in the oven. She didn't mention anything about a pot of water on the stovetop that contained peas. I discovered deep scratches on the front burner knob, but I don't know how or when that happened."

"I'll get this straightened out. Have you emailed me your report for our files?"

"Sure did." Rodney stood. They shook hands. "There's another fire investigation eighty miles from here, so I'd better head out."

The Chief sat, pondering the dilemma. He plopped his hat on his head and left his office. "Butch, I'm going over to the mansion. Be back later."

The *new* Butch documented the chief's plans in his virtual Day Timer. There were no more sticky notes across the edge of the counter for Stephanie, the dispatcher, to collect. Butch's attention to details put others to shame now. He was still in classes at the community college. The chief's threat had opened a new world to him and he could not get enough of technology.

THE CRUISER PULLED UP IN THE CIRCULAR DRIVEWAY OF THE mansion. Chief Price wasn't sure what to expect when he presented the fire investigator's findings. The chief rang the doorbell and Jenkins, ever the professional, opened the door and greeted the chief.

"Is Mrs. Potts, Jimmy, and Brian here? I need to see them," the chief stated.

Jenkins led the chief to a sitting room while he went to check the status of the guests. He returned shortly with Mrs. Potts on his heels.

"Brian will be here shortly. He's just leaving the TIN," Jenkins said as Jimmy tromped down the stairs. "Why don't we settle you in the conference room? Mrs. Diaz might want to attend this meeting."

Jenkins led the way, showed them into the room, then he went to fetch Betty. As the matriarch left her office, the front door opened and Brian called out. "I'm here! Where is everyone?"

Jenkins popped out of the conference room and gathered Brian. Once they were settled, Jenkins went about his business and the chief started.

"The fire inspector stopped by this morning to give me his findings on the fire."

Not a peep interrupted the chief.

"He classified the fire as an accident. From his investigation, he determined that the fire began when the water in the pot on the stove boiled out, which caused the pan to burn. Burning parts of the pan fell to the floor and spread the fire. He said there were some charred peas among the rubble, and deep scratches on the knob for the front burner."

Mrs. Potts looked stricken. "The stovetop wasn't turned on!"

Mrs. Potts cried. "Yes, the pan of peas was on the stove, but I wouldn't have started them until the roast was done."

Brian had a moment. "The peas!" He turned to Mrs. Potts. "Guppy wanted more peas, remember?"

"Oh, lord!" Mrs. Potts gasped out. "After we left for the store, Guppy must have flown to the stove and landed on the knob. It's all my fault for not putting a lid on the pan!"

"Bertha, even if you had a lid on the pan, Guppy knew the peas were in the pan, and his feet turned the burner on." Betty announced. "It was an accident. Luckily, no one—human or animals, were hurt or killed."

Jimmy appeared devastated. To find out his parrot caused the fire was almost too much to bear "This is my responsibility. I'll hire an architect to go over the original house plans and have things added, like the butler's pantry. We'll all sit down and think about what would be ideal."

"You need to explain to the animals the stove is off limits," Betty suggested. "Make a list of dangerous things inside a house. We know they understand what you tell them, otherwise Guppy would not have rescued himself and Maddy in the basket."

Jimmy stared down Brian. "Please don't write that Guppy started the fire. It's best to list it as an accident and leave it at that."

Brian's head bobbed. He understood the ramifications of the mess. "Don't worry. I wouldn't do that to you... us."

CHAPTER SEVEN

J immy climbed the stairs as if he were going to the arena to face the lions. He wasn't sure what to say to Maddy and Guppy. He didn't know if animals suffered from guilt for their actions. Jimmy sat on the next to the top stair and called Celebrity.

Hey, the love of my life, how's it going?

"Oh, Celeb. We just found out that Guppy started the fire." Jimmy couldn't hold back the tears.

I'm on my way!

The line went dead. Jimmy didn't get up. He needed to get his head straight before facing the animals. The front door opened and Celebrity crept in, wondering where Jenkins was. She saw Jimmy on the stairs and bounded up them.

Celebrity embraced him tightly and let him sob quietly. "How did you come to this conclusion?"

"The fire investigator said the fire started at the stove with a pan of peas. Mrs. Potts didn't have the stove burner on, but Guppy wanted more peas. I'm pretty sure he flew over to the stove and landed on the knob. It most likely didn't ignite the burner until he finished getting his peas and then flew away again."

"What should I do? I can't very well punish him. Betty said to tell them the stove is off limits," Jimmy recalled.

"That's good advice. They can understand that, especially if you include the word *dangerous*. Maybe we should drive them over to the gazebo and talk about the fire. Maybe even walk around the wreckage," Celebrity suggested.

"We all want to go over there and see if we can find anything that survived the fire," Jimmy shared. "We should do that now, or soon, so the cleanup can begin."

Celebrity grabbed his hand. "Come on, let's go see Mrs. Potts. Is Brian here?"

"I'm not sure if Brian is here or went back to the TIN."

They stopped at the conference room, which they found empty, and continued on to Mrs. Potts' suite. They found the landlady and Brian staring at each other across the chairs.

Celebrity tapped on the open doorway. "Hey, let's go over to the fire site and see if there's anything to salvage. We're going to bring the animals to the gazebo."

"Good idea," Mrs. Potts said.

"Yeah, let's do this," Brian concurred.

"We'll meet you there," Jimmy said. He and Celebrity climbed the stairs and entered his suite of rooms. Guppy was on his new tree spying on squirrels, and Maddy was curled on the sofa. He whispered to Celebrity.

Celebrity announced, "Who wants to go to the gazebo?"

That brought Maddy's head up fast, and Guppy let loose an ear-piercing shriek. Jimmy went in search of the basket. He put one of the kitchen towels on the bottom of the basket and set it on the table. He grabbed another for his arm. "All aboard the gazebo express!"

Maddy sprang off the sofa and leapt into the basket.

Celebrity picked up the basket while Jimmy offered his arm to Guppy.

"Hang on." Jimmy coaxed. "We have to go in the car and drive over to where we used to live."

Since Guppy didn't have a travel cage yet, Jimmy was stumped about how to transport his parrot safely. "We have to stop at the Wham and see if they have a cage. I haven't found him a sleeping cage yet either."

They stared at the animals when they reached the car.

"Why don't I use the towel on my arm and hold onto the door," Celebrity suggested. "Maddy can sit in my lap, and Guppy on my arm."

"Okay, we can try that, but he's strong, and I don't want him to hurt your arm," Jimmy stated.

"Let's just give it a try. I'll use both towels." Celebrity went to the passenger side of Jimmy's Honda CRV, opened the back door and set the basket on the seat. "Maddy, hop out and wait for me to get in the front seat. I need your towel."

Maddy followed instructions. Celebrity grabbed the towel from the basket and sat in the front seat. She draped the towel over her right arm. Jimmy urged his parrot to climb onto Celebrity's arm, then he saw the dilemma. There would only be one towel protecting her.

"Look, get in the car and let's get over to the Wham-A-Rama!" Celebrity snapped.

With a sheepish expression, Jimmy did just that. He drove slowly to the store and parked. He and Celebrity got out, and she transferred the bird to Jimmy's arm. The second towel went back into the basket and Maddy hopped in. Celebrity wrapped her arms around the base of the basket instead of holding it by the handle. She didn't want any accidents to happen on her watch.

"We're going shopping for your travel cage and a sleeping

cage, Guppy. I want you two to behave yourselves inside. Understand?"

Maddy chirped, and Guppy squawked.

Jimmy approached the door of the store, and the doors slid back, allowing them to enter. People oohed and aahed over the animals as they made their way back to the pet department.

They wandered over to the bird section. Jimmy found one cage that looked like the right size. A clerk approached.

"Do you mind if my bird steps inside this cage to see if it's the right size for him?" Jimmy asked.

"Oh, no problem. You wouldn't believe what people get into over here." The clerk smirked.

Jimmy held his arm out with Guppy. "Gup, see if you like this cage."

Guppy stuck his head inside the cage. He put one foot forward and gripped the wooden rail with his claws, then hauled himself inside. He looked around and seemed happy with the cage.

"Do you have another one like this? I need a sleeping cage and a traveling cage," Jimmy asked.

"Let me check," the kid said. He checked all the boxes above the shelves and didn't find one. "I'll go in the back and see if we have others there. Be right back."

The kid took off. Jimmy and Celebrity looked at other supplies. "Better get some litter since we don't know what your aunt does with the newspaper."

"Have to get newspaper for the floor by his tree," Jimmy stated.

The store clerk returned empty-handed. "That's the only one we have. You can go online and order one. Want me to grab a cart for you?"

"Oh, that would be great. I need to get some litter, a cage cover, bowl attachments, and seeds."

They piled everything into the store cart and headed toward the front to pay when Celebrity had a thought.

"We should get face masks like those we used for Covid, and something to cover our shoes so they don't get wrecked going through the ashes."

"Oh, good idea. Let's go over to the pharmacy area for the masks. I'm not sure about the shoe covers. We may have to use plastic bags and rubber bands to hold them up," Jimmy figured. They found the masks, then asked a clerk about the shoe covers. He suggested Jimmy and Celebrity should check out the sporting goods area, but after searching everywhere, then checking out the shoe department, they gave up.

Jimmy paid at the register and they all returned to the car. Jimmy opened a bag of litter, grabbed a big handful, and spread it on the bottom of the cage. "There you go, Guppy. We'll have to order another cage online, but you can use this one for sleep and travel."

They drove over to the burn site, where they saw Mrs. Potts and Brian walking around the perimeter. Jimmy and Celebrity got out of the car. Jimmy held his arm out so Guppy could step out of the new cage onto his arm.

Guppy was confused. "Where's the house?"

Jimmy sighed deeply. "The house caught fire and burned to the ground. There's no house left. We will have to build a new house." He knew they understood because they stared at him with strange expressions he had never seen before. "Let's go to the gazebo. You can watch squirrels while Daddy and Celebrity walk with Brian and Mrs. Potts."

As they walked to the gazebo, Guppy stretched his neck and kept looking at where the house used to be.

"Here you go. We'll be back in a little while," Jimmy explained. He and Celebrity donned their face masks and used the Wham-A-Rama plastic shopping bags to cover their shoes.

Celebrity figured out how to use the bag handles to tie the bags around their ankles.

Celebrity whispered to Jimmy. "Did you see how upset Guppy was?"

"Was he upset or confused? It's hard to tell." Jimmy didn't notice anything from Maddy.

They headed over to the charred ground, where Mrs. Potts and Brian shuffled about.

"Oh, good, you figured out what to cover your shoes with. We bought face masks. Do you need one? We have extras." Celebrity asked. "It's not a good idea to be breathing in the smell of ash. Tiny particles can get lodged in your lungs."

"I'll take a mask," Mrs. Potts said.

"Me too," Brian added.

Celebrity returned to the CRV, grabbed two more masks and handed them out. "Any luck finding anything?"

Brian shook his head. "Everything's pretty well disintegrated. I was hoping something was salvageable, but so far, I haven't seen anything but ashes."

"Think of how hot it had to be for the entire house to collapse," Jimmy stated.

They wandered around some more, then gave up, stomping the ash off their foot baggies on the grass, then yanking them off. Celebrity pulled an unused bag out of her pocket and stuffed the foot baggies inside and tied the bag closed.

"Let's get someone to clean up the debris, then the four of us can review the house plans and make improvements." Jimmy was ready to get started. "It can take around six months to rebuild."

"Ask Jerry and George if they do this type of work, or if they can recommend someone," Mrs. Potts suggested.

"Good idea," Brian said. He nudged Jimmy. "Give them a call."

EARTH HAULERS, INC. MET JIMMY AND MRS. POTTS AT THE boarding house site the next day. Through their discussions, Mrs. Potts agreed to have the foundation removed because the new boarding house would be larger, and they felt that the fire had compromised the current slab.

The Earth Hauler people unloaded equipment while a huge commercial dumpster was settled at the edge of the property. They explained the cleanup would begin with the removal process that same day. Jimmy told them to call him after they finished, so he could pay their invoice.

They returned to the mansion to sit down with the house plans Jimmy had downloaded from the internet. He went over to the office supply store with a thumb drive and had them print out the plans on plotter paper. The clerk rolled up the plans, stuck them in a mailing tube, and Jimmy cashed out.

"Mrs. Potts, are you ready to look at the plans and make changes to the new place?" Jimmy asked when he tapped on the open door to her suite.

His former landlady popped out of her chair. "Let's go into that conference room so we can spread out. We'll need some colored highlighters. Do you think Betty has extras?"

"I'll ask Jenkins. I know my aunt has an office supply closet around here somewhere," Jimmy recalled.

Mrs. Potts headed to the conference room while Jimmy hunted down Jenkins. The butler showed Jimmy the supply closet, a mini office supply store, that contained everything he could think of that they would need to mark up the house plans.

Jimmy and Mrs. Potts studied the house plans.

"All the closets need to be bigger, and the kitchen needs more cabinets," Mrs. Potts decided.

"Would you want one of those kitchen islands?" Jimmy asked.

"If the kitchen is big enough, an island would be great along with bar stools. But I will always want a kitchen table." Mrs. Potts was adamant.

"A butler's pantry will give you more shelf space for canned goods, paper products, and large pots and cooking equipment. There should be a half-bath somewhere off the kitchen, or in the butler's pantry." Jimmy scrutinized the plans.

"If I'm going to go all out on the new house, I'd like a fireplace in the living room for when it's cold. And, before you say anything, for me, it gets cold here in the winter. It would be nice to have a fire," Mrs. Potts explained.

They studied every room of the house on the old plans and made notations of what new features they wanted.

CHAPTER EIGHT

Celebrity looked over the house plans after Jimmy and Mrs. Potts marked them up to show what they wanted in a new house.

"Ask my dad. Before he joined the empire, he was an architect. He figured he couldn't support himself at that, so when he and my mother got together, he jumped aboard the Katz-Diaz train."

"He was an architect? Wow! I wonder if he would have time to update these plans?" Jimmy asked.

"Let's ask. Grab the plans and we can head to the office," Celebrity instructed.

"The office? I never knew there were offices in Twinkle. I figured everyone in the empire worked from home." Jimmy was baffled.

Celebrity drove them downtown to a four-story office building down the street from the TIN.

"I'll be darned," Jimmy said, "All this time and I never even gave that building a second thought. Are you sure it's okay to barge in without an appointment?" All this time and I never even gave that building a second thought. You sure it's okay to barge in without an appointment?" Jimmy asked.

Celebrity gave Jimmy *a look*. "Honestly, it's my mother and father! You think they'd turn away their only kid?"

"Well, when you put it that way..."

Celebrity parked on the street, and they entered the building. She steered them to the elevator, and they rode up to the top floor. When the elevator doors opened, the glass wall in front of them sported *World-Wide Katz-Diaz Enterprises* in bold letters. Celebrity grabbed the door handle, and they walked inside. She greeted the receptionist with a *hi* and a wave, and didn't stop.

There were two corner offices among a wide hallway of doors. Some closed, others open with people busy at work. Celebrity veered to the corner office on the right, where they found her father reading one of several newspapers stacked on his desk.

"Hey, dad!" Celebrity greeted.

"Well, hello little girl... and hello, Jimmy! What brings you two my way?" Cal asked.

"Daddy, I'm sure you've heard about Mrs. Potts' boarding house burning down to the ground, right?" Celebrity asked.

Calvin Masters shook his head. "That was very sad, indeed. I take it everyone is staying at the mansion?"

Jimmy nodded. "We are grateful for Aunt Betty putting us up. It will take a while to rebuild the house."

Celebrity butted in. "That's why we're here, dad. Would you be able to look over the old house plans and redraw them to include what Mrs. Potts and Jimmy noted?" Celebrity nudged Jimmy. He handed over the mailing tube to Calvin.

"Let's see what you've got." Cal removed the plans from the tube. He re-rolled them in the opposite direction to get them to lie flat, then spread them out on his desk. He scrutinized the box in the lower right corner and tapped it. "I know for a fact the original architect who drew these passed away several years ago. Unless he left the files somewhere, these plans would have to be redrawn from scratch."

"Would you have time to do that?" Celebrity asked. "It's going to take several months to rebuild, and Mrs. Potts is so depressed about losing everything."

Cal studied the plans. "Yeah, I can do this. It will take me two or three weeks."

Jimmy let out a breath he didn't realize he was holding. "Oh, thank you so much, Cal!"

"Once I'm finished, I'll hook you up with a builder that can do the job and follow the plans to the exact specs without any shortcuts." Cal stated. "There's not many builders I trust. Many want to cut corners to line their own pockets."

"Let's go tell Mrs. Potts. This should lift her spirits," Jimmy said.

Celebrity steered them over to the mansion and parked. Jenkins greeted them at the door.

"Would you like some lunch while you're here?" Jenkins asked.

"Oh, that would be great," Jimmy said. "We're going to see Mrs. Potts, then we'll head to the dining room."

Jimmy and Celebrity went in search of Mrs. Potts, and found her in her suite reading. He tapped on her open doorframe.

"Hey, Mrs. Potts. We bring good news!" Jimmy announced.

Jimmy's landlady stuck her index card in the book she was reading and turned to her former tenant. "I'm ready for good news."

He and Celebrity told her about Celeb's father tackling the drawings along with a referral for a builder.

"Oh, that's wonderful! Bless his heart!" Mrs. Potts exclaimed.

Her whole countenance perked up with the news amid a few sniffles.

"Let's grab some lunch." Jimmy and Celebrity led Mrs. Potts to the dining room.

THE ONLY SILVER LINING OF THE DISASTER WAS THAT JIMMY'S meetings with the DDS got suspended. Betty had alerted Pete to postpone the sessions until she determined her great nephew had his head clear. Betty was certain that Bertha was nowhere near recovered from losing everything, and that both Jimmy and Brian were on edge.

While Maddy Zoomed with aunt Betty, and Guppy sang gaily in the tree in the conservatory, Jimmy set up the iPad on the floor in front of the TV, where he had placed tape. He eyeballed the cameras on the ceiling and determined they were perfectly aligned.

Jimmy placed a new yellow #2 pencil beside the iPad, that came from a new package of 40 pencils. He almost forgot the mouse and its pad, and the TV remote.

Once he determined everything was in place, Jimmy trotted down the stairs and checked in with his great aunt and his pets. Guppy was in a tree happy as can be. Jimmy went to his aunt's office.

"Everything okay here?" Jimmy asked. Maddy perched on the back of Betty's chair, looking over her shoulder at everything she typed.

Betty guffawed. "Your cat is very opinionated. Everyone I meet with online enjoys meeting her and listening to her responses. Sometimes it sounds like she agrees with something, and other times when she doesn't, like when she hisses at someone's suggestions." Betty shook her head. "I truly wish I understood the cat language! I could possibly get some advice from Maddy.

Maddy meowed.

"Maddy, why don't you go upstairs and take a nap," Jimmy suggested. He wanted her to discover her very own iPad.

She tried to stretch while on the back of Betty's chair, but discovered there wasn't room to do that, so she hopped onto the desk, stretched, then jumped down to the floor. Jimmy watched as she left the office and headed toward the stairs. He leaned close to his great aunt.

"I set up her iPad," he whispered.

Betty's eyes grew wide. "I can't wait to see what she does next."

"I'm going to go see the chief, then I'll stop in at the TIN," Jimmy whispered, then caught himself and returned to his regular voice.

"See you later," his great aunt said, then pulled up her calendar.

JIMMY PARKED THE HONDA CRV IN A PARKING PLACE IN FRONT OF the police station. He breezed past Butch at the front desk and tapped on the Chief's open door.

"Before you sit down, tell me what's going on with my computer." Chief Price stood and moved aside.

"What's it doing... or not doing?" Jimmy asked.

"Something screwy is going on. When I type in my document, some of the words disappear."

Jimmy sat in the Chief's chair. He grabbed the mouse and highlighted the paragraph. Then he clicked on the font color and chose the standard black color. All the words showed up. "You had some words changed to white, so they looked invisible."

"Huh. I wonder how that happened?" The chief seemed stymied.

"Either you did it, or you have a ghost that plays tricks on you," Jimmy suggested.

"Well, since I don't believe in ghosts, I don't know how or when I did that."

Jimmy took a seat in front of the desk, and the chief settled into his chair. He saved the file.

"Maddy has her own iPad," Jimmy whispered as he looked through the open door to see if anyone heard him.

"Won't that clue her in that you're on to her?" the Chief asked.

"Think about it. She must already know that since she has texted me in the past. I figured having her own device was better than her having to depend on mine. I hope she can figure out how to use it." Jimmy furrowed his brow in thought.

"Don't worry about that. If you leave your laptop open, like you used to, she'll most likely Google instructions for the iPad," Chief Price suggested.

Jimmy nodded. "Instead of leaving scraps of paper with people's email addresses and phone numbers, I'll print a contact list. If she sees that, maybe she'll find it on my computer and email it to herself?"

Chief Price shook his head, mystified. "There's no telling what that smart cat will do next, but if she has her own computer, I don't see her using yours. Just type it up, print it and leave it on the desk."

Jimmy chortled as he stood. "I'm going to drop by the TIN."

"Thanks for helping me with my doc." Chief Price mock saluted, then returned his eyes to his document.

MEATY SAT IN FRONT OF HIS LAPTOP UPSTAIRS IN THE SECURITY office at the Foo. He tapped his fingers on the desk while thinking through a question. His laptop monitor showed Jimmy's apartment at the mansion from one of the secret cameras. Meaty fixed his gaze on the new iPad on the floor. After several minutes of waiting to see Maddy discover the iPad, he gave up and exited the camera system.

He swiveled around to the Foo computer just in time to see a cashier's eyes dart around while she stuffed a bill into her pocket. This called for delicate interference. He called his uncle Brink, the manager.

"Uncle Brink, Trinity just pocketed some cash."

"WHAT?" Brink sputtered a moment. "Every once in a while, her cash drawer comes up short. She convinced me she must have given the wrong bill out in change to a customer. You're security, come do your job."

Meaty hated this part of his security work. Having to catch a thief he's known for a while. He knew his uncle would end up firing the woman. There were just too many shortages to give someone another chance. He quietly descended the stairs and headed toward the checkout stations at the front of the store.

Meaty grabbed a *This Lane Closed* sign and stuck it on the end of Trinity's checkout lane so no one else would get in line behind the current customer.

Uncle Brink commandeered Misty Miles from the office to replace Trinity, along with a new cash drawer that would exchange Trinity's drawer when the customer checked out.

It was unusual to change cashiers in the middle of their transaction with a customer, but Brink let Meaty step in and whisper to the cashier.

"Trinity, Misty will take over. Cameras caught you taking money from the drawer and pocketing it." He guided her out of the small space by the elbow.

Trinity appeared alarmed at first, but her face slumped,

knowing that her game of stealing was up. Brink had Misty take over the rest of the customer's sale, apologizing for the short delay.

As soon as Misty bagged the customer's goods and put them in the shopping cart, she signed Trinity out and swapped out the cash drawers. Brink carried Trinity's cash drawer to the office and set it on his desk. He separated the checks from the bills, set the coupons aside, and counted every penny in the drawer while Trinity looked on with Meaty blocking the exit.

After each bill denomination total, Brink entered the sum into the calculator. All the change was counted and entered into the calculator. Brink totaled up the coupons. What it all boiled down to was the discovery of $47 missing from the till.

Meaty stood in front of Trinity. He looked the part of the security professional. "Please empty your pockets on the desk."

Trinity changed her demeanor. "I don't have to do anything you say!"

Brink chimed in. "Call the police, Meaty. Let them..."

"No!" Trinity dug into her pockets and pulled out every single item, including a paperclip, a cough drop, a crumbled tissue, loose change, and bills in different denominations.

Brink separated her personal property from the money. He counted. He discovered $2.14 over the missing cash drawer amount. Brink set that money aside with Trinity's personal property. Then he skewered her with a hostile look.

"Why? You've worked here for several years. Why steal now?"

He didn't expect to hear what she said.

"It just seemed so easy..."

"You're fired. Do not expect a work reference." He pulled up a file on his computer. Brink typed in her name and details, then printed the form. He slid the printout across the desk to Trinity, along with a pen. "Sign the termination form."

She sniffed back tears as she picked up the pen, signed and dated the form, then stood.

Brink scanned in the signed document and printed out a copy for his now former employee.

"Take your belongings." Brink said.

Trinity pocketed her little pile of possessions that came out of her pockets.

"Meaty, please escort Trinity to her locker, then out of the store."

Several minutes later, Meaty joined his uncle in the office.

"If she had said she was having difficult times, or something was wrong at home, I would have forgiven her. But to tell us it was so easy to steal—that's unforgivable."

Meaty nodded. His uncle was upset and he couldn't blame him. The audacity for that cashier to be so callous.

Brink said, "Good job, Meaty. I hope we never have to go through that again."

"Everyone up front saw Misty taking over, and me escorting Trinity out of the store. They know what that's about. If there was any other secret thieving going on, I'll bet it stops."

CHAPTER NINE

Jimmy entered the employee door of the TIN from the back parking lot. He was still dizzy from the shock of the fire and having to live in the mansion until the boarding house insurance settlement came through. Then the house could be rebuilt. He tapped on Bill Trance's open door. The managing editor gleefully circled mistakes in out-of-town newspapers with his trusty red marker.

"Hey, Jimmy. Come in and have a seat. How are things going?"

Jimmy slipped into a chair in front of the desk. "Better. Cal Masters is redrawing the boarding house architecture plans and adding the things Mrs. Potts would like to include."

"Oh, that's wonderful. I forgot he used to be an architect." Bill set his red marker aside and folded his hands on the desk surface and zeroed in on Jimmy's eyes. "How are you doing mentally? Do you think any of you would benefit from psychotherapy? You've all experienced the type of loss few people do."

Jimmy nodded. "Maybe we'd benefit from that. I'll ask Mrs. Potts and Brian tonight."

"Have you picked up your messages from Milly? They keep piling up, so you'd better return calls." Bill hated to be stern with Jimmy, but he realized he needed a boost to get his head back in the journalism game.

Jimmy shook his head. "I forgot all about that when I was here last." He stood. "I'll get on that right now." He left Bill's office and headed up to Milly's desk.

"Hey, Milly. I'm sorry I didn't pick up the messages the other day. My head wasn't on straight."

"Totally understandable." Milly reached for a clipped stack of pink message notes. "Here's what I've done. Multiple calls got numbered and dated, then trashed except for notes. People can be nuisances."

Jimmy took the messages. "Wow, there's a bunch. Thanks for being my personal assistant! I'll start returning calls today."

"No problem. That's why my desk is at the door. I'm the first line of defense!" Milly gave a toothy smile.

Jimmy headed over to his desk. All the other reporters were out interviewing people to fill up the next edition of the paper. He started with the oldest message first. "Hi, Mrs. Murphy. It's Jimmy Katz returning your call. Oh, thank you for your kind offer, but we're staying with my great aunt over at the mansion."

The next call was to Delia's Flower Shop. "Oh, Delia, Mrs. Potts would love that. Thanks for being so kind. Send the flowers over to Betty Diaz's mansion. That's where we're staying."

Mark Gulliford, the owner of the Tin Man blacksmith shop, was next. *Jimmy, tell Mrs. Potts I'll create a fancy weathervane for the new house when it's built.*

"Mark, that's a wonderful gesture. That will perk up Mrs. Potts."

Jimmy returned ten more calls with more or less the same messages. People offering goods and services, their kindness shining through. The last call was to the Twinkle Stars Gazette, the high school paper. He groaned, remembering the embarrassing photo they printed last year showing his mismatched socks. Hector and Jorge had a meltdown when they saw the photo on the front page of the school paper.

Jimmy gritted his teeth and placed the call. After four rings, someone answered in a noisy background.

"Hello?" Jimmy hollered while cupping the desk phone. "This is Jimmy Katz returning your call. Do you want to call me back from a quieter place?" He couldn't hear anything from whatever was going on in the background, so he disconnected the call. "They'll call back if it's important."

Jimmy left the TIN and drove over to Moses' DoJo. It had been weeks since his last self-defense session, and he knew his very distant cousin would toss him around like a feather blowing up against a tree in the wind. He parked his trusty Honda and went inside.

Jimmy found Moses sitting on a matt in a meditative pose. He quietly sat on a bench and waited for him to "come around." After several quiet moments, Moses stood, stretched, and turned around to see who had entered the building.

"Jimmy! Are you doing okay? I saw the fire video on the TINs website."

The heir nodded.

Moses regarded his student. He recognized the trauma. "Why don't you come back tomorrow and we can start your recovery with workouts?"

"Yeah, I think that will help. Poor Mrs. Potts, she's devastated. Celebrity's father is creating the new house plans with some updates. Let's face facts. It's going to be months before we'll have a house to move into, then there's replacing everything we can recall that we lost." Jimmy stopped. He realized he was rambling, but he couldn't shake the merry-go-round of words.

"Why don't you set up an appointment with Mrs. Trumble?" Moses suggested.

"Who's that?" Jimmy never heard the name Trumble before.

"She's my therapist. You'll like her."

"A couple of people suggested we might need psychotherapy." Jimmy wasn't against therapy, he had never experienced it.

"She's a couple of doors down from the TIN. Stop in and make an appointment. Maybe let Mrs. Potts and your friend Brian know about her."

"Okay. I'll go right now. Maybe she will have a vacant spot..." Jimmy left the dojo, his head in a mist.

Moses pulled his phone out of his pocket and placed a call. "Mrs. Trumble? I'm sending Jimmy Katz your way. He's in desperate need of your services from the fire."

JIMMY PARKED IN FRONT OF THE THERAPIST'S OFFICE AND SAT IN his car for a second. He looked at the yellow door of the place and forced himself out of his Honda, and went inside.

"Hi, I don't have an appointment. Can you tell me when Mrs. Trumble has an open spot on her calendar?"

The receptionist, a young man in his early thirties dressed in a suit and tie, greeted him. "Welcome! We've just had a cancellation – measles!" Oren, from the nameplate on his desk, shuddered. "I thought measles had been obliterated?" He moved the mouse and opened the calendar. "What's your name? I'll let Mrs. Trumble know you're here."

"Jimmy Katz. Yeah, I didn't realize measles was still around."

"Why don't you take a seat. It should only be a minute."

Oren texted his boss. Before Jimmy could grab a current magazine from the coffee table, the inner door opened and an elderly woman greeted him.

"Jimmy? I'm Agatha Trumble. Won't you come in?" She

moved a lot quicker than Jimmy expected, which made him rush to catch up with her.

They entered an inner space that was much like he expected it to look like, with the exception of a treadmill and a stationary recumbent bike.

Agatha gestured at an assortment of chairs, a sofa, and the exercise equipment. "Sit wherever you feel most comfortable. You can change your mind at any time." She winked at him.

He chose a wing-back chair in a nice gold-colored upholstery. It was super comfortable.

"How can I help you today, Jimmy?"

He stammered and stuttered, then blurted out what had been tormenting him. "My bird and cat were almost killed in the house fire. We've lost everything—Mrs. Potts, Brian and myself. Mrs. Potts lost all her memorable possessions. We were just told by the fire investigator that Guppy, my parrot, was responsible for turning the knob on the stove that started the fire."

Jimmy sat there staring at Mrs. Trumble with wide eyes.

"That is quite a lot for a body and brain to assimilate. I understand that the three of you and your pets are staying with Betty at the mansion?"

He nodded, his words spent.

"Jimmy, all you can do now is to move forward. It won't do you any good to dwell on the *what if's*. Your pets made it out of the fire alive. For you, that is the most important thing. Those are some smart little creatures from what I saw in the videos on the TINs website."

"There was a fire in our neighborhood and that made me scared. I explained the dangers to them—"

"You talked to your animals, and they understood you?" Mrs. Trumble tried hard not to look perplexed.

"They're very smart from watching children's programs on TV. They seem to understand more than people give them credit for." Jimmy made himself stop before he got into secret information.

"Well, your parrot—Guppy, did you say his name was?"

Jimmy nodded.

"Your bird screaming out *Fire* while flying down the street was a sight I'm sure the whole town will never forget. Your animals saved themselves. But now you have to move forward. The investigation is over. Flush the guilt down that proverbial toilet because you can't do anything about what Guppy did. He's an animal, and even though he's smarter than the average parrot, you can't hold him responsible for the fire. Get a squirt bottle to teach him not to go near dangerous things."

Jimmy nodded. He agreed, but still had the *what if's* zooming around inside his head.

Mrs. Trumble read the expression on his face. She knew it would take some convincing before he stopped blaming himself for the fire.

"Mrs. Potts needs to decide what to do... rebuild or move somewhere else, so you and Brian can make plans."

"Oh, we're rebuilding. Cal Masters is updating the house plans, and he knows the best builders."

"Excellent! Now you can order things you want for your new space. Rent some storage units for the three of you and start shopping."

"Yeah, I thought about that. I'll talk to Brian and Mrs. Potts and see if they want to pick things out. I don't know how long it will take the insurance company to pay our claims." Jimmy hadn't received a response to his claim, and he knew Mrs. Potts hadn't either. He'd have to check with Brian.

"Has the adjuster contacted Mrs. Potts about the house claim? That would come first, then the homeowners claims for personal possessions," Mrs. Trumble stated.

Jimmy thought for a moment. "I'm not sure if anyone other

than the fire investigator has contacted my landlady. I'll ask when I go home."

"Well, now. You have some things to think about, and to talk about with your roommates. Why don't we get together next week around this time? You can stop at the front desk and have Oren set up an appointment." Mrs. Trumble stood.

Jimmy stood. He shook the therapist's hand. "Thanks, Mrs. Trumble. I feel a lot better for having talked with you. I'll see you next week." He stopped at the front desk and set up his appointment. Oren promised to text him a reminder an hour ahead of the appointment, which would give Jimmy time to make any adjustments to his day.

He drove back to the mansion and let himself in, then went in search of his landlady. Jimmy found her in her suite, and worried about her turning into a recluse.

"Hey, Mrs. Potts. I just had a session with Mrs. Trumble. Moses recommended her, and she helped me out of my funk. Why don't you make an appointment with her?"

"I've never met her, but I have heard nice things about her." Mrs. Potts looked thoughtful.

"By any chance, has the insurance adjuster contacted you about the house insurance? The contents should be under the homeowners policy. I had renter's insurance, but I haven't heard from anyone about my claim." Jimmy tried to remember everything Mrs. Trumble suggested.

"No, I haven't heard from anyone other than that fire investigator. I'd better call them and see where they are with the claim."

"Mrs. Trumble said we should rent some storage units for when we order furnishings and other things for the new place. I think that's a good idea. What about you?"

"Well, the only problem I see is if something I've ordered doesn't fit in with the new place, or I don't like something about it." Mrs. Potts tapped her lips with a pencil. "Most places have a specific return timeframe."

"I guess we could hold off until the new house is framed. Everything in the interior should go pretty fast. If you look at appliances for your kitchen, then you can give the exact manufacturer measurements to Cal to make sure they're going to fit in their spaces."

Mrs. Potts wore a daydream expression on her face. "I have always wanted one of those refrigerator drawers! Wouldn't it be fantastic to have the produce on hand where you need it? Oh, Jimmy, this is a good idea!"

"Give Cal a call and tell him so he can work it into the kitchen plan." Jimmy was happy to see his landlady uplifted. "Brian hasn't really talked about the fire. I think he's more traumatized than he's letting on."

"Give him a nudge to make an appointment with Mrs. Trumble. He needs to open up about his losses and how he is handling —or not handling his emotions." Mrs. Potts became concerned for Brian. "I'll be able to start shopping for my kitchenware and linens as soon as the insurance money shows up."

MADDY CIRCLED THE IPAD ON THE FLOOR NEAR HER CUSHION, sniffing. "Is this a computer, Guppy?"

The parrot sat on his new fake tree. "Looks like one."

Maddy studied it for a moment. A keyboard was attached to the iPad. She reached out a paw and touched the keyboard, and the monitor came alive. "Look, Guppy!"

Maddy snatched up the brand-new yellow pencil in her ultra-strong jaws and whacked the search area. "Oohh, what should we look up, Gup?"

"Fires! Everyone is so sad."

Maddy went about whacking keys and moving from one side of the keyboard to the other. She typed in letters to form a word and hitting the space bar to enter another word. She finally had *house fire* typed in, then hit the search key.

Guppy fluttered to the floor and balanced on Maddy's cushion. His talons gripped the pillow. He and Maddy stared at the list of items associated with a house fire.

- What is the #1 cause of house fires?
- What is the definition of house fire?
- How would a house fire start?
- What should we do if the house is on fire?
- Structure fire death toll
- What are some of the deadliest structure fires?
- What causes a structure fire?
- What to do after a house fire?

"Let's begin at the top of the list," Maddy suggested as she clicked on the first bullet.

"Look! Cooking is number one! The stove is dangerous!" Guppy gawked. He recalled scooping peas into his beak from the pot on the stove. "I'll never go near the stove again!"

"What's smoking?" Maddy asked.

"Oh! I know what that is. People put white or brown sticks in their mouth, but not sticks from trees. Then they use fire to start the sticks to burn. They smell awful afterwards, especially their clothes, hair, and their mouth." Guppy remembered the sea captain who smoked cigars.

Maddy stared at her friend. "Sticks? Don't they worry their hair would burn? How stupid!"

She skipped down to the last bullet to find out what to do after a house fire. "Look at this, Guppy. I wonder if Mrs. Potts or Daddy did these things?"

- Get an advance from your insurance company for necessities.
- File your claim right away.
  - Get a three-ring binder to keep track of all communication, permits, invoices and estimates.
- Make sure the insurance company acts promptly.
- Keep track of your living expenses.
- Get the right repair estimates.
- Keep paying your insurance premiums.
- It's not over until you say so.
- Consider hiring a public adjuster.
- Don't worry about losing your insurance.

"We have to send them this list!" Maddy exclaimed.

"Google how to do that on this computer." Guppy stared at the keyboard. It was slightly different from Daddy's laptop keyboard.

Maddy scrolled up to the search bar. She whacked it with her pencil. The website address lit up. She hit the Back arrow and was returned to Google.

"Maybe we can get a picture of the list. I'll ask Google." It took a lot of whacking keys and running from side to side to get her question in the Google search bar. "Okay, here it is. We have to hit the top button and the Home button. Let me go back to that page we need." Maddy hit the back button and the list of items appeared.

"Ready, Guppy? I'll get the top button. You use your beak on this Home button right here."

Maddy's pencil pressed the top button, and Guppy pecked on the Home button. They heard a CLICK.

"There it is!" Guppy squawked.

"Okay. Now we need to send this to Daddy. I don't think Mrs. Potts knows what to do." Maddy looked over the icons in the system tray. She recognized the green message button and whacked it. There wasn't anything there. Then she noticed Contacts. She whacked the icon and discovered some names.

"There's Daddy's name—Jimmy Katz," Guppy pointed out.

"Okay. I think all I need to do is hit that. Hold on..."

Maddy aimed her pencil at Jimmy's name.

"Hit Message!" Guppy demanded.

Maddy hit the green Message button, and sure enough, it opened the familiar message area. "Okay, but now we need to get that little picture in that message place." She fretted, which sounded like mewling growls.

Maddy gripped the pencil and jammed the eraser on the photo in the bottom left corner of the screen. She moved slightly to her right, and the photo followed. Guppy had to scoot out of the way, so Maddy could keep moving to the right to get the photo into the green box.

"Wow! That was a lot of work! Now I can send this to Daddy, Guppy." She whacked the green arrow, and the photo appeared to be sent. It was in the window where Jimmy would see it.

"Do you think Daddy heard a message ding?" Maddy asked. "I remember how it dings on his phone and his computer when Celebrity texts him."

"Yes! Daddy's phone will ding!" Guppy announced.

Maddy yawned. "I need a nap."

CHAPTER TEN

J immy pulled up to the Biggem Diner at the same time Brian arrived. Shortly thereafter, Danny, Ramirez and Celebrity arrived. They goofed off in the parking lot for a bit, then went inside to grab a table.

Oatie, Danny's girlfriend and a server at the diner, waved them over to her section. "What are you bunch up to?"

"Oh, you know... as little as possible." Danny chortled. He sported black ink-stained fingers on his right hand.

"Speak for yourself," Ramirez ribbed Danny. "You aren't out on the streets dealing with the depraved."

Brian scoffed. "Depraved? You mean kids making out behind the bleachers?" He and Celebrity chuckled.

"What happened to your fingers?" Oatie asked.

"Ink leaked from my favorite pen. I've tried everything and it won't wash off." Danny looked at his fingers in disgust.

"Have you tried Dawn dishwashing soap?" Oatie asked. "It gets practically everything out that I've tried in the past. I even add some to my laundry load for anything greasy."

"Huh. I'll see if we have some at home," Danny said.

"Okay, who's having what today?" Oatie asked.

Four *the usual's* were called out. Oatie waited for Ramirez to make up his mind.

The detective looked up at the Specials board. "Let me have the meatloaf special."

"Okay. I'll be back with your tea in a sec." Oatie took off to the order area and called out her orders. She returned with a pitcher of iced tea and a bucket of ice and filled glasses.

Lunch arrived. They ate, talked, then paid, leaving their tips on the table. When they arrived in the parking lot, Ramirez was the first to take off, followed by Danny, who had to run out to Derrick and interview someone and take pictures.

Jimmy's phone dinged a message. He glanced at the screen and was surprised to see it was from Maddy. "Look! Maddy sent me a text!"

Brian and Celebrity gawked at Jimmy, then they looked over his shoulder at the text message.

"Oh, look! They must have looked up information about fires!" Celebrity said loudly, but lowered her voice while glancing around the parking area.

The three of them read the list.

"Oh, this is good information! Can you forward this to me?" Brian knew he needed to get moving on his insurance claim.

Jimmy forwarded the text, then stared at his long-time friend and roommate. "I talked to this woman named Mrs. Trumble. She's a therapist that Moses recommended. I feel so much better, as if a huge weight has been lifted from my shoulders."

Brian studied his best friend. There was no getting around the stress they were going through. *Maybe I should go see that woman.* "Send me her info."

"Should I send a text back to Maddy?" Jimmy tried to think about how his cat would react, but it was impossible to read her thoughts.

"Might as well," Celebrity said. "Even though she doesn't

know the ins and outs of electronics, she's smart enough to know that messages go both ways."

"Okay, here goes." Jimmy sent a simple message saying thanks for sending this. There was no immediate response.

"She may be napping, or downstairs," Brian suggested.

Celebrity walked to her cop car. "See you later."

Brian headed out.

Jimmy got inside his Honda and decided he was up to learning more about the empire. He steered toward the DDS offices.

MEATY SCRUTINIZED THE AISLES IN THE GROCERY STORE FROM HIS security domain upstairs. All was well. No one was stuffing steaks or cans of soup in their purses, down their pants, in their backpacks, or pockets. He swiveled over to his laptop where the *real work* took place. Meaty pulled up the app to check on Maddy's iPad.

He noticed how difficult it was for the cat to copy and paste items, and to take screenshots while her best friend helped using his beak. Meaty thought about that difficulty for a minute, then drilled down into the iPad and put together some code that would appear as instructions on the home page. He added one purple button and a pink button on the system tray near the green Message button. In the future, all Maddy had to do was click on one of his newly made buttons to perform those functions with one or two clicks.

Meaty set an alert so he could see if Maddy succeeded by using the new buttons. Then he took the stairs down to the floor of the grocery to find lunch and a couple of snacks. He stood in line at the bar-b-cue area and ordered a mixed plate with roast pork, beef, and chicken with a choice of two sides. Meaty opted for the mac and cheese, and baked beans.

He slid his tray to the cash register, which was an unnecessary step since his food was free with the job, and being the manager's nephew was a bonus. But he didn't want others in line to think he was stealing a tray of food. The workers understood his reasoning and waved him along. Meaty climbed the stairs and dug into his food while monitoring the shoppers going about their business. He checked his personal laptop for any *government jobs*—those private snooping contracts that paid for all his toys. He enjoyed helping lock up the bad guys and getting them off the streets where they preyed upon people.

Meaty was about to congratulate himself for not slopping food on his keyboard when a blob of baked beans with mac and cheese fell off his fork. His chin dipped to his chest. This was a big mess.

Brink Hellman, the Foo manager and Meaty's uncle, clomped up the stairs with a tray holding his lunch. "Thought I'd join you so we could spend some time together." He shook his head when he saw the mess his nephew made on the keyboard. "Why, exactly, do you eat over your keyboard when you know you're sloppy?"

"I don't know." Meaty shrugged.

"Looks like we sent a message to employees and shoppers when I fired Trinity." Brink was sure shoplifting was finally under control.

Just as the words left the manager's mouth, Meaty's system sounded an alert. He spun his chair back to the monitor and saw an old lady stuffing soft packages of food in her giant purse. He groaned.

Brink stood and looked over his shoulder. He groaned along with his nephew. Brink recognized Mrs. Malone. "I'll go talk to her." He hurried down the stairs and joined the woman in the canned meat aisle.

"Come with me, Mrs. Malone." He led her over to where the gift cards hung on a rack. He pulled a Foo Visa gift card and walked over to a cash register that had just finished up with a customer. "Ring this up with my code." When the sale went through, Brink handed Mrs. Malone the card. "Use this for those things you're carrying in your purse. In the future, take one of those red carryall's so we don't think you're stealing."

Mrs. Malone kept a straight face, but knew the manager caught her. "Thank you for your kindness. My Social Security check won't arrive for another week."

Brink patted her back. "Don't worry about it." He left her at the register and hurried back to his now cold lunch.

MADDY WOKE FROM HER NAP AND STRETCHED OUT HER BACK. With great effort, she twisted and turned, grooming herself until ready to face her public. She gave herself another stretch, then lightly batted the mouse to wake her iPad. Maddy stared at the Home screen. There were white words on the normal black background. She noticed two new buttons on the system tray.

"Hey Guppy, the system updated our computer. There's some new words here and two new buttons."

Guppy fluffed out his wings from his nap, then fluttered over to his best friend. He landed on her pillow and leaned in to read the screen. "Where'd they come from?"

"Remember when we heard Daddy talking about these updates with Mrs. Potts? He said if you don't accept the updates, your computer can get out of date, then everything might not work together." Maddy explained, although she didn't quite understand what she said.

"I wonder what's supposed to work together?" Guppy asked.

"I don't know. We need to learn more." Maddy saw there was a 1 on the green Message button. "Hey, we've got a message!" She snatched up the yellow pencil and whacked the message button.

They read the thank-you message from Jimmy, then stared at each other.

"Guppy, we can talk to people!"

Guppy nudged Maddy. "Let's look at Contacts. See who's there."

Maddy grabbed the pencil between her teeth and whacked the Contacts icon. There were seven people listed with cellphone numbers and email addresses: Jimmy, Celebrity, Mrs. Potts, Brian, Aunt Betty, Chief Price, and Meaty.

"Meaty is a computer guy," Maddy mentioned.

"Like Boris?" Guppy asked. They learned a lot from the Russian on his YouTube channel.

"Yeah, I think so." Maddy wasn't too sure what exactly Meaty did, or where he worked.

Mrs. Potts sat at the small desk in her suite at the mansion, drumming a pen on the desk while lost in thought, staring at the laptop monitor. She noted several items on the screen, then thought about the presentation. Mrs. Potts had a thought, then typed away. She typed in headings with several blank lines between:

- Kitchen
  - Butler's pantry
  - Half bath
- Living room
  - Half bath
- Dining room

- Small office
- Laundry room/area
- Master bedroom
  - His & Hers closets
  - Big bathroom
  - Linen closet
- Three more bedrooms with bathrooms

Once she had the room categories noted, she thought about the contents of those rooms from the old boarding house. She sighed deeply, trying to move past the horror of losing everything. After she had a grip on her emotions, she did a mental inventory of each room, beginning with the kitchen.

Mrs. Potts highlighted new things to be included. She would have to contact Cal and let him know if there was anything new that she and Jimmy hadn't placed on the marked up old house plans.

Counter space was required, especially on each side of the stove. Countertop appliances, cooking tools, and cleaning supplies which included the bottle of hand washing soap and the manual dishwashing soap, required more space. One of the first things she would replace would be that wonderful little do-it-all oven Jimmy had given her. The Breville Smart Oven not only replaced her toaster, it dehydrated, air fried, had a pizza button, and a bagel button.

It baked, broiled, had a cookie button, a roast button, a proof function for bread making, reheat, warm, and slow cook button. She snorted a chuckle. That one appliance was king of the kitchen. Too bad it didn't wash up after itself.

Mrs. Potts mentally went through her old kitchen and typed items using bullets. She required all the gadgets and hand tools, an excellent set of knives, steak knives, silverware, wooden spoons, spatulas... the list went on and on.

One decision she made was not to buy any black coated

cookware or utensils. She would go with ceramic and stainless-steel frying pans and pots. Those would not peel or chip off bits of plastic into food. She tried to recall when she had switched to that dark coating on pans and why.

Mrs. Potts figured she probably had consumed at least a half a cupful of plastic bits and pieces in all that time. She shuddered at the thought.

She added the refrigerator drawer and the kitchen island to the list. Cal already knew about those two items because Jimmy penciled them on the old plans.

The landlady had a thoughtful moment. Where she had noted half-baths, she made sub-bullets about the size. Her old half-bath was so cramped her knees hit the toilet paper roll. The new half-baths would be twice the size, which would give ample room for supplies.

A special cabinet, like a bookcase, was for her baking supplies. So it had to be tall and wide to get all the spices and baking ingredients stored. That brought up another issue. Where to store pizza pans, baking sheets, and cupcake pans? A cabinet with separate vertical storage spaces was called for to keep those things in order. That's where she could also keep the chopping mats and the cork hot plate holders. She scratched out plastic for the mats and typed in metal and wood.

Oh, she was having so much fun!

CHAPTER ELEVEN

Marty the mortician answered the phone at the Twinkle Funeral Parlor. His face scrunched as Mildred Jingle announced herself.

Gene's dead again, Mildred stated.

"He wasn't dead the first time, Mildred. He was in a medically induced state, most likely from one of his prescriptions. Are you sure he's dead this time?"

He died at six this morning. I've been waiting for him to wake up, but so far, no luck.

"Well, that sounds like true death. It's three o'clock in the afternoon. He should have come around if he was going to. I'll send the hearse for him."

Okay.

Marty hung up the office phone, then clutched his head. He picked up the phone and dialed a number he knew by heart. "Chief, Marty here. Listen, Mildred Jingle just called and said Gene's actually dead this time. She said he died at six this morning, so she's sure he's really dead. I'm going to send the car for him. I'd like to know if you could verify he's dead."

We sure don't want a repeat of that! I'll head over to the Jingle's. Do you want me to bring you anything while I'm there?

"Would you ask Mildred for all Gene's medications? I want to see if he was taking some combinations that could have caused the reaction he suffered the first time."

Good idea. I'll see if she'll hand them over.

They ended the call, and Marty hung up the phone. He opened a file folder and found Gene Jingle's first unfinished death certificate and pondered how to resume.

THE CHIEF ARRIVED AT THE JINGLE'S HOUSE AT THE SAME TIME AS the hearse pulled up. Edgar and Troy stepped out of the sleek, black vehicle and retrieved the gurney from the rear of the car. The three approached the front door, and Chief Price knocked.

Mildred yanked the door open, eyes filled with anxiety. "He's really dead, Chief Price. I even tried holding a mirror under his nose. Nothing."

She finally stepped back and opened the door fully, allowing the chief, Edgar and Troy to enter.

"Show us where he is," the chief asked.

They followed Mildred to the main bedroom. Gene was on his side. He looked peacefully asleep. The chief approached the bed and placed his hand on Gene's forehead. It was stone cold to the touch. Chief Price nodded.

"He's very cold, so I'll agree that this time it looks like your husband has passed away."

Mildred sniffled. Now that she knew for sure Gene was dead, she allowed herself to lose it. "I can't believe I have to make all those calls again!"

"Why don't you hold off until tomorrow?" Troy suggested.

"Yeah. Wait until tomorrow. Then you'll know for sure he's not going to recover like last time," Edgar stated.

"Mildred, Marty would like me to bring him Gene's prescriptions. He wants to see if there's something that would have caused that false appearance of death," the chief said.

"I'll sue those bastards into the next century!" Mildred spit out.

The chief patted the distraught woman on the back. "We don't know for sure that's what happened. Marty will determine things when he does what he does." The chief just couldn't put his words together to address the situation. He followed Mildred to the kitchen, where Gene's medications were on the counter with sticky notes of instructions taped to the counter in front of each bottle.

"Are all these Gene's?" Chief Price was astounded.

"Uh-huh. Blood pressure, cholesterol, anxiety, arthritis, thyroid, fibromyalgia, prednisone, and ibuprofen."

The chief picked up each bottle and looked at the prescribing doctor. "Looks like four different doctors. Do you know if he told each of these doctors what the other doctors had prescribed? I'm wondering if he was over-medicated?"

Mildred had a thoughtful moment. "I'm not sure how open Gene was. He never wanted me to go with him. Probably because he thought I was a big mouth and would say something he didn't want to share."

"He wouldn't share things with his doctors?" The chief looked perplexed. "Well, do you have a bag I can put these in? I'll drop them off and talk to Marty."

Mildred opened a drawer and brought out a paper lunch bag. "This should do it." She dropped all the plastic RX bottles in the bag and handed it to the chief.

They left the kitchen and returned to the bedroom. Troy and Edgar had Gene on the gurney and covered with a white sheet-like cloth.

Mildred rushed to the gurney and pulled the sheet down to Gene's chest. "Let's not smother him if he's not really dead."

Troy opened his mouth to say something, but the chief elbowed him and gave a slight shake of his head. Troy swallowed. "Sure thing, Mrs. Jingle."

"We'll take Gene to the funeral parlor, and Marty will check him out," Edgar said, his voice filled with sympathy.

They rolled the gurney out of the house and loaded it into the back of the hearse. Mildred stood at her opened front door, the chief beside her. She waved as the hearse took Gene away, as if she expected him to sit up and wave back.

Chief Price patted Mildred on the shoulder. "I'm sorry for your loss."

BETTY TYPED LIKE A TORNADO WITH MADDY WATCHING EVERY stroke. A message beep sounded and Betty checked her Messages on the computer.

Are we still meeting? One of her business associates sent.

"Did I forget a meeting?" Betty clicked on her calendar and saw nothing she had scheduled for the day with this person, but an upcoming meeting at the end of the week.

She typed: *My calendar doesn't show a meeting for today, only Friday. When was this scheduled? Did you send me a meeting confirmation?*

There was a long pause, then she saw the three dots of typing.

Oh! I'm so sorry. It's a good thing you said Friday. I accidentally showed today.

Betty thought about it a minute. *We can have a brief meeting now, since I'm here and available. I'll send a Zoom link.*

Are you sure this isn't an inconvenience for you?

Betty turned to Maddy. "People just don't get it sometimes." She typed. *I'll send you the link.*

The Zoom screen popped up, and she clicked on one of the many names listed on the left.

Maddy saw Betty's image on the screen. She loved online meetings.

In a short blink, the man who had contacted Betty appeared. Maddy surprised Betty by meowing loudly and taking a step toward the monitor.

"Maddy, what on earth is the matter with you?"

"Hello, Mrs. Diaz. I'm sorry for the confusion."

"Arturo, we're here now. What can I help you with?"

"The women's shelter is short of funds. I don't know what happened."

Betty frowned. She distinctly remembered issuing a transfer of funds for all expenses.

Maddy lifted her paw to touch the screen.

Betty leaned over to the cat and whispered. "I'll take care of this." She turned back to the Zoom meeting. "Arturo, what exactly was short changed? You sent me the budget, and I transferred the funds."

Arturo stammered and shifted about in his chair. "I don't know what happened. The bank sent me an overdraft notice..."

"How much are you short?"

"Around twenty-five *thousand* dollars." Arturo was wide-eyed, as if in shock.

"I'll call the bank and my security people. Once we straighten out what happened, I'll release money to the women's shelter's account to cover the shortage. Was there anything else?"

"No, thank you very much." Arturo hit the Leave Meeting button and was gone.

Betty closed the Zoom app, turned to Maddy, and said, "There's something fishy going on." She pushed the speakerphone option and the speed dial button on the office phone, and waited.

Hey, what's up? Meaty asked.

"Meaty, I need you to find out what's going on over at the women's shelter I support." She explained what took place on the call, the money that she had already transferred for the entire month, and her reluctance to send more. And, furthermore, Maddy had an issue with Arturo.

Well, that settles it. If Maddy had comments, there's something funny going on. He was joking, but he knew full well how smart that cat was. She had learned a lot from Boris, the Russian guy on YouTube when she and Guppy were researching identity theft. *I'll get into the accounts and get back to you.*

Betty disconnected the call. She turned to Maddy. "Thanks for letting me know something was wrong. Arturo never struck me as a thief, but if you see easy money, sometimes it's just too tempting to stay honest."

Maddy purred and rubbed against Betty's shoulder.

Jenkins appeared in the doorway with a small tray that contained a sandwich on a plate, a glass of iced tea, and some minced ham in a small bowl. "Lunch is served."

He served Betty first, knowing Maddy would devour her food before Betty took one bite of her sandwich.

"Oh, thank you, Jenkins. You read my mind." Betty got in one good bite of her ham sandwich when she saw Maddy licking her lips, her bowl empty. "Don't eat so fast, Maddy. No one is going to steal your food. If you slow down, it will last longer and you'll have much more enjoyment from eating."

Jenkins threw in his ten cents' worth of advice. "And your body will digest the food better." He cupped a hand at his mouth and whispered to her. "Digestion means you'll have better poops."

Maddy stopped licking up mid lick. She stared at Jenkins, thinking about what he said. She gave him a little meow.

Jenkins didn't know if she was agreeing with him or insulting him.

The butler returned to his duties, all the while thinking about Maddy. He had noticed that everyone talked to the cat as if she understood everything, so he decided not to be left behind. Jenkins thought it was uncanny how the cat responded. She was opinionated. She liked, and disliked people and things and didn't hesitate to add her advice or suggestions. He couldn't figure it out.

Betty noticed how Jenkins acted and responded around Maddy. She wondered if someone told him about the animals. She went in search of Bertha Potts and found her in her suite, reading.

Betty tapped the opened door frame. Bertha looked up from her book.

"Do you have a minute?"

"Come on in!" Bertha said.

Betty entered, then shut the door behind her. She took a seat across from Bertha and whispered, even though the door was closed. "Have you told Jenkins?"

Bertha scrunched her brows in alarm and shook her head. "No! Why?"

"I've noticed the way he communicates with Maddy. I don't know if he talks to Guppy, but he seems to know about Maddy."

Mrs. Potts looked panicked. "We need to call the other pact members and find out if someone let the secret slip! I'll text the chief, Meaty, and Brian. You text Jimmy and Celebrity."

They got busy on their phones. They sent messages. Phones rang. Explanations were given and shared. Betty and Mrs. Potts put their heads together.

"Okay, it seems Jenkins has noticed how we communicate with Maddy, and he's mimicking us. Should we just include him?" Betty couldn't decide about what to do.

"Think about it, Betty. He's your trusted employee and has been for years. And he lives here. If we include him in the pact, he'll be the first line of defense of anyone coming through your front door."

Betty nodded. "Okay, we should text everyone for a meeting." She stood.

"I'll send out an email to the entire pact asking for RSVPs," Mrs. Potts said.

"Okay. I'll get back to work then." Betty left Mrs. Potts, the official pact leader, to complete her task to set up the meeting.

MEATY CRACKED HIS KNUCKLES, SWIVELED HIS HEAD, ROLLED HIS shoulders, then got to work on the latest problem with the Katz-Diaz conglomerate. He pulled up the bank account for the women's shelter and gasped. The account was in arrears to the tune of twenty thousand dollars. He saw where the first draft was for five grand.

"How the heck would the bank allow an account to get twenty grand in arrears? I don't believe it!"

The security expert pulled up several websites, logged into them and began his snooping. Arturo's bank account had a grand total of $4.32. Like Betty, Meaty didn't think Arturo was the culprit. He engaged his super snooper app, connected it to the women's shelter bank account and clicked GO. The race was on. The map attached to the app showed the scammer zigging and zagging all over the globe, trying to lose anyone who wanted to discover the actual user.

Those crooks didn't know Meaty, and they sure didn't have the same app he did. The security expert had found an app and modified it into his super snooper. The Feds were impressed by Meaty's results from using the app on contracts they gave him. As far as Meaty was concerned, if his program was better than what the US Government could produce, he was *In Like Flint.*

Within seven minutes and fourteen seconds, a name and

location flashed on the screen. Obviously a fake name. Waylen Morrongo. He dug deeper and discovered the idiot used his real name, and he discovered everything about him, including Waylen's D.O.B.: February 12, 2000 at Charity Sisters hospital in Memphis, Tennessee.

The guy's driver's license (Memphis address confirmed) and Meaty found an abysmal credit report score (430).

Well, Waylen, looks like you won't be buying a house anytime soon.

He discovered where Waylen stashed the money. There were five bank accounts set up in different banks in and around Memphis. All used fake names but the same address. *This bozo gives professional bank robbers a bad rap.*

Meaty perused his list of detectives and law enforcement people he had gathered from the various online meetings and in-person seminars throughout the past five years. Bryan Whitger was a detective in Memphis. He hoped he was still on the job. Meaty called the number. It went straight to voicemail, so he left a brief to the point message.

"Bryan, this is Arthur Hellman. Uh, you probably remember my nickname, Meaty. Anyway... we met several years ago at a law enforcement conference and I need some help with a perp in Memphis. Give me a call when you get a chance. If you can't grab a hold of this case, let me have the name of someone who can." He left his phone number.

Meaty did more snooping on the life and times of Waylen Morrongo. There was a lot to discover. He had several convictions of low-level crimes, most involving money theft. He wondered how he came across the women's shelter account? His cell phone rang with a number he didn't recognize, but it showed Memphis.

"This is Meaty. Who's calling?"

"Meaty! It's Bryan Whitger. You still in Twinkle, Texas? I love the name of that town!"

"Hey, Bryan. Thanks for calling. Yup. Still twinkling away. Listen, I've got a situation that I hope you can help with. I think you've most likely dealt with this doofus before. Waylen Morrongo bilked money from a women's shelter bank account online. I've found five bank accounts where he deposited the money into. Different aliases, but stupidly used the same address for all five."

Bryan moaned. "This guy has been in and out of jail so many times I've lost count. What's the amount of money?"

"25 grand. He grabbed five grand, which dropped the balance down to pennies. Then he snagged another twenty grand, which put the account in arrears. I'm going to have to contact the bank and find out why they didn't report the amount to the organization. Our matriarch, Betty Katz-Diaz, provided the funding. Someone should have contacted her immediately. But, I'll get to the bottom of that."

"This is good news for us! We'll haul this fool in. With a 25 grand heist, he's looking at hopefully five years or more." Bryan sounded happy.

Meaty verified the detective's email, then provided all the information he found on the thief in an email.

"Looks like a different address than what we show for him. I'll go pick him up after I get a search warrant. Might as well put my time to good use. Thanks so much, man. Getting one more creep off the streets is a good day's work."

"Let me know if you need any other information. Be happy to send it to you."

They ended their call and Meaty spun his chair. Then he called Betty.

"Arturo is in the clear. A guy in Memphis hacked the bank account. I've turned his information over to a detective I know there. I'm driving over to the bank to find out why the first hack went unreported. It began with a five thousand withdrawal that left a smidgen amount in the account. Then the Memphis guy figured he could get more, so he withdrew another twenty grand."

Betty was stunned. "The bank never contacted Arturo? No one contacted me!"

"I'm going to go see FeBe," Meaty explained. "She'll sort this out." Meaty ended the call with Betty and tromped down the stairs. "Uncle Brink," Meaty called out. "Have to run to the bank for a client. Be back soon."

CHAPTER TWELVE

Celebrity, her mom, and dad, arrived at the mansion at four in the afternoon. Cal carried a mailing tube. Jenkins greeted them and showed them inside. Geenie headed straight to Betty's office.

"Hey, Jenkins," Cal greeted. "We need to round up Jimmy, Brian, and Mrs. Potts to go over the new house plans. Can we use that small conference room?"

"Sure, you head that way while I fetch Mrs. Potts. Brian isn't here right now, but I'm sure Jimmy is upstairs." Jenkins shut the front door.

Cal went to the conference room. Celebrity climbed the stairs to Jimmy's suite, and Jenkins went to gather Mrs. Potts.

Celebrity tapped on Jimmy's open door. She didn't see him, so she called out. "Jimmy? Are you here?" Guppy and Maddy were missing, so Celebrity backtracked and went downstairs. She found Guppy in the conservatory on his favorite tree, singing away.

Jenkins took it upon himself to attach a seed tray to a limb, and he papered the floor for parrot messes. He regularly used the easy-clean-up vac to keep things in order.

Celebrity headed to Betty's office. She found Maddy on the desk supervising the matriarch, Jimmy looking over Betty's shoulder. Geenie sat in a chair in front of the desk.

"Hey, I wondered where you were." Celebrity smooched her fiancé on the cheek. "What are you doing?"

"He's helping me with a corrupt document," Betty said.

"My dad's here with the house plans. We're in the small conference room." Celebrity left everyone to carry on with their business, and she walked over to the conference room.

Cal had the house plans unrolled and re-rolled in the opposite direction so they would lie flat and not curl up. Mrs. Potts was eager to see the new house on paper.

"Jimmy will be here in a sec. He's helping Betty with a document."

Celebrity sat by Mrs. Potts. "Are you excited?"

Mrs. Potts dabbed her eyes with a tissue. "I can't wait until the foundation is laid!"

Jimmy rushed into the room followed by Maddy. "Sorry I'm holding things up."

Maddy jumped onto the conference table.

"You're here now, so let's get started." Cal showed them the ground floor first. "Mrs. Potts, you'll notice the additions to your kitchen you requested. Your refrigerator drawer, the kitchen island, counter space galore, and a butler's pantry. All lower cabinets have pullouts, so you won't have to crawl into the cabinet to reach something in the back. You'll notice all the drawers are wider than what you had."

Mrs. Potts patted her chest. "Be still my heart!"

"Also, the builder I like doesn't use plastic shelf clips. He has his people to install wooden slats to hold up shelves. There's nothing worse than those shelves collapsing when the plastic clip gives out. There goes anything that's breakable."

Celebrity and Mrs. Potts shared a look of surprise.

"Oh, I've never given that any thought," Celebrity said.

"Me neither. I've always trusted my cabinet shelves to stay put!"

"There's a half bath in the butler's pantry, and your knees won't hit the wall," Cal gave a goofy smile. He pointed out the dining room, living room, Mrs. Potts' suite, Brian's suite, and a spare room. He showed them where the tankless water heaters were located and explained they would get better use with them and less water waste. There was also a long covered back porch off the kitchen, like the previous house had.

"Oh, this is so wonderful!" Mrs. Potts exclaimed. "My suite looks double the space I had before!"

"If you want, I can create a separate room for an office in your suite." Cal pulled the first sheet and pointed.

The landlady pondered that change, then shook her head. "I don't have any need for an office, just a desk and credenza for the printer."

Cal pulled the second story floor plan on top of the first. He nodded to Jimmy and Celebrity. "I made the upstairs one full apartment with three bedrooms. Figured you'd live there for a couple of years once you're married, and I made allowances for one or two children. Guppy has window options for his tree, and I included deep window sills for Maddy."

Jimmy and Celebrity hunched over and went over their space. Maddy joined them, touching the plan here and there.

Cal pulled another sheet of paper. "I've included a four-car garage with access through the kitchen. You have enough land and it won't crowd your lot."

"Oh! That sure is a bonus. I've always been concerned about parking out in the weather, especially when there's hail or a torrential downpour."

"I'll leave the plans so you can look them over for a couple of days. Make sure you have everything you require," Cal said. "Then we'll go talk to Norris Trusty, the best builder in the county."

"I'm so excited!" Mrs. Potts fanned herself.

Jimmy tapped the top sheet of the plans. "Thanks so much for doing this, Cal. We're looking forward to moving back into the boarding house!"

MEATY DROVE OVER TO THE TWINKLE BANK & TRUST AND tapped on FeBe Morales' open door. The president looked up from her monitor and gave a huge smile to her visitor.

"Hi, Meaty. What brings you my way?"

Meaty entered the office and closed the door behind him.

"Uh-oh," FeBe knew something was off when the top Twinkle security expert wanted a private meeting.

"FeBe, the women's shelter account has been hacked to the tune of twenty-five grand."

The bank president's jaw dropped. She attacked her keyboard and pulled up the account. "I don't believe this!" She hit her speaker button on the desk phone and jabbed a number.

"Hi, FeBe, what can I do for you?"

"Stuart! Someone hacked the women's shelter account!"

There was a silent pause, then, "Couldn't happen!"

"Get in here!" FeBe disconnected the call.

Stuart, a middle-aged man who had been in the banking industry for a quarter of a century, opened the door and barged in. When he saw Meaty, he stilled. "How did this happen, Meaty?"

The expert was quiet for a bit, then came to a conclusion. "The guy in Memphis had help. He sure didn't do this on his own. Trust me, he's just too stupid. Let me make a call..." He pulled up Bryan Whitger's phone number in Memphis. "Hey, Bryan. Your perp had help."

Meaty explained what had happened at the bank. The Memphis detective agreed that their guy didn't have the smarts to pull off this operation on his own. From his past convictions, he didn't have the knowhow to jumble the accounts to disable the alerts.

"We've got him in lockdown," Bryan stated. "I'll see what we can get out of him, then I'll let you know."

Meaty stood and nodded to FeBe and Stuart. "I'll let you know what we discover." He drove back to the Foo and went upstairs to his domain. He twisted his chair back and forth while mentally following a trail of the events. "Had to have help."

His cellphone rang. He recognized the Memphis number. "Hey, what's up? Did you find someone?"

I sent the team back to the apartment and they discovered the brains behind this heist. Fellow by the name of Reginald Armbruster who is currently in prison."

Meaty's mouth dropped open from the shock of hearing that name. "Reggie Armbruster? You're sure?"

Found some correspondence between them. Not quite sure how Mr. Morrongo connected with him, or how Armbruster managed to get a hold of a computer while in prison."

Meaty almost lost the ability to speak. "Wait until I pass this along. People here are going to go into an apoplectic shock. Thanks for passing this along. I've got to do damage control on my end." They said their goodbyes. He thought delivering the news in person was better, so he rushed back downstairs.

MEATY PARKED IN FRONT OF THE POLICE STATION AND WAS greeted by Butch. He only had enough spare energy to raise a hand in greeting as he rushed to the chief's office. Just as he arrived, Kenton Price raised his eyes away from his computer monitor to be visually greeted by a very distressed friend and colleague.

"What's up? I can tell something's wrong," Chief Price said. Meaty closed the door, then slipped into a chair in front of the chief's desk. "I'm not even sure how to begin to explain the enormous problem I've just uncovered."

Meaty went through the basic information. The call from Betty. What his snooping super program found. His calls to Memphis. Then he dropped the bomb that he just learned from detective Bryan Whitger.

Police Chief Kenton Price was stunned. "Reggie Armbruster?"

Meaty nodded.

"He's still in prison, isn't he? No one has notified me about an early release." Chief Price was flabbergasted. He pulled up the Texas Department of Criminal Justice (.gov) website. He typed in Reggie's name and waited. The system returned the information. "Reggie is still incarcerated. The system updates daily, so there's no mistake."

"That's a relief, but we need to find out how he's helping this Waylen Morrongo in Memphis."

REGGIE ARMBRUSTER SAT ON HIS NARROW COT IN A WHITE cotton pullover and white pants with an elastic waist in his prison cell. He was glad it wasn't the orange jumpsuit the county jail used. Orange was not his best color. Reggie hovered over his prison-issued tablet checking his email. There was no email reply from Waylen Morrongo. The update was two days overdue. He wondered what Morrongo was doing.

Maybe the petty thief had absconded with the money? Reggie recognized a numbskull when he first spoke with Waylen. It had been easy to get the Tennessee guy on board with Reggie's offer of a 55/45 cut, in Reggie's favor. He had instructed him how to set up offshore accounts for the money, and how to go about hacking the women's shelter bank account.

Reggie had upped his bank hacking expertise thanks to the Texas prison system. There was a plethora of experts sitting only a couple of cells away whose bragging educated anyone who would listen. Granted the *expert* was incarcerated, but sometimes after long careers of not getting caught. One slip-up and their extensive livelihood ended.

Having only the meager amount of money in his personal checking account, Reggie worried he would run out of funds. Social Security was suspended for anyone convicted and serving twelve or more consecutive months. Furthermore, there was no lump sum payoff at the end of your sentence. He thought about all the money he threw away on that loser son of his.

Caleb's drinking had wrecked Reggie's heart. If his wife or his parents were still alive, they would have blamed everything on Reggie for poor parenting skills. But, truth be told, Caleb secretly began drinking with a rotten bunch of teens, then didn't quit throughout his twenties. By the time his son turned thirty, he was considered the town drunk.

Reggie blamed himself for bailing his boy out every time he was picked up by the cops. If he had let him rot for a week or two in a Twinkle jail cell, his kid may have straightened out. That was a lost cause and his money evaporated from his poor decisions. But, now, Reggie was in dire need of cash. If he didn't pay the past due mortgage and taxes on his house, it could be foreclosed and/or have property liens attached. That house was all he had left.

Taking a deep breath, he checked his email again, then decided to send another. It was imperative that he keep anxiety out of the message and maintain a strong vocabulary to assert his being the boss. He had to word it in a way so that the prison snoops didn't catch onto the scam he was pulling.

He wrote his message, editing, rewording, deleting things along the way.

Hey, Waylen, I haven't heard back from you. There's a lot to plan for our trip to the Caymans when I'm released. Keep focused on sunshine, beaches, and women in bikinis. – Reggie

He pressed the Send button, his stomach grinding with anxiety.

MEATY STOMPED UP THE FOO STAIRS AND PLOPPED INTO HIS chair. He reached down and retrieved his canned air to blast his keyboard of debris, then quieted himself to think about the current problem. Waylen Morrongo hooking up with Reggie Armbruster, or the other way around, was a huge anomaly.

He wondered how Reggie came across Waylen's name to begin with. First things first. Meaty searched for an email account for both men on the main email companies: Gmail, Yahoo, Outlook, Hotmail, AOL, Mail.com, and iCloud mail. There were other companies who provided email accounts, but he figured these morons would use one of the most popular services. He figured correctly. Reggie had an AOL account, and Waylen had a Hotmail account.

Meaty hacked Reggie's email and noted his login credentials. He had a long history in that account, which showed his outgoing emailing ceased at the time of his arrest. Meaty thought about it for a long minute and decided he'd better check and see if Reggie had one of the prison tablets.

Sure enough, the inmate had a tablet and a prison email account. Meaty bypassed prison security, discovering four rejections in Reggie's sent emails.

He discovered one of the four recommended Waylen. Then Meaty read through their correspondences. *Boy oh boy, Reggie's going to be upset that this doofus didn't open that offshore account.*

CHAPTER THIRTEEN

Celebrity thought about the animals. She had watched over a dozen videos on Jimmy's computer. *They must communicate with each other to do these things. They seem to coordinate actions when it's needed.* She wondered if they would communicate with her. After her father left the mansion, Celebrity stayed behind in the little conference room. She pulled out her phone and clicked on Maddy's name in her Contacts. Her finger hovered over the message button while she thought about what to say.

Celebrity clicked the message button and composed her message. She started, deleted, backspaced, then finally sent a simple message. *Hi Maddy. Hi Guppy. This is Celebrity. Let's be friends.*

She wondered how Maddy would respond... and if she would respond. She wondered why Guppy didn't use the computer. It would be a lot easier using his beak to peck the keys instead of Maddy having to run back and forth with the pencil. Celebrity figured Maddy's jaw must get tired from all that whacking on the keys. Maybe she would suggest that if they got a conversation going.

Her police communicator squawked a message from Stephanie, the dispatcher. *Teen boys fighting in the gym parking lot.* Celebrity left the room and hurried out the front door to her car. She suspected these idiots were fighting about a girl. Celebrity sped down the driveway, onto Diaz Circle, then turned onto Stonerich Blvd, then turned right onto Schuster Street. She cut through Andrajulas Street, then turned onto Ruddy Duck Drive and into the gym parking lot.

Two boys were duking it out with a small crowd encouraging them. Celebrity hit her siren, making a *whoop* noise to get their attention. She got out of her car and stood tall.

"What's going on here?"

The fighters separated, and the spectators were slinking off.

"Come back here!" Celebrity commanded to the crowd of teens and older boys. She glared at the two fighters. "You have two minutes to explain your actions before I haul you in handcuffs into my car." She glared at the people who had done nothing to stop the fight. "You encouraged this fight instead of looking for a peaceful way to stop it. Explain yourselves."

The fighters sputtered out what the fight was all about.

The teen in the blue shiny shorts and contrasting black shiny tank started the dialogue. "He started it. Called me a name."

"What'd he call you?" Celebrity asked.

"Jew-boy. I'm not even Jewish!"

Celebrity's eyebrow rose. She swung her eyes over to the other fighter. "Why did you call him that if he wasn't Jewish?"

The second teen with longish black hair in a ponytail practically growled his answer. "He's a cheapskate. Borrows money from everyone and never pays it back."

"Do not!"

"Do so. Want a list of people you owe?"

Celebrity huffed. "First on my list of things to get you on the right track of your lives is never, ever use racial slurs. Understand?" She looked over not only the two boys, but the young crowd as well. "Next up, never ever borrow money and not pay it back. In the world of adult finance, you would have a low credit score which means you will never get a loan for a car, house, or anything else. A debt is a debt. You owe money and it should always be paid in full using good faith."

She stared down the teen in blue. "Do you have a job?"

He shook his head. "I'm still in high school."

Celebrity had no sympathy for him. "Kiddo, I hate to be the one to explain this to you, but a lot of high school students, and even students in middle school have parttime jobs. Is there a reason why you can't get a job?"

"I'm focusing all my attention to my grades so I can get scholarships to college. All I do is go to school, go home, help around the house, and do my homework. I'm in advanced classes and have a heavy load for high school."

"You'd better ask your parents for money to pay back all the people you borrowed from," Celebrity suggested.

"I can't. My father was just diagnosed with advanced MS, and my mom doesn't work. There's no extra money," he wailed.

"Okay, you come with me." Celebrity gently took him by the upper arm and led him to the car. She placed her hand on his head while getting him in the back seat. She closed the door which could not be opened from the inside. She returned to the crowd and focused on the black-haired kid. "Did you ever think to ask him why he couldn't pay you back?"

The kid dropped his chin, shook his head, then looked up to be eye to eye with the detective. "I had no idea there were family problems."

"What did you learn from this?"

The teenager stammered and stuttered. "I guess I shouldn't jump to conclusions."

Celebrity put on her stern face. "You might consider asking questions. You can leave now."

The small group of spectators started to drift away. "Not you. Get back here."

There was a look of fear and uncertainty among the small crowd.

"I don't ever want to see any of you urging someone on to fight ever again. Do you understand? Do you know why?"

There were no volunteers.

"We live in a world of sporadic violence. It can get out of control very quickly. You were lucky no one had weapons. It all starts with something offending someone. People taking sides without even knowing why they're doing that. Then fists fly. Things get broken. Property destroyed. Before you know it, someone is dead or injured gravely, and someone arrested. You'd better make sure you understand the consequences of your actions. Any questions?"

People shook their heads, no one wanting to be first in responding.

"Go about your business and think carefully about what happened here today." She left them disburse, returned to her car and drove back to Betty's. She parked at the mansion, got out of the car and opened the rear seat door for her passenger to get out. "Come with me."

Jenkins opened the door, lifted one brow in question, but saw Celebrity's tightened jaw and didn't ask. "Go on back."

Celebrity led the boy down the hallway to Betty's office. They heard Guppy singing away in his real tree, a happy and content parrot. Celebrity tapped on Betty's open door.

"Got a minute? This boy needs help." She nudged him into the office and over to a chair in front of the desk.

Maddy quit her grooming and looked the boy over.

Betty saved her file, then turned to the teen seated on the other side of her desk. "I'm Mrs. Diaz. And you are...?"

"Elwood James, ma'am, but people call me Woody."

"Who are your parents?"

"Curtis and Mami."

Betty thought a moment. "I seem to recall meeting a Mami. That's not a typical name, but I don't know where or when I met your mother." She turned to Celebrity. "What brings you two here today?"

"It appears Woody borrows money from classmates but doesn't pay them back. There was a fight in the parking lot at the gym that I had to break up."

Maddy walked to the edge of the desk closest to the guest chairs, then stepped down onto Woody's knees. She made herself comfortable in his lap. He subconsciously petted the silky coat.

Celebrity and Betty knew Maddy was a good judge of character, and the cat must have tuned into the teenager's stress at being in the hot seat.

Betty turned to Woody. He figured it was his turn to explain.

He told her about his studies and what he was putting into his education. Then he mentioned his father being diagnosed with advanced MS.

"Do you read the TIN?" Betty asked.

Maddy's ears perked up.

Woody nodded.

"Do you recall reading about the fund my great-nephew, Jimmy Katz set up? Why didn't you or your folks apply for aid?" Betty patiently waited for an answer.

"I think we were all stunned by my father's diagnosis. Maybe my parents didn't consider it, or forgot they read about it." Woody wasn't sure of the answer.

"Who do you owe money to, and how much?" Betty asked, her eyes zeroed in on the teen.

He looked ashamed. "I'll have to make a list."

"You get back to me as soon as possible. I will loan you the money until you graduate from college. Then I expect you to pay me, or the estate, back."

Woody's eyes clouded with tears. He sniffled. "I promise to pay you back, Mrs. Diaz. Thank you for helping me. I'll try to get a ride back over here with my list."

Betty handed him a business card. "No need. Email me the list. Have your parents apply for help through Jimmy's fund. They more than qualify."

Maddy realized the meeting concluded, so she stepped back onto the desk again.

Woody stood. He reached out to shake Betty's hand and her strong grip surprised him. "Thank you, Mrs. Diaz." He stroked Maddy, then turned to the detective.

Celebrity led Woody out of the office, house, and into the car. "Sit up front with me."

She dropped the distraught teen off at his home

BETTY TWIDDLED HER FINGERS ON HER DESK. MADDY SAT LIKE A queen close to her.

"That boy has been through a lot, but he didn't have a clue what to do to pay people back, or what steps to take to solve his problem. Instead of fighting, he should have talked to the people who loaned him money to let them know what was going on."

Maddy paid rapt attention to Betty.

"That's the problem, Maddy. People don't take logical steps. It's like their brain goes haywire and they take extreme actions."

Maddy made some low-based meows and twerps, adding in her two cents.

"Well, we'll wait and see if he comes through."

Half an hour later, an email notification arrived from Woodywoodpecker. "How original," Betty groaned and clicked the message open. She scanned the message. "He owes a dozen people between $20-$25 each. That's not a lot of money to get into a fight over, but they're teenagers, so I guess their funds are short most of the time."

Betty stared into space for a moment. She turned to Maddy. "I'll loan him a thousand dollars. He can pay off these people and he should have enough left over to float until his circumstances turn around."

Maddy looked very serious as she sounded her opinion.

MEATY HAD ALL THE BANK ACCOUNT NUMBERS AND LOGIN information, which included the fake name for each account Waylen Morrongo used. He methodically went about logging into each account and transferred every drop of money back to the women's shelter account. Then he closed those accounts.

Next up, he changed the login information for the women's shelter bank account when his phone rang. He saw it was the Twinkle Bank and Trust and answered.

"Hey FeBe."

Did you just transfer the money back into the shelter's account?

"Yup, and I changed the login information. I'll get in touch with them and let them know what the new credentials are. Our friendly crook won't be needing those bank accounts, so I closed them. He'll be in jail for a while."

Thanks for taking care of this and letting me know what happened. Sneaky thief to be able to go around our security system.

"People learn a lot of tidbits when they're in prison. I'd better get on the ball and get the shelter people on the phone."

FeBe disconnected the call and Meaty called Arturo. He passed on the new bank credentials and had him read them back to him so the man could update the account.

"Arturo, you can't use easy passwords. They have to be complicated, and you need to maintain a password list."

After that phone call, Meaty contacted Betty. "The funds are back in the shelter's bank account."

Meaty figured he'd have a little fun. He sent both Waylon and Reggie an email. He didn't know if Waylon had access to his email account, but Reggie had that prison iPad and the prison email address, so he wrote an email to him.

Hey, Reggie. It's Meaty. So sorry about Waylon going to jail. He's most likely going to be out of circulation for a few years. Don't worry, I closed the five local bank accounts he set up in Memphis and returned the money to the shelter. Nope, he didn't follow your advice to set up an offshore account. When you deal with stupid people, you get what you get. I've got my eyes on you...

Meaty left it at that and pressed the Send button. Then he cracked his knuckles.

MADDY LEFT BETTY'S OFFICE AND RACED UP THE STAIRS. A NAP was calling. A few minutes later, Guppy flew upstairs and landed on his fake tree. He took his squirrel monitoring seriously and couldn't go for long without getting a treetop view of the activity.

"I'm taking a nap," Maddy announced.

"I'll keep us safe," Guppy declared.

Maddy pulled on the sofa throw from over the top of the couch until it flumped down on the cushions. She burrowed under the throw and hunkered down and dozed off. A couple of hours later, Maddy stuck her head out from under the throw. She saw Guppy in his sleep cage, his beak nestled under a wing snoozing.

The cat stretched out her long body and jumped to the floor. She moseyed to where her food and water dishes were, lapped up some water, nibbled on some kibble, then set to grooming herself. When she felt she was presentable, she sauntered over to the iPad on the floor and woke the device by nudging the mouse.

Maddy saw there was one new message. She forgot her parrot friend was sleeping when she called his name. "Guppy! We have a new message!"

Guppy startled awake with a loud squawk. "Aacckk! What's wrong?" The bird stepped out of the sleep cage onto his fake tree limb. He checked the windows to make sure no squirrels had come close to entering the room.

"We have a new message, Guppy!" Maddy could hardly contain her excitement that someone wrote to them.

The parrot fluttered to the cushion on the floor at the iPad. "Let's see!"

Maddy grabbed her yellow number two pencil in her strong jaw and bashed the green message icon. There should only have been five names present, Jimmy/Daddy, Mrs. Potts, Chief Price, Betty, and Meaty. Now there was another name: Celebrity.

"Guppy, look! Celebrity sent us a message!"

"Click it!" Guppy demanded.

Maddy whacked Celebrity's message. She and Guppy read the message. *Hi Maddy. Hi Guppy. This is Celebrity. Let's be friends.*

"Celebrity wants to be friends with us!" Maddy was giddy with excitement.

"Let's be friends!" Guppy flapped his wings.

"What should I say?" Maddy seemed frozen, unsure what to say back in their message.

"Just tell her we want to be her friends too," Guppy suggested.

"Okay. That sounds good." Maddy whacked out the message. They both stared at the screen and read the message.

"Looks good. Send it," Guppy demanded. He was excited with this human technology.

Before Maddy could whack the Return key to deliver the message, Guppy pecked the key sending the message on. Maddy dove into a fit of grooming to relieve the stress of excitement. Guppy flew over to his fake tree to spy on squirrels.

CHAPTER FOURTEEN

Meaty heard footsteps stomping up the stairs of the Foo to his domain. Two seconds later, Celebrity popped into view.

"Hey, Meaty. How's it going?"

"It's going." Meaty squirted canned air at his keyboard, clearing the clutter from snacks. He wore goggles, so bits of chips and other things flying in the air didn't blind him.

Celebrity watched him, "I heard you were giving Reggie Armbruster a hard time." Celebrity giggled, thinking about what the chief told her.

"Yeah, I'm waiting to hear from him. What does he expect when he's dealing with a brainless bozo? The prison will most likely confiscate his tablet, so there goes his entertainment, communications, and scam projects."

"Honestly, prison has come a long way. Who would have thought prisoners would have tablets? Next thing we know, they'll have subscriptions to Netflix and Prime with deliveries to their cells!" Celebrity plopped down into one of Meaty's guest chairs.

She glanced over at the staircase, then leaned in toward

Meaty. "I texted Maddy and Guppy and asked if they wanted to be friends!"

Meaty gawked at the detective. "You're kidding!"

"They've got the iPad, which has a contact list. I figured, why not? We know they communicate. I want to know what's going through their heads and this is the only way to find out." Celebrity smirked.

Meaty stilled, thinking about what she said. He nodded. "Yeah... I think you're right. I'll wait until you get a response, then I'll send them a message."

"Keep it very simple. I told them I wanted to be friends." Celebrity's phone dinged an incoming text. She glanced at her phone and her eyes lit up. "They wrote back!" Celebrity zoomed her chair around the desk to sit beside Meaty. She opened the text list, and they saw Maddy and Guppy's text. She clicked on the message.

Hi Celebrity. Guppy and I want to be your friend too!

"Oh, wow," Meaty exclaimed. "What should you reply with?"

"It has to start off with simple messages until we can determine how much they understand." She wasn't too sure what their comprehension was, but everyone HAD watch them reading the newspaper in one of the secret videos.

Meaty shook his head. "I don't think you have to dumb down the messages. Look at everything we know. They learned a lot from children's programs on how to communicate, use the computer, and all the rest of it. Then they stumbled on that Russian guy on YouTube and watched all his videos about identity theft. They solved that case and communicated with the chief and Jimmy, who had to figure out a way to lead me by the nose to the solution." He shook his head again. Bested by a cat and bird. Who would have thought?

Celebrity stared at Meaty, thinking about what he said. "Yeah, you're right. We should just use our regular language. They'll pick it up." Her fingers flew over her phone message keyboard. *Maddy, Guppy, you can always contact me or the chief if you discover something bad going on. Even if you THINK something isn't right. We will help you solve the problem and keep safe.*

She shared her screen with Meaty. "What do you think?"

"Yeah, that looks good. Who knows what they'll get into next?" Meaty was clueless about what the animals would discover that required their help.

"Now that Jimmy is living with his aunt, Maddy spends a lot of time with Betty, watching her type and listening in on her phone and Zoom calls." Celebrity wondered if Maddy would text Betty questions, her thoughts, or suggestions.

"What about Guppy?" Meaty wondered what the parrot was doing while Maddy was conducting business.

Celebrity guffawed. "That bird! Now that they have a wider range to explore, Guppy fell in love with a tree in the conservatory. He literally sings when he's on the tree. He's so happy."

CHIEF PRICE WAS CLUNKING THROUGH A SPREADSHEET WHEN HIS phone rang. He didn't recognize the number. "Kenton Price, Twinkle Police Department." He listened, eyes growing wider by the moment. "Wait a minute. Are you telling me one of your inmates has filed a complaint?" He listened, growing angrier by the second.

"First of all, Reggie Armbruster is a convict. He has no business contacting someone without his communications being monitored. You would have caught his scam in the making if you had been watching. Our investigator, Arthur Hellman, also known as Meaty, isn't a fly-by-night dumbbell harassing your prisoner. He's a contract federal investigator and has ways to stop fraudulent transactions and reverse the damage."

The chief listened to the sputtering on the other end of the phone. "I'd advise you to confiscate that tablet and place Reggie Armbruster in solitary confinement to think over his actions."

The chief listened some more. "No, I will take no action on my end unless it involves hauling Reggie Armbruster back to court to lengthen his sentence."

He disconnected the call and huffed out in exasperation. "The nerve of some people!" He pressed an auto-dial number. "Meaty, seems like your interference stopping the scam between Reggie Armbruster and Waylen Morrongo hit the hot button."

What's going on? What does that mean?

"Reggie registered a complaint with prison officials that you interfered with his transaction!"

You've got to be kidding me! Who's in charge over there, the prison officials or the inmates?

"Just wanted to let you know in case you receive something in the mail. If you do, call me right away and I'll speak with the DA and see if we can haul him back here to add to his sentence."

Thanks, I'm not good at checking the postal mailbox, but will check and see if they've sent me something.

"Okay. Let me know." Chief Price disconnected the call with a huff.

"What was that all about?" Celebrity asked as Meaty set his iPhone on his desk.

"You're not going to believe this..." He explained the call from the chief.

Celebrity stared at Meaty, trying to comprehend how this could happen. "Wait a minute. No one monitors those prison issued tablets?"

He stared back.

"I guess some bleeding-heart liberal determined prison was just too difficult and inmates deserved some entertainment in the way of tablets. Paid for by us, the citizens in the free world who pay their salaries through taxes."

Celebrity stared a minute longer. "What's next? Gourmet meals? Amazon deliveries?" She stood. "Guess I'd better get back to the real world and my desk."

MRS. POTTS WAS OUT OF HER FUNK AND HAVING A BLAST. JIMMY had set up a MasterCard debit card for her with a shocking, refillable limit. She crawled through places she didn't think she could afford to shop at online previously. Presently, she was on Le Creuset's website ordering stainless steel cookware. She made comparisons with the same offerings at Williams Sonoma, Sur La Table, and Crate and Barrel.

After reading that chefs and professional cooks avoided the black-coated cookware she had used for at least a decade, she went with stainless steel. She had thought about ceramic coated pans, but didn't want to chance they would chip.

One package sat on the floor of her suite that contained a wooden cooking utensil set from The Cutlery Collection. It wasn't the cheap wooden spoons she had bought plenty of times from the Wham-A-Rama. These were top of the line BPA and toxin free utensils.

Tomorrow she expected a delivery of stoneware for everyday meals. Mrs. Potts hadn't decided on what she wanted for special holiday meals. She was leaning towards white place settings so they would not clash with whatever napkins and tablecloths she chose for the occasion.

When packages piled up in her suite, she would grab Jimmy and Brian to haul them to the storage unit Jimmy had rented for her. It would be several days before she moved on to other rooms with her shopping. The kitchen held more items than any other room. Mrs. Potts was glad she mentally went from cabinet to cabinet in her old kitchen and saw what needed to be replaced.

All the do-dads in drawers, cabinets, and on shelves were for specific purposes. She used some only a few times a year, but she learned a valuable lesson years ago. Mrs. Potts had donated many of those things she didn't think were necessary that were taking up space only to discover she needed them. She ended up paying much more to replace them.

Exactly how many times did she ever use a melon ball thing? There were so many odd things in those junk utensil drawers. Mrs. Potts made a note to find some baked potato nails. They really sped up the doneness for sweet potatoes. She remembered to order a small needle-nosed plier for the silverware drawer. Those was necessary to pull off the annoying aluminum foil from the lactose intolerant milk container, and those vitamin bottle sealers with the tiny tabs that needed to be pulled up to peel the seal off.

Mrs. Potts went down her list of cabinet items.

- Stainless drainers of various sizes
- Small pizza pans, the eight-inch size
- Baking dishes in various sizes
- Stainless steel and plastic mixing bowls
- Roasting pans in multiple sizes
- Knife block and sharpening steel
- Soup bowls and cups
- Coffee and tea cups in all sizes with large handles
- Several sizes of glasses
  - Juice glasses came from the small glass jars of dried beef
- Gravy boat for festive occasions
- Baskets in all sizes for breads, muffins, etc.
- Salad spinner ??
- Wood chopping blocks

- Straw container
- Mandolin slicer
- Cooling racks

Then she began a new list for the different electric gadgets:

- Coffee maker & grinder
- Electric tea kettle
- Crockpots in 3 or 4 sizes
- Chopping devices
- Smoothie maker
- Waffle maker
- Salad shooter
- Hand mixer
- Stand mixer
- Bread maker

She saved her file and called it quits for the day.

THE DOORBELL RANG AND JENKINS CHECKED THE FRONT DOOR monitor to see who was there. He wasn't taking any chances and just opening the door for anyone unless he knew who they were and what their business was. Ever since the *stair case incident*, he kept a steely eye on the staff and the doors.

Jenkins recognized George and Jerry Potts and greeted them.

"Hey, Jenkins. How's it going?" Jerry asked.

"Same old, same old. You?" Jenkins threw back at them.

"Business is booming," George acknowledged. "Is Mrs. Diaz busy? We need to talk to her about the shacks in Clem's Corner."

"Come on back." Jenkins led them to Betty's office.

"The Potts boys are here to see you, Betty."

Betty stood and came around her desk. She grabbed them both in a hug. "How wonderful to see you in person this time."

Maddy stopped in the middle of her grooming session to assess the situation. She sounded off a meow that, for all intents and purposes, sounded like a question.

Betty introduced them. "Maddy, this is George and Jerry Potts, Mrs. Potts nephews."

George and Jerry had thoughts that Betty finally reached the end of her brilliance.

Betty caught their odd looks. "Boys, this is Maddy, Jimmy's cat. She's quite the character and seems to comment on people and conversations. Ask anyone in this house and they'll agree. So, let's get down to business, shall we?" Betty returned to her chair and the Potts boys sat in the guest chairs in front of the desk.

Jerry slid a clipped set of papers across the desk. "Here's the assessment of the shacks. They're specific addresses with the proposed business name and business owner."

"They more or less all require the same upgrades. There's two that need a little more tender love and care than the others, but nothing major," George pointed out.

"We're looking at what you mentioned at the start of this project: electrical upgrades, plumbing, internet, a/c and heat. The extras include a new front door on one and replacing the steps to the front door on the other one. We figured the new owners would want to choose their own paint and interiors, so we're not including that."

Betty looked over the paperwork as the Potts brothers talked. They had each service type billed separately, so she could see the expenses for each shack. "I guess I should stop mentally and verbally calling them shacks." She mulled over what Jerry said about interior paint and came to a decision. "I think it's a good idea to refresh the interiors with white paint. The shop owners can change the colors, but this gives them a head start to open their doors for business. Once you're finished with these upgrades, they'll be ready to move in."

"We're ready to get started," Jerry said.

"Once we have your approval, that is," George stressed.

"Everything looks good. Add the interior paint to each of the buildings. You can begin anytime you want. Which service will you begin with?" Betty asked.

George jumped in. "We're starting with the two most important upgrades, electrical and plumbing. Bruce's brother, Mule Wojkenski, is a licensed electrician and he'll inspect and approve each of the places as we finish up the work. We've got our plumbing licenses, so we're all set there."

"Excellent! Do you need starting funds?" Betty asked. She knew there would be out-of-pocket expenses, and she didn't know what their finances were like.

"Thanks, Betty, but we've got it covered. We will invoice you for each completed project." Jerry stood, followed by his brother. He patted Maddy on the head.

"Don't be strangers," Betty said as they left her office. She turned to the cat. "Another project underway."

Maddy sneezed.

CHAPTER FIFTEEN

Three cars parked at the side of the road. Jimmy, Mrs. Potts, and Brian stood at the edge of the property and stared at the huge vacant lot. The Earth Haulers had removed the burnt debris and charred foundation at the old boarding house site. Nothing stood between the gazebo and the road. It was strange.

"I'll call Cal and have him introduce us to his builder-friend so we can get this house up again." Jimmy had a standing appointment with Mrs. Trumble dealing with his extreme guilt over Guppy causing the boarding house to burn to the ground.

Mrs. Potts patted his arm as if reading his mind.

"It looks so small," Brian commented as he stared at the place where he pictured the front door used to be.

While everyone was grateful for Betty offering them a place to live while they were in limbo, they missed what they used to have. Mrs. Potts missed cooking and baking in her own kitchen. There was no way she could waltz into Betty's kitchen and ask Duncan Carver if she could prepare a meal or bake some goodies.

Brian missed his comfy suite where he could chill out, and eating meals with Jimmy and Mrs. Potts.

Jimmy missed his own place, where he enjoyed spending time with his animals and having Celebrity and his friends pop in. He knew Maddy and Guppy most likely missed their trips to the gazebo.

After long, sentimental moments, the three returned to their vehicles and took off. Brian returned to the TIN. Mrs. Potts headed over to her storage unit. Jimmy was ready to get down to business with Cal to move the building forward.

The Honda CRV parked in front of the office building and Jimmy took the elevator up to Cal's office. He tapped on the open office door to get the former architect's attention. Cal bounded to his feet.

"Hey, Jimmy. Come on in and have a seat."

"Earth Haulers finished the cleanup. Everything's gone."

Cal eyed Jimmy. "They removed the foundation, didn't they?"

Jimmy nodded. "Yup. There's nothing there except the gazebo across the yard. Looks so strange."

"Let me give Norris Trusty a call." Cal looked up a number on his contacts list and used the office phone to place the call using speaker phone. After four rings the call was answered.

"Trusty. Who's calling?"

"Hey, Norris. It's Cal Masters. Do you have a few minutes?"

"Oh, hey, Cal. What's up?"

"I'm referring a client to you. Jimmy Katz is representing Mrs. Potts and her boarding house. I've recreated the house plans, and the lot has been cleaned up, foundation removed, and they're ready to get the boarding house building underway."

"Who's paying? Insurance or private lender?" Norris asked.

Cal eyeballed Jimmy, who leaned forward.

"Hi, Mr. Trusty. Jimmy Katz here. Mrs. Potts is waiting for the insurance settlement, but I'm footing the bill, so we don't have to wait for any settlement. Would you be available to meet with Mrs. Potts and me?"

"Sure. Hold on while I pull up my calendar." They heard him clicking on his keyboard. "How's tomorrow at 9:30 look?"

"We've available. Where do you want to meet? We're living with my great aunt, Betty Diaz. We can come to your office. Either way works for us." Jimmy knew Mrs. Potts would cancel a meeting with the pope to get her house underway.

"Why don't you drop by my office? Cal, email me the plans. Look forward to meeting you and Mrs. Potts."

Jimmy whooshed out a sigh of relief. "Thanks so much, Cal."

NORRIS TRUSTY'S OFFICE WAS BETWEEN THE BIGGEM DINER AND Bottoms Top. Jimmy parked the Honda on the street, and he and Mrs. Potts stood on the sidewalk in front of the building for a moment.

"Ready?" Jimmy asked.

His landlady nodded. "I'm so excited!"

They went inside and a receptionist greeted them. "May I help you?"

"We have an appointment with Mr. Trusty," Jimmy stated.

The receptionist pulled up her calendar. "Jimmy Katz?"

"Yes, and Mrs. Potts," Jimmy affirmed.

"Have a seat. I'll let Norris know you're here." The receptionist texted her boss.

They settled on chairs in the waiting area. Mrs. Potts took in the room. Current magazines. The TIN and two other newspapers. A coffee-table book of architectural wonders, including some Frank Lloyd Wright homes and buildings.

An inner office door opened, and a large man approached them. "Jimmy? Mrs. Potts? I'm Norris Trusty. Come on back."

They shook hands, and he led them into his office and closed the door. The room was the size of two or three offices. A desk and a credenza where a regular printer stood were not the main focal areas.

Plotter drawings and files filled the work area's two large tables. A huge plotter printer, a commercial copy machine, and an industrial shredder was against a wall, with an open supply case nearby.

Another table held large books of some kind, along with boxes of material examples people could choose from.

Norris offered them the guest chairs in front of the desk. "Can I offer you water, coffee, or iced tea?"

"Oh, thank you, but we're okay," Mrs. Potts said. She didn't want to waste time with beverages.

"I've studied the house and garage plans Cal sent over and went to the property to see the layout." He focused on Mrs. Potts, since it was her property. "Let's go over the exterior and interior materials. Were you thinking of wood, brick, or concrete? I'm not sure if you have given any thought to the exterior?"

"Concrete? I've never thought of that, but I know a lot of homes are made with concrete these days," Mrs. Potts stated.

"Many builders consider concrete the strongest option, and it is fire resistant. It's typically reinforced with rebar. Another good point for concrete is that it absorbs heat in the daytime and releases it at night." Norris stated. "You can choose your exterior colors and features, such as shutters, solar panels, and storm doors. I'd like to suggest some things you may not think about, like an expansive and wide covered porch with ceiling fans, plant hangers, solar LED lights, and electrical outlets including under the eaves for Christmas lights, and water faucets for plant watering."

The builder noticed his new client's eyes glossing over. "I know it's a lot to take in, but when you have all these options in front of you before the building starts, it saves time and money.

You'll want storm rated windows that insulate against the cold in winter and the hot summer weather. I suggest the type that tilt for easy cleaning. You'll also want screens, and storm doors for each exterior door."

"You've thought of everything," Jimmy stated. "What about gutters and downspouts?"

Norris nodded. "Would you want to consider a water-collection system for yard watering? That could be set up along with a sprinkler system. I'd also suggest installing a whole-house automatic generator, and a water filtration system to get rid of chemicals, minerals, heavy metals, and fluoride."

"Oh, yes, getting rid of those chemicals in the water is extremely important," Mrs. Potts exclaimed.

"Some things that I include in a home building project include continuous structure wrap and window and door tape to reduce air and water infiltration, radiant barrier roof decking to reduce attic temperature, continuous soffit and ridge vent system for superior attic ventilation. Also, pipes in the attic, inside the house and the exterior pipes are protected against freezing and excessive heat."

"When can you begin?" Mrs. Potts asked.

Norris pressed his intercom button on his office phone. "Jeanette, print up a contract for Mrs. Potts' house."

"Just so you understand, I'll be footing the bill for the house," Jimmy stated. "We're still waiting to hear from Mrs. Potts' insurance company on the settlement from the fire."

Norris buzzed Jeanette again. "Jeanette, change the name on the contract for the payment part to Jimmy Katz. Mrs. Potts remains the property owner."

He turned to Jimmy and his landlady. "We can get the foundations laid for the house and garage. Then we'll go over all the interior details. I know your brains are most likely at the limit of absorbing anything else."

Jeanette, the receptionist, tapped on the closed door, entered and presented Norris with three copies of the printed document.

As Norris pointed to where Mrs. Potts should sign, she brought up something for confirmation. "Cal said you made sure all cabinet shelves didn't use those plastic support things. I want to make sure my glassware doesn't come crashing down."

"When I build a house, it never get shortcuts. You're paying for a solidly built place and that's what I'll deliver." He winked. "That's why my houses do not come cheap. I use the best materials and the best contractors who know their stuff and understand their work is on the line. If they screw up to line their own pockets and I catch them, they're blackballed from ever working for me again. Plus, word spreads."

Norris pointed to where Jimmy should sign. Jeanette entered carrying her notary stamp. "All set?" she asked. She stamped the documents and signed her name.

"We'll get the foundation poured. A lot of builders start the framing within seven days, but we wait the full twenty-eight days for the full curing. You really don't want to add a lot of weight until the foundation is solid."

Mrs. Potts was all atwitter as she and Jimmy left Norris Trusty's office. Jimmy drove them over to the ice cream shop, where they celebrated with hot fudge sundaes.

GUARDS RETURNED REGGIE ARMBRUSTER TO HIS NONDESCRIPT prison cell, where he seethed and spewed venom after a guard locked the door behind him. His visit to the warden's office to file a complaint against Meaty backfired. They confiscated his prison-issued tablet, and he barely talked his way out of solitary confinement. It was back to square one, wondering where the money would come from for his incidentals, mortgage and property taxes.

Once again, he mentally spewed invectives at Caleb, his only child and the town drunk. Never would he ever admit he was Caleb's biggest enabler, paying untold amounts for bail and rehab to the point where he had nothing left. He would lose his house if he couldn't pay the taxes.

It was difficult to admit that he was not much better. His attempts at bank theft were not about to get him to the French Riviera, where books, TV and movies showed where the best criminals lived in luxury. Hell, he didn't need luxury. All he wanted was to save his house and have enough money to be comfortable again. He thought about his empty house. All the furniture sold off to pay his son's legal expenses. For what? Caleb was still in jail and would be for a while longer.

Reggie collapsed on his cot. His head throbbed, and it wasn't like he could waltz over to the medicine cabinet and grab an aspirin bottle. He had to admit he was royally screwed.

Jimmy worried the romance had deflated with Celebrity. All the trauma and drama seemed to evaporate or change their bond. Maybe now that rebuilding the boarding house was in the capable hands of Norris Trusty, he could focus on moving forward and they could have a romantic getaway. There were enough babysitters for Maddy and Guppy at the mansion, so that wasn't anything he had to worry about. He'd have a chat with the animals and let them know his plans.

He parked in front of Life Adventures on Pincher Street and went inside.

"Hello, may I help you with a fantastic getaway?" a middle-aged woman asked while arranging brochures in a rack for Hawaii and other places. She was a looker with deeply tanned skin, a little too much on the toasty side, as far as Jimmy was concerned. The streaked hair wasn't attractive. The purplish tint through her ash blonde locks clashed with the chartreuse shirt. Her stretchy jeans must have been spray-painted on, which showed every single bulge of fat.

Jimmy shuddered as he pulled his gaze up to her face. Those cats-eyes staring back at him would have Cleopatra breaking the mirror. There was so much black eyeliner that it got lost in the fold between her eyes and brows. He didn't know where to look and was positive his face showed an urgency.

The woman stuck her hand out. "Hello. I'm Doreen Hickenlooper."

Jimmy shook her hand. "Jimmy Katz. I'd like to take my girl-friend on a short getaway."

He swore he saw dollar signs light up her eyes. She most likely recognized his name and figured *the heir* would pay big bucks for a vacation.

"Have you ever been to San Antonio?"

Jimmy shook his head. He couldn't believe he lived in the big city for so long and never visited neighboring cities.

Doreen continued her sales pitch. "There are wonderful places to experience, like a trip to the Alamo, the River Walk, the Hopscotch immersive light art, Natural Bridge Caverns. Then you can drive just 29 miles west to New Braunfels where you can enjoy authentic German food and everything German. The Sophienburgh Museum is quite remarkable which details Prince Carl Solms crossing the ocean, trekking across the USA and settling in New Braunfels."

As she spoke, she handed Jimmy various brochures. He flipped through them as he listened to her chatter on and on. The places she touted looked interesting. He thought he and Celebrity would like the trip.

"If this is to your liking, I could make all the reservations, so all you would have to do is show up with your toothbrush and enjoy." Doreen raised her eyebrows in question.

"Yeah, this sounds like a good idea," Jimmy said, still flipping through brochure pages. "I'll have to see when my girlfriend can get off work for three or four days. Maybe we should plan two days in each town. There's a lot to do."

Doreen steered him toward her booking desk. "Do you think you would want to try for this week or next?"

"I'd like to go this week, but I don't know her schedule." He pulled his phone out and sent her a text. He saw the three dots of her typing an answer.

There's nothing going on right now that Ramirez couldn't handle. Why?

Jimmy texted. *Want to get away on a 4-day mini vacation?*

Where to?

Jimmy texted back. *San Antonio and New Braunfels.*

He waited; figuring she was thinking about it.

We can go Wednesday. I'll have to pull our clothes together this afternoon and tomorrow. Are we taking Maddy and Guppy with?

Jimmy read a lot into the *"our clothes"*. He assumed she wanted them not to clash, and thinking about Doreen, he understood all about clashing.

He texted back. *Just us. I wouldn't want to take a chance that they would get lost, stolen or something.*

Do you have luggage?

He thought about his beat-up old wheeler. *We might have to buy something better than what I have.*

I'll take care of that. I'll put in a vacation request with Stephanie and the chief. I'm sure we can plan to leave early Wednesday.

His wide smile was all Doreen needed. Her fingers flew over the keyboard. She took down the required information: names, addresses, phone numbers, email addresses, credit card number, and emergency contact information for both of them.

"Let me get on this right away. I'll make all your reservations. When everything is in place, I'll email you both the itinerary. You'll have such a wonderful time!"

After Jimmy signed the credit card authorization, he stood.

"You'll have to present this credit card at the hotels and other places I've reserved for you, so make sure you bring it with you," Doreen explained.

"I'm so glad I stopped by, Doreen. Thanks for putting this all together for us."

"My pleasure! Now, go pack."

CHAPTER SIXTEEN

Jimmy dozed in the passenger seat while Celebrity drove. They swapped at 200 miles when they made a pit stop. There were still 250 miles to go, so Celebrity figured they'd swap again somewhere around 150 miles. She and Jimmy had gathered Maddy and Guppy and talked to them about the trip. They went into detail about their babysitters. Jenkins, Brian, Mrs. Potts, and Aunt Betty. No one would let them go hungry, thirsty, or be lonesome.

Those animals, she thought. She and Jimmy figured Maddy and Guppy talked about things. Since Guppy had a voice, he was the one who squawked their questions or opinions.

"Accidents!" Guppy belted out.

"We're not going to get into an accident," Jimmy said in a firm voice.

"Kidnapping!" was Guppy's next statement, followed by, "Volcano! Boom!"

Celebrity stifled a snort of laughter. "Look, nothing is going to happen! Where exactly do you think we're going to get hit by a volcano? We're only going away for four days. We'll be back Sunday."

Jimmy went to his desk. There was a calendar on the wall with pictures of birds. He grabbed it and brought it to the table, where the discussion was taking place. "Here's the calendar." He tapped Wednesday. "This is Wednesday, tomorrow morning. We will leave bright and early because it's a very long drive in the car." He tapped Sunday. "We will be home Sunday sometime. That's four days away. Home on day five."

Maddy sniffed the calendar.

Guppy pecked Wednesday.

"Yes, Guppy. That's Wednesday. Tomorrow morning. We will drive away after breakfast," Jimmy explained.

Maddy hopped down from the table and curled up on her comfy pillow on the floor and settled in for a nap.

Guppy flew back to his tree and took up window vigilance.

"Well, that went well," Celebrity stated. "Let's go pack your clothes." She grabbed the handle of the new rolling suitcase and headed toward Jimmy's bedroom.

THEY WERE STILL OUT IN THE MIDDLE OF NOWHERE ON TEXAS 55 when traffic slowed, then stopped altogether. Celebrity gently nudged Jimmy.

"Looks like there must have been an accident or something. Traffic's come to a halt."

Jimmy grogged awake, sat up straight, rubbed his eyes and stared out the windshield. "Huh. Wonder what's happened?"

"Probably one of those high-flying 18-wheelers. They're so dangerous!" Celebrity said. She couldn't see anything except for the cars in front of her. "I'll go see what's happening. You stay here."

"Bring your badge in case cops try to give you a hard time." Jimmy suggested.

Celebrity dug into her purse. "Good idea." She grabbed her

badge, stuffed it into her pocket, and she and Jimmy got out of the car. He slid in behind the wheel while she took off down the road.

After at least twenty minutes, Celebrity trotted back to the car and slipped into the passenger seat. "Looks like we're going to be stuck here for hours. Two 18-wheelers collided. There's some kind of liquid all across the lanes, so the hazardous waste crew has to clean it up."

Jimmy contemplated. "Let me call home." He pulled up Jenkins number. "Hey, Jenkins. We're stuck on 55." He reiterated what Celebrity said.

"Hang tight. Toombs will grab the helicopter and we'll pick you up and take you to San Antonio. I'll sit with your vehicle."

"Okay. See you soon." Jimmy turned to Celebrity. "I guess we have a helicopter? They'll be here soon."

Celebrity snickered. "Helicopter, private jet, limo—why should anything surprise you?"

"Wait until the kids hear about this. Might not be our accident, but at least it wasn't a volcano!" Jimmy chuckled.

Twenty minutes later, they heard the chopper approaching. They got out of the car and waved until they were spotted. There must have been a mile of cars behind them. Toombs was behind the controls. He landed the bird in the grass on the side of the road.

Jimmy popped the trunk and grabbed their bags while Jenkins headed their way.

"I've got your spare key. There's a turn-around back around a quarter of a mile. I'll get across the lanes and head back to Twinkle. We'll pick you up in the chopper on Sunday, or whenever you want to go home." Jenkins pointed in the direction of the turn-around.

"Whatever you do, make sure you carefully explain what happened to the kids. They were worried about accidents, kidnappings, volcanos and boom," Jimmy said.

"Volcano's?" Jenkins asked. "How'd they come up with that?" Celebrity elbowed the man. "Who knows?"

"Thanks, Jenkins. Be careful that no one crashes into you getting across these lanes," Jimmy stated, worried.

"No problem. Have fun." He waited until Jimmy and Celebrity stowed their luggage into the chopper, climbed in, and Toombs lifted off.

Jenkins got into the SUV and maneuvered it amid angry honks and middle finger waving trying to get across the lane to the opposite direction, which was empty. He headed back up Texas 55 and finally drove back to Twinkle with a dozen or more vehicles following him.

CELEBRITY TOOK CHARGE OF THE ITINERARY. AFTER TOOMBS landed the chopper on the hotel's helipad, he waited until Jimmy and Celebrity were in the clear before he took off. After waving to Toombs, they rolled their luggage toward the stairwell.

Doreen Hickenlooper had arranged for the penthouse suite in the 5-star hotel. It had a huge bedroom, a living room and a dining room with a full kitchen. Once inside, they wandered around the enormous suite. They took in the beautiful view from the floor to ceiling windows.

They had an hour to relax before getting ready for their dinner reservations at Chama Gaúcha Brazilian Steakhouse.

"We have enough time for a half-hour nap and a shower," Celebrity stated. She rolled her luggage into the large room and flopped onto the bed.

Jimmy eyed the sofa and that was that. He removed his shoes, pulled his phone out of a pocket, and set an alarm. Thirty minutes wasn't enough, but a quick nap before dinner would revive him somewhat. It had been a long drive. He was grateful for Toombs and Jenkins coming to their rescue.

He was out like a light and woke to Celebrity shaking his shoulder. "Your alarm has been going off for a while. You were really out. Go jump in the shower. I laid out clothes on the bed."

Jimmy struggled off the sofa, slipped his feet into his shoes, and shuffled to his temporary bedroom.

THE LYFT DRIVER DROPPED THEM OFF AT THE RESTAURANT. THERE was a long line that stretched down the sidewalk. Jimmy and Celebrity approached the door guard. "Jimmy Katz. We have reservations."

The guard looked them over, then checked his clipboard. He nodded and opened the door. "Enjoy your meal."

Once inside, the maître d' greeted them.

"Jimmy Katz. Reservation for two."

"Ah, Mr. Katz, my lady, we have your table ready," the maître d' said. "If you will follow me?"

The maître d' led them to a table by a large artwork on the wall. He helped Celebrity into her chair and draped a napkin across her lap. He handed them each a menu and discretely slipped away.

A server poured water in their glasses, then whisked away to another table.

They studied the menu.

"I'm going to get the picanha. Looks delicious." Jimmy said. He pointed to where it was on the menu. It was described as USDA Prime that was aged 45 days and served with a sprinkling of sea salt.

"Oh, that looks good. I'll have the same. Why don't we try the fried polenta and garlic mashed potatoes?'

"Look at those desserts!" Jimmy's eyes were lit with temptation as he read about the offerings.

"Better wait until we know we'll have room," Celebrity suggested.

"We can always get it to go for later. There's a fridge in the kitchen."

A server took their order and Jimmy staved off ordering dessert. Another server approached with two wine bottles. "May I offer you some wine?"

They accepted the wine and let their eyes wander the restaurant. They noticed interesting wall art. The restaurant buzzed with conversations. Warm bread wrapped in white linen arrived. Celebrity buttered a slice of bread, then sipped wine.

"This has to be the nicest restaurant I've ever been inside," she stated.

"Let's hope the food is as good as the atmosphere," Jimmy said.

Two servers delivered their meal. The steaks were mouthwatering, and the sides were delicious. After they finished, Jimmy sat back. "I think we'll get those desserts to go."

They left the restaurant with their desserts in a bag that Celebrity held. "Why don't we walk around for a little while?" she suggested.

"Good idea. We can walk off the sleepiness that comes after a great meal. I'm going to have to send Doreen flowers. She really took care of us."

Celebrity smooched him on the cheek. "That would be a nice gesture. So far, the hotel and this restaurant are 5-stars."

Jimmy called Delia's flower shop and ordered flowers and a note to be delivered to Doreen Hickenlooper. The note thanked her for such great accommodations, including their first restaurant experience. Jimmy mentioned they would both leave reviews on her website when they got home.

They cut their walk short and called for an Uber. They were

still beat from the long drive and the backed-up highway. Tomorrow would be a full day of planned activities, and they wanted a fresh start.

THE HOPSCOTCH IMMERSIVE LIGHT ART BLEW THEIR MINDS. They wandered the gallery with open mouths gawking at the incredible works of art.

"I've never seen anything like this," Celebrity stated. "I can't wait to tell my mom and dad about this place."

"That travel agent really did me a favor with this vacation!" Jimmy stuttered out while looking at an eye-widening display of lights.

"Let's go get something to eat," Celebrity said, nudging him.

"K."

Celebrity steered Jimmy to the doors and pulled him outside. "I'm going to tell everyone I know about this place. It just has to be experienced!"

They stood on the sidewalk and looked around.

"I saw an Indian food restaurant down there." Celebrity pointed.

"Let's go. It's been a while since I've had Indian."

Jimmy had no sooner spoken when a black sedan screeched to the curb in front of them. The doors opened and hands grabbed him. He hollered. Then the fighting skills he learned from Moses kicked in.

Celebrity jumped into the fray. "POLICE! UNHAND THAT MAN!" She grabbed one of the kidnappers and whacked him about, leaving him in a sniveling lump on the sidewalk where a crowd had gathered, cellphones recording the action.

A siren approached, and a police car angled itself so that the kidnapper's vehicle could not take off. Two police officers jumped out of their vehicle and jumped into the struggle. Jimmy was released from the grip of the guy he was fighting.

After handcuffing the three kidnappers and putting them in the back of the police car, the officers approached Celebrity and Jimmy. Celebrity presented her badge.

"This was not a random kidnapping attempt," she explained. "We only arrived yesterday afternoon. These people must have learned who we are from someone at the hotel where we're staying."

The cops waited for an explanation to her statement.

"This is Jimmy Katz, the heir to the Katz-Diaz empire."

Now there was some interest. One of the police officers whipped out a small notebook and a pen. He took down their information, Celebrity's badge number, and the name of the hotel. The other stood by the police car and was talking through the communication device on his shoulder. When he was finished, he joined them again.

"The captain has dispatched a team to the hotel. We need to find out who worked in collusion with these guys. Can't have hotel guests fingered for these types."

"Where exactly is Twinkle in Texas? I've never heard of it."

"It's several hours north and west... way west of here," Jimmy explained. "You should come for a visit."

"Huh. I'll look it up on the map."

"Uh, you may not find it on any map. It's small and out in the middle of nowhere," Jimmy said with a chuckle. "When I moved there, I didn't think I'd ever get there."

"We're sorry this happened to you, but we'll get this sorted." The officer handed them his card. "Call if there's anything else we can help you with." The officers returned to their vehicle and carted off the kidnappers.

"What do we do now?" Celebrity didn't know if they should pack up and get out of the hotel, or what.

"Let's go back to the hotel and see what they have to say for themselves," Jimmy suggested. "I'll get an Uber."

Celebrity was busy on her phone searching for something on Google.

"What are you looking for?" Jimmy leaned in on the back seat of the Uber and saw what Celebrity was searching. "Volcanos? Get real."

She looked up from her phone and ground her eyes into his. "You might recall what Guppy said: accident, kidnapping, volcanos, and... boom."

Jimmy stared back, thinking about the parrot's declaration of warning. "Where in the world would we be threatened by a volcano around here?"

Celebrity held her phone for him to see what she discovered. "There's a bunch of volcanos in Texas. They just haven't erupted in millions of years. The internet says they're extinct, but this group of geologists say it's possible they could become active again."

Jimmy was lost in thought when the Uber stopped in front of the hotel. It pulled up next to three police cars.

"I'm wondering if we should cut our trip short and get back home," Jimmy stated. "There's no telling if my animals have some hidden knowledge about a volcano."

With a mildly freaked-out expression regarding Maddy and Guppy's predictions, Celebrity agreed. "Call Toombs! I'll pack!" She yanked the car door open and sprinted into the hotel, and headed to the elevators.

Jimmy entered the hotel and approached the police and the hotel manager. "We're leaving. It's not safe here. Please check us out. We'll turn in the keycards when the helicopter arrives."

The hotel manager sputtered apologies following Jimmy to the elevator.

CHAPTER SEVENTEEN

"What happened?" Toombs asked as Jimmy and Celebrity climbed into the helicopter after storing their luggage.

"Toombs, you're not going to believe this, but before we left home, Guppy warned us about accidents, kidnapping, volcanos, and boom." Celebrity nodded her support as Jimmy explained to the security specialist for the Katz-Diaz property.

Toombs shifted his glance to his passengers, eyebrows raised. "Volcanos?"

"Look, there's a bunch of extinct volcanos all over Texas, especially West Texas. We didn't want to take any chances of being away from home if something like that occurred."

"No volcano is going to erupt, Jimmy. Where on earth did this come from? You're not getting your news from a parrot now, are you?" Toombs snorted a chuckle.

"Listen, Toombs. There was an accident on the highway which brought you and Jenkins in the chopper. Then Jimmy was almost kidnapped in San Antonio. Do you really think we were going to laugh off a volcano erupting?" Celebrity snarled.

She leaned over and whispered into Jimmy's ear. "We need to include Toombs in the Pact."

Jimmy whispered back. "When we get home we'll gather everyone." Celebrity nodded. They didn't engage in any other conversation until twenty minutes later when Toombs landed the chopper on the helipad at his great aunt Betty's property.

Jimmy helped Celebrity out of the helicopter, grabbed their luggage and rushed to get into the house, not waiting on Toombs. They abandoned their luggage near Mrs. Potts suite, entered her rooms and closed the door.

Mrs. Potts saw the stress on their faces. "What's wrong? You weren't due back for another couple of days."

They took turns explaining the experiences in San Antonio, and Toombs.

"We need to include Toombs in on the Pact," Jimmy said. "Right now."

It was Mrs. Potts' turn to look stressed. "Oh, my! I'll send a text to the group and tell them we need to meet ASAP!" She got busy on her cellphone. "Go get your laptop and we'll all meet in the conference room. Don't call Toombs until you explain the whole thing to the group."

LESS THAN A HALF HOUR LATER, THE PACT GROUP SAT AROUND the conference table. Jimmy and Celebrity took turns explaining the problems they had while on vacation, and how Toombs needed to be included.

"Well, he is Betty's head of security," Chief Price said. "After Jenkins as the door stopper, Toombs has unbelievable skills. Yes, we should include him."

Betty looked over to her great nephew and Celebrity. "I can't believe the problems you experienced! I would have run back home if that was the only way to get here."

"Call in Toombs so we can get him on board," Mrs. Potts stated.

Betty messaged Toombs and asked him to come to the small conference room. Jimmy had his laptop ready to show the videos of the animals.

"I can't wait to see these videos again," Jenkins stated.

A tap sounded on the closed door, then Toombs entered. He glanced around the table at the occupants. "Everything okay?"

Betty started. "Have a seat, Toombs. There's something you need to know which is a high priority that everyone in this room is privy to."

Toombs raised an eyebrow. "If this is a security issue, why wasn't I included to begin with?"

"At first, the group only consisted of four people," Jimmy explained. "Mrs. Potts, Brian, the chief, and myself. Each time we added someone, they were important in the chain of events. Now, we feel you need to be included in The Pact."

"The Pact?" Toombs questioned, grinning like a loon while thinking this was some kind of a prank.

Chief Price nodded. "The Pact. It's a situation that we all guard with our lives. It's no joking matter, as you will see shortly."

"When we mentioned what Guppy said about the accident, kidnapping, volcano... and boom, it was no funny-ha-ha thing," Celebrity stated.

Toombs glanced around at the faces in the room. No one was smirking. They all wore very serious expressions.

"This all goes back to the incidents at the boarding house shortly after I moved to Twinkle," Jimmy began. "Remember the break-ins?" He went into the details while others in the room joined in. Then he clicked on one video after another.

Toombs sat stone-faced while he watched what the two culprits did when they thought no one was around. He couldn't believe Maddy whacking the keyboard and running back and forth to send messages, do searches, watch YouTube programs.

"Never, ever look up to the ceiling in Jimmy's suite," Meaty warned. "We don't want them to know there're cameras up there. They think they're motion detectors like what was in the boarding house in case someone tries to climb in a window."

"How did they learn these things?" Toombs just couldn't get his head around Maddy's computer skills.

"When Jimmy brought Maddy home after taking her to the vet, she was around five or six weeks old," Mrs. Potts explained. "He turned on the TV to a children's program. Maddy and Guppy watched those shows every day, different programs that taught children all sorts of things. She also learned by watching what Jimmy did on the laptop."

Toombs sputtered. "But she's a CAT! He's a PARROT! These things should be impossible. And I take it they talk to each other... Maddy and Guppy?"

"Guppy is the voice. His limited vocabulary explained things out loud until Maddy discovered she could send texts," Jimmy added.

Toombs shook his head, shocked at what he witnessed on the dozen plus videos.

Meaty took the floor. "Listen, Toombs. Remember the Reggie Armbruster problem with the bank? Maddy and Guppy solved the case after subscribing to and watching this Russian guy's YouTube channel about identity theft. The Chief had to lead me to the problem, so a human was the one to solve the case. It takes a while to get used to the fact that these gifted animals are clever enough to figure things out way before we do."

"But how did they know to go to YouTube? And how did they find this Russian?" Toombs was stuck in a quandary.

Mrs. Potts patted Toombs' arm. "I know this is a stretch to understand, but you have to understand that Maddy watched every children's TV show you could imagine. She and Guppy learned computer skills. They learned how to Google, and go to YouTube to learn other things."

"I'll add your info to their Contacts," Meaty said.

Toombs wondered how he'd react to getting a text from the animals.

Chief Price stood, hand outstretched. "We are including you in The Pact, Toombs. You are never, ever to speak of this to anyone other than the people in this room. Do you understand the ramifications? If the government were to find out about these animals, they would confiscate them and dissect their brains."

Toombs practically jumped to his feet. He stretched his hand out and placed it on top of the Chief's hand. Others joined in.

"I swear I will never breathe a word about this to anyone!" Toombs was shell-shocked from this discovery.

The Pact was sworn to. All the members sat.

"So, accident, kidnapping, volcano, and...boom?" Toombs studied the faces around the table.

As they all stared at each other, wondering about that last prediction, they felt the building shake ever so slightly under their feet.

"Was that an earthquake?" Celebrity squealed.

Phones were out around the table. Everyone Googled earthquake in Twinkle and volcano eruptions nearby. Jimmy discovered the U.S. Geological Survey website and passed on the link.

"It looks like tremors don't necessarily lead to eruptions," Betty pointed out.

"How did they know?" Toombs was stuck in his head.

"Well, they're animals, so they have different instincts than we do," Jimmy said. "Never dismiss what comes out of Guppy's mouth, or Maddy's texts. Sometimes it may not make sense, but if you wait it out, what they mentioned manifests into fact."

"Thank God there was no boom!" Meaty exclaimed.

Mrs. Potts, Brian, and the Chief nodded. Everyone stood and went about their business. Toombs threaded his way through the house. He noticed Guppy on his favorite tree in the conservatory with Maddy grooming herself on the floor amid some violets that were just blooming.

He stopped, stared at the critters deep in thought. Toombs cleared his throat, more of a nervous reaction than having something stuck in his throat. "Maddy, Guppy, you can text me anytime you think I need to know something, especially if you see or think there's something wrong or dangerous. Jenkins and I are the closest protectors of you, Betty, Mrs. Potts, Brian, Jimmy, the kitchen people and the house staff. We try our best to keep this house and property safe."

Maddy meowed.

"Gotcha," Guppy squawked.

Toombs rocked back and forth from heel to toe, digesting that response. He studied the two animals and figured Maddy said something in animal speak to Guppy, then the parrot made the audible affirmation. He almost couldn't get his head around the whole business of these two animals having the capacity to do what they have done.

The videos from the hidden cameras were authentic. He watched how they read the newspaper, for crying out loud. It was a team effort. Guppy turned the pages. Maddy scrunched over the page, sometimes using her paw to go across a line of text. He wanted to cry for the unfairness of it all, that these two animals had to be protected at all costs.

Toombs came to grips with himself and nodded at the animals. "Back to work for me."

Jimmy walked Celebrity, the Chief, Meaty, and Brian outside to their cars.

"Well, that went okay," Jimmy stated. "Toombs was a little flummoxed, but overall, I'd say he grasped the situation."

Chief Price nodded. "I've known Toombs for as long as he's been Betty's security man. It may take time for him to digest everything he witnessed, but there's no way he'd ever let out one peep about this. He'll take this Pact to the grave."

BETTY ENTERED HER OFFICE AND SETTLED INTO HER CHAIR. SHE brought up her calendar and discovered she had just enough time to use the restroom before her next appointment online. When she returned to her desk, Maddy hopped up to her spot, did a fast grooming of her face, then mewed as if to say she was ready.

Betty patted Maddy, then grabbed her mouse to get the link sent to the parties for the meeting. Suddenly, Guppy was hollering out squawks and flying out of the conservatory in a mad dash.

"What in the world?" Betty was on her feet and out the door. She almost bumped into Mrs. Potts. "What's wrong, Guppy?"

"BOOM!" he squawked.

Maddy jumped down and joined Betty and Mrs. Potts outside the office. Maddy's hair bristled.

Jenkins came running. "What's going on?"

"Don't know. Guppy said *boom* and now Maddy's all upset. Has everyone left?" Betty asked.

Jenkins took off to the front door. He saw the cars taking off. He ran, jumped and waved his arms. The chief's car ground to a halt with everyone else's cars squealing to a stop. People jumped out of their cars and ran back to Jenkins, who met them half way.

"What's happened?" Chief Price boomed.

"Guppy is frantic and Maddy's upset. He called out BOOM,

but we don't know what that means. I thought it was the volcano!" Jenkins explained.

Everyone barreled up the driveway and into the house. They heard the bird and saw the commotion.

"Upstairs! Come on, Guppy, Maddy. Send a text so we know what boom means," Jimmy shouted.

Maddy dashed up the stairs with Guppy's wings flapping overhead. The humans followed. Maddy slid to a stop by her iPad and her pal landed on her cushion. With the yellow pencil gripped in her strong jaws, Maddy whacked the text icon. Then she whacked Jimmy's name to bring up the message area.

Guppy leaned in and pecked at keys. *Strange noise in sky. Danger!*

Chief Price pulled his phone out and made a call. "Toombs, do you see or hear anything from the sky? Drones? A Plane?" He listened. "Guppy senses danger from the sky." The chief headed out the door, down the stairs, then out the front door, followed by everyone else except Jenkins. He stayed behind to see if there was any other information forthcoming from the bird.

Jenkins squatted and talked calmly to the animals. He held his phone. "Text me if you feel any other information would help. I'm going to stand at the front door and I'll yell anything you send me to the others, okay?"

"Gotcha!" Guppy agreed.

Jenkins rushed out of the room and down the stairs. He opened the front door, walked outside a few feet away and saw everyone standing in the middle of the front lawn, eyes to the sky.

In the distance, everyone could see a small jet flying low with smoke billowing out behind it. Chief Price barked out instructions.

"Celebrity, call Stephanie and have all units get over here on the double. Have her call in the fire department."

"Jimmy, call the airport air traffic controller."

"Meaty, call the NTSB or FAA, whichever one is the easier to get through to."

"Jenkins, have Duncan Carver prepare food for emergency responders."

Toombs drove the property Jeep to where everyone was on the front lawn. He had to wait until the jet was on the ground before he could drive anywhere.

"Looks like a Cessna," Toombs said.

Brian, always in reporter mode, sent a group text to Danny, Bill Trance, and Sylvan Stoneridge.

They assumed the pilot had somewhat of a control of the jet because the trajectory and speed changed. What could have been a close hit to the mansion changed to what looked like the main street, Stonerich Boulevard.

Chief Price belched out to his deputies, "Clear Stonerich Boulevard! That jet's going to land!"

The chief and Celebrity ran to their cars and took off, sirens screaming. Ramirez must have come to the same conclusion. They found him using the microphone in his car to get people and vehicles out of the way. As people saw what headed toward them, they ran screaming for cover or ducked into their vehicles and raced in the opposite direction of the jet.

Fire trucks from Twinkle, Derrick, Dime Water and Pancake screeched into place along Stonerich Blvd. The plane's wheels hit the pavement beyond the old boarding house location, bounced a few times and sped down Stonerich Boulevard.

"There's not enough street for that jet to stop!" Mrs. Potts screeched in panic.

As the plane slowed, everyone watched, praying for no casualties or damage. The Cessna stopped a hundred feet back from the fire engines.

The pilot, copilot, and two passengers scurried out of the plane and ran toward the police and spectators while smoke engulfed the area. An explosion occurred in the rear of the plane that shook the ground and caused a passenger to stumble and fall. Two first responders charged toward the fallen passenger and hauled him to safety.

The fire departments raced equipment to the jet, cautious of any possible new explosions. The pilot and copilot were questioned about any cargo, and what, if anything, was in the hold that would cause the explosion.

Chief Price, Jimmy, Brian, and Toombs made eye contact.

"That's the BOOM!" the chief whispered.

They were all thinking similar thoughts: this disaster would have been much greater without Guppy's early warning.

Betty steered everyone from the burning plane to the mansion.

Jenkins led the airport authorities to the small conference room, where they could conduct interviews and discuss the crash.

The kitchen staff brought out trays of beverages: coffee, iced tea, and bottled water.

Chief Price took control of the first responders on the property, barking out orders.

Toombs surveyed the area and made sure none of these strangers wandered where they shouldn't go. While they may be first responders, the Katz-Diaz empire was no secret. It was Toombs' first duty to protect Betty and everyone in the mansion.

Jimmy rushed up the stairs to his suite to check on the animals. Mrs. Potts huffed up after him. They found Maddy on the windowsill and Guppy in his tree, watching the activity down on Stonerich Boulevard.

"It's a good thing you two warned us," Mrs. Potts exclaimed. She stared at the Cessna burning on the street.

Jimmy fluffed Guppy's feathers, then patted Maddy.

CHAPTER EIGHTEEN

Hours and hours later, everyone not belonging to the mansion left. The Cessna still took up space on Stonerich Blvd., waiting to be hauled away, but cars could squeeze past it and get on their way. Experts would examine the jet and all the parts that had broken away, from one end to the other, to determine what caused the first fire, then the explosion on the ground.

The front page of the TIN contained a photo spread with articles by Brian and Danny. The website contained video segments from people all over Twinkle. Eddie Garcia, the website guru, provided links to government explanations of what happened during an investigation when a plane crashed.

Breakfast with Jimmy, Mrs. Potts, Betty, Brian, Jenkins, and Toombs began as a silent affair the next morning. Then, after people had their orange juice, café mocha, eggs, bacon or ham, and toast, conversations launched.

"I can't believe that jet was heading straight for the mansion," Betty stated.

"It's a good thing the pilot could maneuver the aircraft to the street," Brian said.

Toombs let loose a deep sigh. "It's a good thing the Chief, Celebrity and Ramirez cleared Stonerich Boulevard of vehicles and people in time! I can't imagine what that disaster would have looked like."

Jimmy drummed his fingers on the table. "It seems sort of odd that these three disasters..."

"Four," Brian piped up.

Jimmy silently counted with his fingers. "You're right. I discounted the volcano because it was only a rumble."

Mrs. Potts shook her finger. "Don't test it, Jimmy."

They all thought about what she said.

Jimmy piped up again. "Let me rephrase that. The accident on the highway and the kidnapping attempt were not disasters. Even the *volcano* wasn't a disaster because we only felt an insignificant movement. The jet crash—that's the big disaster."

The men nodded knowingly. Betty and Mrs. Potts shook their heads, trying to shake off the event that could have flattened the mansion. Mrs. Potts was stuck in her head about almost experiencing losing a home twice.

"What's there to think about?" Brian challenged. "There's no way on earth you will ever be able to understand how the animals know these things. There's no second guessing them, Jimmy."

"Animals see, hear, feel, and sense things humans lost the ability to detect eons ago," Betty reminded them.

Toombs stood. "I should find out if the Chief needs our help with anything or anyone from the crash." He turned to Jenkins. "Make sure all the doors are secured. While I made sure no one was wandering the grounds, there's no telling if reporters are sneaking around."

"I'll make sure the kitchen staff and the help don't leave that kitchen door unlocked." Jenkins admitted to himself that he was also guilty of stepping out briefly and returning to the house and maybe, just maybe, not locking the door behind him.

Everyone stood to go about their business. Jimmy took the stairs two at a time and entered his suite. He found Guppy eating his fruit and veggies in his fake tree. Maddy was washing up after her breakfast.

"Any messages for Daddy today?" Jimmy asked.

"Nope!" Guppy squawked out, along with food spewing from his full mouth.

Maddy stopped her grooming and mewed to Jimmy.

"Okay. Daddy's going over to the TIN, then the dojo. Send a text if you need something."

"K." Guppy belched out.

MOSES DIAZ SAT ON JIMMY'S CHEST. "CELEBRITY TOLD ME YOU defended yourself from those kidnappers in San Antonio. I need to teach you more defenses."

Jimmy wheezed. "Get up! Please!"

Moses remembered where he was sitting and jumped up. He held a hand out and hauled Jimmy to his feet. "You realize there's hundreds of videos that show self-defense on YouTube, right?"

Jimmy stumbled to the chair where his water bottle sat. He guzzled water, then plunked into the chair. "Uh huh."

Moses shook his head at his client's nonchalance. "Have you watched any of them?"

Jimmy shook his head. "No, haven't given it much thought... until now."

Moses stared at Jimmy. "Do you mean to tell me that since moving here and experiencing the robbery attempts and people trying to kill you, you never gave protecting yourself much thought? What's wrong with you?"

Jimmy huffed in aggravation. "I liked to think that I was a regular person, not the *heir* of billions. It's kind of difficult to change perspectives when you came up from so broke that you lived in a storage unit for a while."

"Well, that's long gone. You've had a couple of years to accept your new status. If you can't protect yourself, you'll have to hire guards to accompany you everywhere. Including the bathroom." Moses hoped Jimmy *got it*, but he wasn't going to hold his breath.

MRS. POTTS AND BRIAN STOOD AT THE EDGE OF THE PROPERTY where her beloved boarding house had sat for decades until the fire. The new foundation was settling. Lumber and supplies were stacked on the premises.

"Once that foundation is solid, the builder will begin the work. The house will be up and ready before you know it," Brian encouraged his landlady.

"I can't wait to cook in my new kitchen!" Mrs. Potts exclaimed.

"Want to sit in the gazebo?" Brian asked.

Mrs. Potts gazed at the structure her nephews built. "Sure."

"Maddy and Guppy love the gazebo," Brian said as they trekked across the lawn. "I'll bet they'll be happy when they can return to their schedule to visit the gazebo every day."

He opened the door and held it while Mrs. Potts entered the space and plunked down on the bench. Brian closed the door after himself.

"I'm surprised Guppy didn't fly them to here when the house caught on fire," Mrs. Potts said.

"They probably couldn't get the door open." Brian remembered all the videos the TIN received of the parrot flying down Stonerich Boulevard carrying Maddy in the basket. "It's a good thing Guppy flew them to the police station. They saved themselves, though the house was beyond saving."

Mrs. Potts studied her vegetable garden, which was overgrown with weeds since it hadn't been tended to since they all moved to the mansion. "I'm not sure how I feel about peas now."

"That's understandable, but it could have been any vegetable that Guppy hadn't gotten his fill of. So, don't blame the peas."

A knock on the gazebo door startled them. Danny opened the door and plopped down on a bench. "Whatcha doing? Commiserating?"

"Yeah," Brian acknowledged. "We came over to see how things were coming along, and we're happy to see the foundation is curing."

"Before you know it, you'll be in the new house and ordering furniture and stuff," Danny said with a nod of his head.

"I've been ordering things for the kitchen. Jimmy set up a storage unit for me. I haven't ordered any furniture yet. I really need to walk the inside of the house before I can do that," Mrs. Potts explained.

"It looks like the builder is getting ready for the framing," Danny suggested as his eyes took in the stacks of lumber. "The house should go up pretty fast if everything he needs is readily available. Once the framing is done and the windows are installed, it's a piece of cake."

"I plan to come here every day to see how things are progressing," Mrs. Potts said. "Watching my dream house rise from the ashes."

MADDY AND GUPPY EXPLORED THEIR IPAD. THEY FOUND THE profile and Guppy pecked at their names. That opened a screen that showed Payment and Shipping. They saw Payment Method and Card. There was a Visa card listed. They read what was under the heading Shipping Address.

"Is that our address here?" Maddy asked.

Guppy flew over to Jimmy's desk, snatched up an envelope in his beak, and flew back to the pillow and the iPad. He dropped the piece of mail. Maddy eyeballed the address on the envelope and compared it to the address on the screen.

"It's the same address. I guess this is where we live here at Aunt Betty's house," she informed Guppy.

"Look up that VISA card and find out what it is," Guppy suggested.

Maddy exited the profile and headed over to Google. She laboriously typed in VISA CARD and whacked the return button. The screen filled with dozens of offers for credit cards.

"Credit card. I wonder what that's all about?" Guppy asked.

Maddy hunkered down and read several of the first lines of the many ads. She turned her head and stared at Guppy, straight in the eyes. "Gup! We can buy things! The Visa card is like our bank account!"

"Are you sure?" Guppy didn't think that made sense.

"Here's what they say. A Visa card is a payment card you can use to make purchases and withdraw cash." Maddy stared wide-eyed at the screen.

"We can go shopping!" she all but freaked out.

Guppy was stumped. "We can't go to the Foo or anywhere."

"We don't have to!" Maddy was about to come out of her fur. "We can buy things on Google and have them delivered to us!"

"What would we buy?" Guppy was still confused by the whole concept that they could buy anything at all.

"I don't really know," Maddy admitted, "but we can buy something when we know we need it."

"Do we have an email address?" Guppy asked. He pecked on the envelope in the system tray. It opened and they found that they had an email. Guppy pecked the email icon and it opened. "Look, we have an email from Meaty! He says we need an email address for a lot of places online. Look at this! Here's your email address and here's mine!"

"What's that little "a" with the circle?" Maddy asked.

"I don't know, but it's a part of the email address." Guppy stared at the keyboard. "There it is. It's part of the number 2."

"We've got to study up on this." Maddy yawned. "I'm going to take a nap."

Guppy fluttered over to his tree. He checked the windows and didn't see any squirrels trying to get inside, so he tucked his beak into his wing and settled in for a nap.

JORGE DROVE THE MINIVAN UP STONERICH BLVD AND TURNED into Ding Circle. He steered the van into Betty's driveway and parked close to the front door. He rang the doorbell and the door sprung open before the chimes finished their sound throughout the downstairs of the mansion.

Jenkins eyeballed Jorge, surprised to see him. "Hey, what can I do for you today?"

"I have a delivery for Brian," Jorge stated. "Can you help unload the bags and packages?"

Jenkins stepped outside. "Sure."

He and Jorge walked to the rear of the minivan. Jenkins was about to lay a suit bag across his outstretched arm when Jorge had a conniption fit.

"NO, NO, NO!" the clothier all but squealed. "Dangle by the head of the hanger! You'll crease the clothes the way you were going to carry the bag!"

Jenkins almost dropped the bag. He recovered his calm façade. "Oh, I wasn't thinking." He grabbed another bag, careful to only carry one in each hand for fear of a repeat performance. Jorge was well trained by Hector.

They walked into the house and up the stairs to Brian's quarters. Jorge gasped in horror as he spotted what could only be men's clothes from the Wham-A-Rama. "NO! Oh, this poor man! I'm so glad Hector isn't here. He'd have a stroke!"

Jorge balanced both his bag hangers on one hand, then used his free hand to slide the offending clothes into the dark shadows of the rack. He deposited the bags on the rack in the closet and stepped aside for Jenkins to unload his bags.

Jenkins and Jorge returned to the van. Jenkins allowed Jorge to grab the remaining bag, and he grabbed the handles of two paper sacks. He didn't think he could be called out for a wrong way to transport paper bags.

The final trip was for six boxes of shoes. Jenkins and Jorge divided them up.

"Where do you want to put these? In the closet, or on the bed?" Jenkins asked.

Jorge looked over at Jenkins as if the butler had sprouted another nose. "On the bed? Why on earth would we put these shoe boxes on the bed?" Jorge settled his three boxes on the floor of the closet, then stepped aside for Jenkins to do the same.

Jorge took mental inventory of the contents of the closet. He practically sneered at the offensive items hanging on the dark side of the closet. "Well, that's all. Thank you for your help, Jenkins." He studied the butler, grabbed the shoulder seams of Jenkins uniform jacket, and tugged a pinch. "That's better."

Jimmy and Brian arrived back at the mansion at the same time. They parked in the circular driveway away from the front door and met at the rear of Brian's car.

"Let's go see what Duncan prepared for supper," Brian said. The food the chef prepared was scrumptious, but he missed Mrs. Potts' home cooked savory meals. "I hope Mrs. Potts replaces that checkerboard cake pan!"

"We'd better remind her. She's been ordering kitchen things," Jimmy recalled.

They went inside and up the stairs to their suites. Brian walked to his bathroom, ran the water until it heated up, then splashed water on his face and rubbed vigorously. "Ah, that feels better," he said through the towel while drying his face. He returned to his bedroom and noticed the closet doors were open.

"What the...?" He looked at the suit bags, then glanced down to the shoe boxes lining the closet floor. He popped the lids off the boxes and stared, surprised. Loafers in three colors: navy, black, and brown. Another box held two pairs of slippers. The fifth box held sandals. The bigger box held a pair of boots.

"Oh, wow!"

Next, he stood in front of the suit bags and unzipped one open. Two tailored suits. The next bag held an assortment of shirts, ties, and belts. All told, the bags held jackets, coats, long and short-sleeved t-shirts. He discovered one bag contained a bag inside on the bottom, which contained briefs and under-shirts. Another bag contained a similar bag that held socks and, he realized, handkerchiefs.

Brian lowered his head and shook it. He left his suite and walked down the hall to Jimmy's domain. He heard Guppy through the door, giving the squirrels hell. He tapped on the door and it sprung open. Jimmy had a container of cat treats in his hand.

Brian grabbed his best friend and pulled him into a hug. "Oh, Jimmy. I'm so grateful, and I'm sorry if I was too prideful to accept your offer and you had to go behind my back."

Jimmy patted Brian's back. "Sometimes it's difficult to accept a simple gesture of help. Like when I didn't accept your help and Guppy and I ended living in a storage facility."

Brian nodded. "I'll be the best dressed reporter, after you, that's for sure."

CHAPTER NINETEEN

Meaty watched Maddy and Guppy through the hidden cameras on the ceiling in their suite upstairs in the mansion via his laptop at his security desk at the Foo. He assumed they were trying to understand the VISA gift card and had Googled it. The security wiz noticed they looked at each other a lot. Exchanging silent information he'd never be privy to... but he'd pay a fortune to listen to one of those conversations. There was a lot going on in those brains light years past eating, grooming themselves, and looking out windows.

Maddy and Guppy did not understand how the human world worked regarding getting things. What were banks, really? What were these plastic cards? As animals, super intelligent animals at that, all they knew was their Daddy brought things home in bags. A delivery person brought the pizza. Celebrity, Brian, Danny, and Ramirez brought things. Even Aunt Betty, Jenkins and Toombs brought things. Things seemed to magically appear.

They knew nothing about payments or purchases. They had been to stores such as the Wham-A-Rama and the Foo where

Jimmy had bought things. Maddy and Guppy had watched from their places in the shopping cart as the cashier slid each item over the counter. The cashier or a bagging person bagged his items, then they saw their Daddy hand over the little plastic card. The cashier handed him a piece of paper. But they didn't know what it all meant.

Meaty wondered how much they needed to know. He decided to create information on the iPad home page explaining about the name, date, and code on the back of the card for when those were required during the purchase process. Then he shook his head, remembering this was a gift card, not an actual credit card, so there would not be a personal name on the back of the card.

Meaty almost deleted what he had just coded. Then he stared into space for several moments, thinking about the process. All he ended up deleting was the part where he mentioned the name on the back of the card. He screen-shotted a VISA gift card's back online and used his graphics program to outline the date and code required to complete purchases.

When Meaty returned his eyes to the monitor on his laptop, he saw the wily animals had ventured over to YouTube. He stared at a picture of Boris, the Russian. He assumed this guy would be in his 50s, but a much younger man stared back from the picture. Meaty guessed Boris was at most thirty.

He watched as Guppy used his beak to scroll down the page. Boris had recorded videos about everything anyone could want to know about fighting spam, scammers, identity theft—there were rows after rows of short videos to choose from.

Meaty hopped over to YouTube on his work machine and looked up the Russian. He found Boris Ivanov's page and perused his profile. Boris had created this YouTube channel to educate people so they could avoid scams. Boris apologized on behalf of his fellow countrymen and women for the viruses, money scams, romance scams, and all the rest of the trash his fellow Russians dished out.

"Huh."

Meaty turned back to his laptop and watched what the animals were up to.

MADDY WATCHED AS MRS. POTTS SEARCHED THE WEB AND FOUND the special cake pan for what the boys called her checkerboard cakes. She ordered two. She always thought of Jimmy and Brian as boys, but tried to adjust her thinking. Mrs. Potts also found the potato nails, which sped up the baking time, especially for baked sweet potatoes, and added those to the cart. Her old potato nails were four bound together, which didn't work well with the big potatoes. This time, she purchased six individual nails.

Mrs. Potts opened the bottom desk drawer where she kept her purse. She pulled her MasterCard debit card out of her wallet that Jimmy had set up for her and set it on the desk. Maddy reached out a front paw and pulled the debit card to her, and sniffed it. It didn't say VISA on the front of the card. She read what was printed on the card carefully. There were two unfamiliar words she had not come across before: MasterCard and Debit.

Maddy crept closer to the monitor and watched the entire process of how Mrs. Potts ordered these two items as a guest. She stuck her paw out and touched the word Guest.

"Guest means I'm not setting up an account, Maddy. I don't normally visit this website. If I find myself here again, I'll fill out the information to create an account. That makes it easier because the store saves your basic information, which is your name, address, and sometimes your payment information. Either a credit or debit card." Mrs. Potts felt that was a thorough explanation, but she had no way of knowing if this smart kitty understood everything.

Maddy jumped down and sauntered out of Mrs. Potts' suite. She raced through the ground floor to the staircase and charged up the stairs. Her pal was giving the squirrels *what for* from his fake tree.

"Gup! I watched Mrs. Potts buy some things online. She explained about important things!"

Guppy squawked. "What did you learn?"

Maddy licked her chest while thinking. "When we want to buy something, we can either be a guest, or fill out information to set up an account. That would be easier for us, so we don't have to fill in information every time we visit that website—if we have to go there again."

"A guest? What's that?" Guppy asked.

Maddy stopped her grooming. "I don't know. Let's look it up."

"How do you spell it?" Guppy asked.

"I don't know. It's not like we can say the word out loud and have someone find it for us!" Maddy spit out.

"No, but you can text someone!" Guppy wasn't put off by Maddy's bad attitude for not understanding something.

"Okay, who should we text?" Maddy asked.

"Meaty! He knows everything." Guppy said.

Maddy hunkered down in front of their iPad and grabbed her yellow pencil, which was covered with bite marks. She whacked the green Messages button and looked at the list of names. "There he is." She whacked Meaty's name.

Guppy fluttered down to the pillow. He used his beak to type the message, so Maddy didn't have to go back and forth with the pencil.

What is a gest?

❖ ❖ ❖

MEATY WAS ABOUT TO DOZE OFF IN HIS CHAIR AFTER LUNCH WHEN a text dinged him, alert. When he saw it was from Maddy and Guppy he straightened up in his chair. He read it out loud. "What is a gest?" He thought they meant a jest, but stopped himself from answering. He didn't think they meant a joke. After going through several scenarios in his head, he realized this must have something to do with their VISA gift card and ordering online. "Guest," he said out loud. Then he typed into the text area.

You mean G U E S T. A guest is a visitor. If you're shopping online, you can be a guest instead of opening an account. If you're at home and people arrive, they are guests.

The animals stared at their iPad screen and saw Meaty's message arrive.

"Visitor," Maddy said. "Oh, I get it now."

"We have visitors all the time," Guppy acknowledged. "We can be a visitor when we find something we need to buy."

"Daddy feeds us. We live here and have everything we need," Maddy thought out loud.

"I miss going to the round house," Guppy admitted.

MRS. POTTS LIFTED HER PURSE STRAP OVER HER HEAD AND DRAPED it across her chest. Her keys dangled in the front pocket of the many-pocketed bag as she headed out wearing one of her smart outfits from Amanda Jane's Fashionable Clothing store. It was like wearing something from one of her favorite catalogs, where she circled her choices.

She approached the front door of the mansion and spotted Jenkins. She waved goodbye.

"See you later," Jenkins called out.

Mrs. Potts drove over to the boarding house site. Her heart fluttered as she saw the progress of the framing going up. "Oh, it won't be long!" She watched as the builders worked. She daydreamed about cooking in her new kitchen. Her cellphone rang, startling her out of the scenario she created in her new kitchen.

Caller ID showed it was the insurance company.

"Hello?" she inquired.

"Mrs. Potts, It's Jason with your homeowners insurance company. I'm calling to let you know that the claims for your house and belongings have settled. You should receive two separate checks this week. Your boarders should check their claims from their insurance providers for their personal belongings," her agent informed her.

"Oh, Jason! Thank you so much. I was just visiting the site, and the framing seems almost finished. I can't wait to furnish the house and move in!"

"That's good to hear. Let me know when you are ready to move in so we can write a new policy," Jason said.

"Do you need to see the house plans? It will be larger than the original house, and includes a four-car garage." She wondered if there was anything else she should tell him, but couldn't think. "Oh, and there will be a fireplace."

"When you're ready to move in, you can walk me through the rooms over the phone and let me know what each contains structurally. We'll do the same for your personal property. I don't have to be there in person."

"Oh, good to know. Thanks for calling about the claim. I'll be on the lookout for the mail carrier."

When the call ended, Mrs. Potts called Jimmy's cellphone. "Jimmy! The insurance company just called and said they've settled the claim for the house and my belongings. I will get two checks this week!"

Oh, Mrs. Potts, that's good news! I'm glad they didn't have any problem with anything and they didn't haggle. Brian and I shouldn't have any problems with our claims either.

"I'm over here watching the builders frame the new house. It looks like they're almost finished with the framing, but I don't really know."

MADDY DECIDED TO EXPLORE MORE OF THE MANSION. SHE wandered from room to room, jumping up on surfaces to get a better view of what the room contained. She found herself in the kitchen and discovered the outside door slightly ajar.

Guppy! I'm in the kitchen and the outside door is not closed! I'm going to see who's outside and if everything is okay.

Guppy belched out a squawk. *Don't get locked outside!*

I won't. I'll only be a minute.

Maddy nudged the door open with her right paw. She stuck her head out and looked around, but the door was in the way, so she stepped outside. A kitchen helper was smoking a cigarette. Maddy knew Betty and Chef Duncan didn't allow smoking on the property.

She didn't recognize the man, but since she rarely ventured into the kitchen, Maddy didn't know who worked there. She walked up to him and tried to read the name embroidered into the jacket. It was one of Duncan's jackets. Maddy's hair rose, and she hissed, backing away a couple of steps.

The man reached down and snatched up Maddy. "Well, look at you. What a pretty cat!"

Maddy tried to get out of his grips and away from his smoker's breath.

Guppy! A kitchen worker is out here smoking. He's wearing one of Duncan's jackets, so I don't know if he's a new person or someone who doesn't belong in the house! He's got a hold of me!

Scratch him and get back inside! Guppy was distraught.

The kitchen worker hurried over to where the staff vehicles were parked. He opened the door on an old blue Volvo and got inside with Maddy squirming in his arms. He started the car and drove away.

GUPPY! I'M BEING KIDNAPPED!

Guppy almost fell out of the tree. He flew into Betty's office and landed on the back of her chair, flapping his wings wildly and squawking his terror.

"Guppy! What on earth is the matter with you?" Betty ducked out of her chair to avoid the onslaught of his wings.

Guppy fluttered down to the vacant chair and studied the computer screen. He saw the green Messages button and tapped it with his beak. He carefully tapped letters into the message area: MADDY KIDNAPPED!

Betty leaned in and read the message. "WHAT? Who has her and what happened?"

Guppy typed in all caps: KITCHEN. BLUE VAR.

"Blue var? Oh, typo, you must mean blue car! Hold on!" Betty grabbed the phone and called chief Price. "Kenton! Maddy has been kidnapped!"

What? When did this happen? Do you have any details?

"Guppy typed a message. Someone from the kitchen left in a blue car."

Maddy must have told Guppy what had happened to her. Get Toombs immediately. He may know the details of the vehicle! I'll be there in less than five.

Betty called Toombs. They met in the kitchen and almost plowed into Duncan.

"Who's the worker with the blue vehicle?" Toombs asked Duncan.

"Are there any new workers?" Betty asked, not giving Duncan a chance to answer Toombs' question.

Duncan held up a hand. "Slow down! What's going on?" He looked around his domain. Everyone who was supposed to be there was there. "Everyone's here."

Toombs checked his parking lot cameras. He saw someone hurrying to a blue Volvo with Maddy squirming to get free.

"Who is this? He's in a kitchen coat," Toombs showed Duncan his phone screen.

"No one I know!" Duncan looked around the kitchen again. "Does anyone know who this is on Toombs phone?"

The kitchen help took turns looking at the phone.

"Yeah, I don't know his name, but he was here yesterday and today," someone said.

Toombs checked another camera and just caught the license plate as the car zoomed off. He forwarded a screen capture to Chief Price.

Chief Price hit the button on his shoulder and blurted out the license plate number to his deputies and detectives. He sped away from the police station as his lights blazed on the top of his police car and the siren screamed. "Stop this Volvo immediately! The driver has kidnapped Maddy, Jimmy's cat! He just left the mansion!"

Maddy was not going quietly. She growled, hissed, scratched and bit the kidnapper on his arm and hand with every bit of strength she had. The Volvo screeched into Stonerich Blvd., then onto the main highway leading away from Twinkle. She knew it was a matter of time that this vehicle would disappear into the traffic and she may never see her loved ones again.

The man held her on his lap while driving with one hand. Maddy sunk her teeth and claws into his thigh. The driver screeched, grabbed her by her scruff, but she wouldn't let go. The car went flying off the road, into the deep ditch, and flipped one, two, three times. The impact flung Maddy through the windshield on one of the flips. The Volvo ended upside down with the driver impaled on the glass from the windshield.

Police cars screeched to a halt. Ramirez arrived first, followed closely by Celebrity and the Chief in their cars. Jimmy's Honda came close to bashing into a police car. He was out of his car with wide eyes, running with the police to the wreckage.

"MADDY! Where's Maddy?" Jimmy was about to jump into the ditch among the wreckage, but Ramirez grabbed his arm and stopped him.

"STAY HERE! We'll find her. You may end up doing more harm than good!"

CHAPTER TWENTY

Chief Price and Celebrity carefully made their way down the steep bank of the ditch. An ambulance arrived at the scene, sirens screaming and lights flashing.

Danny and Brian arrived on the scene in Danny's car, iPhone cameras snapping photos as soon as their feet touched the ground.

"Holy Smokes!" Danny exclaimed as he viewed the wreckage.

Brian ran over to Jimmy. "Have they found Maddy?"

Jimmy was beyond speech. He shook his head, eyes never leaving the site of the car wreck.

They watched as the chief made his way to the driver's side of the vehicle. When he spotted a long shard of glass through the kidnapper's neck, he knew there was no hope of this man being alive. The hood of the car was a bloodbath. Still, the chief reached out to the man's limp wrist and checked for a pulse.

Nothing.

The chief shook his head to those on the scene.

Celebrity deftly combed the area for a sign of Maddy.

Ramirez joined her, and they widened the area. The surrounding area of the ditch and the embankment did not have tall grass, so there wasn't anything to hide Jimmy's cat.

They returned to the car and peered through the vehicle windows. No cat.

Celebrity climbed the ditch back to Jimmy. "There's no sign of Maddy."

Jimmy came unglued. "She has to be down there somewhere! The cameras showed her taken away in this car!"

Ramirez and the Chief joined them.

"Maybe... just maybe, she escaped out a window before the crash, or at the time of the crash! She could be anywhere!" Ramirez suggested the only other explanation.

They all took in the car and the area. All the car windows were closed.

Jimmy cupped a hand around his mouth. "MADDY! MADDY!" He wandered the side of the road for a distance before the crash, hollering his cat's name.

Meanwhile, Marty the mortician arrived in the hearse with Edgar and Troy. Marty climbed down the embankment, followed by his employees and Chief Price. Troy carried a black body bag.

They studied the victim's position.

"This isn't going to be easy, or pretty," Marty told the chief.

"I think Troy and I will have to climb up on the hood of the car," Edgar said, his eyes taking in all the blood.

"Go ahead and try. Get him down on the ground and into the body bag," Marty said.

The chief studied the driver's door, which was bashed closed. "Maybe we can pry the door open. I think if one of you can get inside and lift the body through the windshield, the other can pull the victim free. What do you think, Marty?"

Three tow trucks arrived at the scene. Celebrity removed her hat and had the drivers toss their identifying coin into the hat. She swirled the coins in the hat, grabbed one, held it up for the other two to see, and awarded the job to the winner. The other two tow trucks drove away.

"This may be a little while," she told the driver.

"Is that glass through that guy's neck?" the driver asked, astonished.

"Yes. Not a pretty sight up close." She left the driver and hurried over to Jimmy, Danny, and Brian.

Jimmy was like a zombie, bereft over the whereabouts of Maddy. Celebrity engulfed him in a swaddling hug. "We'll find her." That only made Jimmy cry more.

Troy spoke up after studying the situation. "I think we're going to have to break the glass around the windshield and just pull him out over the hood." He shrugged. The way he was thinking was this guy was already dead and a few more scrapes from broken glass was not going to do any harm.

The chief and Marty concurred, nodding their heads.

Edgar and Troy spread out the body bag and unzipped it.

"What about that glass through his neck? Do we try to break that off?" Edgar asked.

"Anyone have some plyers?" Chief Price called out.

"Got some!" the tow truck driver called out. He rushed to where his toolbox was in the back of the truck and produced a pair of plyers.

Celebrity left Jimmy and ran back to the tow truck driver. She stuck her hand out and the driver plopped them into her hand. She took off to the accident vehicle and handed the plyers over to Ramirez. Celebrity pressed her hand to her mouth as she watched Edgar, on his tiptoes, stretch his arm to break off the glass empaling the victim with the pliers.

The chief thumped her on her back.

"I'm typically not squeamish, but this is something else." Celebrity swallowed down bile.

Chief Price nodded. "This is a terrible situation. I'm not sure if we're going to be able to figure out why this man was at the mansion, and why he kidnapped Maddy."

Ramirez joined them. "Horrible way to die. Wonder if hitting the windshield knocked him out before the glass..."

All the onlookers watched Troy and Edgar climb onto the bloody hood of the car. Edgar used the plyers to break the shards of glass around the windshield. When he had the glass sufficiently removed, he stuck the plyers in his back pocket. Troy and Edgar grabbed the body and pulled it through the broken windshield. When they had the body free from the windshield and out of the car, they stopped to rest for a moment.

Troy slipped on the bloody hood, taking the body with him to the ground.

Edgar screamed in alarm as he jumped to the ground. "Troy!" The body was half on and off Troy.

The glass projecting from the victim's neck had missed impaling Troy by an inch.

Marty, the Chief, and Ramirez rushed to the scene. They helped Edgar carefully lift the body off Troy. They flipped the victim onto his back on the ground.

Ramirez held out his hand and helped Troy to his feet. "That was a close call."

Edgar grabbed the pliers from his pocket. "I think I'd better break that glass down on his neck. It's too dangerous leaving it extended like that, and it's going to rip the body bag." He got to work breaking off the glass. When he finished, and the glass was less dangerous, Troy and Edgar lifted the body and settled it into the body bag. Edgar zipped the bag.

"Can you give us a hand getting him out of this ditch?" Troy asked the assembled people.

Marty watched as Ramirez and the Chief each grabbed a corner of the bag while Troy and Edgar grabbed the remaining corners. They struggled up the embankment and loaded the body bag into the back of the hearse. The men shook hands. Then the hearse drove away with the body of the kidnapper.

The Chief motioned for the tow truck driver to join them. When he arrived, the driver assessed the situation of the car in the deep ditch.

"I'll get my truck in place up here. Should be able to pull the car up and onto the flatbed with the boom." The driver took off to his truck.

Chief Price called out to people. "Move your vehicles out of the way so the tow truck can have access here." The chief went to his vehicle and moved it further down the road, then walked back to the scene.

The tow truck pulled onto the shoulder as close to the edge of the embankment, leaving enough room for safety's sake.

Everyone stood around, watching.

The driver climbed back into the ditch while hauling the huge side puller hook on a steel cable. He wove the cable through the front passenger tire and hooked it into the tire rim. The driver went back up the embankment and hit a button on the flatbed.

The side puller cable slowly pulled the car up the embankment sideways, clearing the bottom of the deep ditch where it had landed.

"MADDY!" Jimmy screamed when he saw his beloved cat splayed on the ground where she must have been under the vehicle. He launched himself down the steep bank, followed by Celebrity, Brian, Danny, Ramirez and the Chief.

Jimmy knelt beside Maddy and assessed the situation. She was bloody and unconscious. He didn't know if she was dead or alive.

"Don't touch her," Celebrity cautioned.

"Need to see if she's alive," Jimmy choked out.

"Look, her chest is moving slightly," Danny said.

Jimmy was going to gather her up into his arms.

The Chief placed a hand on Jimmy's arm. "Better not. Don't know if there's broken bones or organ damage."

"Be right back." Ramirez took off up the side of the ditch and ran to his car. He returned holding one of his floor mats. "Let's slide her onto this mat. We can carry her up the wall of the ditch."

Jimmy, Celebrity, and the Chief pondered this.

"Yeah, I think that will work," Chief Price said. "She'll get jostled, but I think it's a safer bet than carrying her."

Celebrity spread her arm across Jimmy's shoulders in a hug. "Why don't you call Doc Halliday? He needs a heads up about Maddy."

Jimmy nodded, coming out of his head where the trauma replayed. He pulled his cellphone out, took a picture of Maddy on the ground, then placed the call to the vet.

The front desk put the call through to Doc Halliday. "Jimmy? There's been an accident?"

"Yes. Maddy was kidnapped by some guy. He drove recklessly, causing the car to flip into a ditch. The impact threw both of them through the windshield. We just found Maddy under the car when the tow truck pulled the car out of the ditch. I can send you a picture I snapped just now." Jimmy said by way of an explanation.

"Send it to my cell number." Doc Halliday gave Jimmy the number.

Jimmy sent the photo. He heard the ding of the text received on the vet's phone.

"She's breathing?" Doc Halliday asked.

"Yes." Jimmy explained what Ramirez suggested they do.

"Using that floor mat should work to get her up that wall of the ditch. You need to make sure she stays as stable as possible. There's no telling what condition she's in. Cats are pretty flexible. I've seen one fall from a three-story building and act like it was no big deal with a grooming campaign."

The tow truck driver maneuvered the vehicle onto the flatbed. He secured it in place.

Chief Price approached the driver. "Get that car to the police impound immediately. Do not touch the inside of the vehicle. If we find your fingerprints inside, you'll have to answer to me. We consider this vehicle a crime scene. Understand?"

"Sure, Chief, no problem. I'm not one to steal from the vehicles I tow like some of the other tow truck drivers."

The tow truck drove away.

Ramirez slid the floor mat up to Maddy's back. Celebrity pushed down on the front of the floor mat to get it underneath Maddy. Ramirez inched it forward. They got Maddy onto the mat while not causing a lot of jiggling.

"Jimmy, gently place your hand on Maddy while we climb that wall. I'll drive you to Doc Halliday's. Danny can drive your car back to the mansion." Celebrity and Ramirez firmly held the ends of the mat while the Chief supported the bottom. It was awkward climbing out of the ditch, but they made it to the cars.

Jimmy fished his keys out of his pocket and tossed them to Danny. "Thanks, man." He turned to Celebrity. "Where should we put her?"

Celebrity opened the rear driver's door of her police car while the Chief supported the bottom of the mat. "I think it would be best to place this mat on the seat so we can carefully get her out at the vet's office. You sit beside her and make sure she doesn't roll."

Ramirez took over the mat and placed it on the back seat. Maddy rolled with the move, but never opened her eyes. Celebrity opened the passenger rear door so Jimmy could scoot into the back seat.

"Okay, let's go." Celebrity got into the driver's seat, buckled up, started the car and engaged the siren and lights. "Better buckle up, Jimmy!"

Jimmy used the middle seatbelt. Eight minutes later,

Celebrity pulled her police vehicle up at Doc Halliday's office. She disengaged the rear door locks. Jimmy climbed out, went around the car, then carefully arranged his hands under the mat and pulled it from the car.

Celebrity ran to the office door, held it open for Jimmy and Maddy, then she returned to her vehicle and secured it.

Jimmy entered the reception area. "I'm Jimmy Katz and this is Maddy. I spoke with Doc Halliday about this emergency!"

One of the assistants rushed around the counter and led Jimmy to an examination room. "We've alerted the doc you're here, Mr. Katz."

Jimmy carefully settled the floor mat on the exam table just as the interior door opened and Doc Halliday emerged.

After the vet acknowledged Jimmy, Doc Halliday belted out instructions to his team. Xray's were required. Sedation was required. Cleaning the blood off Maddy's fur was required so Doc Halliday could assess the injuries.

An assistant gently steered Jimmy by the elbow out of the exam room. "I know how difficult this is, but you'll have to wait up front. It's going to take a while to see the full extent of Maddy's injuries."

Jimmy looked like he had slammed into an 18-wheeler. He was definitely feeling the shock of the whole incident.

"Perhaps you should go home and rest? This is going to take a while and you're not going to want to sit here on an uncomfortable chair."

Celebrity joined Jimmy and the assistant. "I'll take it from here. You'll call as soon as Doc Halliday has a prognosis?"

"Yes." The assistant returned to the exam room.

Celebrity led Jimmy through the door to her police vehicle. She opened the front passenger door and guided him onto the seat. "It'll be okay."

She drove them to the mansion. Jenkins opened the door

and Celebrity helped Jimmy inside. Guppy was on the newel post at the bottom of the staircase.

"He won't go to the tree in the conservatory and he won't go upstairs," Jenkins explained.

"Where's Maddy?" Guppy hollered out when he saw Jimmy. "Where's Maddy?"

Betty hurried out of her office and joined them in the foyer.

Jimmy lurched over to Guppy and cried into the bird's feathers. "It'll be okay. It'll be okay, Guppy. Maddy's at Doc Halliday's. He'll get her fixed up."

His parrot stared at him. "Where's Maddy?"

"Until he sees her with his own eyes, he most likely will keep asking," Betty said.

"Does anyone know who that guy was, or what he was doing here?" Celebrity asked.

CHAPTER TWENTY-ONE

Celebrity walked up the stairs with Jimmy. Guppy didn't want to budge from the newel post, so Jimmy carried his parrot up the stairs to his fake tree.

"Celebrity, close the door. Guppy's traumatized and it won't do either of us any good to stare at the front door." Jimmy had calmed significantly. He knew it would be a couple of hours before he heard from the vet.

"Why don't you try to take a nap, or just rest on your bed," Celebrity suggested. "I've got to get back to work."

"Okay. Should I put Guppy in his sleep cage?"

"If you think that will help calm him down, go ahead. Put the sleep cover on the cage." Celebrity didn't know if that would help, but it was worth a try. The Amazon parrot was worried about his friend.

Jimmy walked over to the sleep cage on the fake tree. "Gup, take a nap. Maddy will be okay. She's with Doc Halliday. Remember him? He's taking care of her. She'll be home soon." He lifted Guppy into the cage onto the rod Guppy's talons gripped as he slept. He closed the cage door, then slipped the covering over the cage.

Celebrity hugged her fiancé. "Get some rest. Let me know when you hear something. They will most likely want to keep Maddy overnight."

They smooched, then she shut the door behind her when she left Jimmy's suite.

Celebrity entered the kitchen and was not surprised to find Ramirez and the Chief grilling everyone about the dead kidnapper. They had a photo of his face in death, but that was all the identification available until his fingerprints were run through the system. Stephanie, the dispatcher, along with Butch, the greeter at the police station, were searching through databases to discover who the man was.

No one had a clue why the man was at the mansion or in the kitchen. They were pretty sure he was not working alone, and all the usual suspects were sitting in prison cells, but as luck would have it, not one of them were excluded from suspicion in cooking up this drama.

Toombs entered through the kitchen door. "I followed the wrecker to the impound lot. Your people are going through the vehicle, taking prints, and searching for any information about the kidnapper or who might have hired him. They said they'd report to you when they finished tearing the car apart." Toombs indicated Chief Price was their contact.

Chief Price nodded. "Standard procedure. We'll sort this out."

Doc Halliday sat in his office after normal business hours to make phone calls about his patients. He began with Mrs. Paulson to let her know he had to remove GoodBoy's toenail, but the Sheltie would be okay after his foot healed. *Yes, he would limp for a day or two, but he'd be fine. She could pick him up in the morning.*

Next, he called the Lerners with the bad news that Crystal's cancer had spread throughout her organs and there was no sense in spending good money on prolonging the cat's life. She was in too much pain to endure any treatment, which would not relieve the pain.

He saved Jimmy Katz for last. "Jimmy? Doc Halliday. I've got Maddy sedated to get her through the night. She has a dislocated right shoulder, a broken left front paw, a bruised liver, and lacerations from the glass."

Oh, No! Will she be okay?

"I want to keep her here for a couple of days to make sure her liver is functioning properly. I'll sedate her for most of that time to give her body a chance to recover from this tragedy."

Jimmy was quiet on the other end of the phone. He stared at Guppy's cage wondering how he would explain this to his parrot. "I know this sounds crazy, but could I bring Guppy there so he can see her? He's been so upset."

"If you can wait until tomorrow after hours, say arrive around 6:30, you can see her. I know how difficult it is for an animal to miss his companion."

"Oh, good. Guppy and I will be there tomorrow afternoon. Thanks, Doc Halliday."

Jimmy sent a group text to the pact letting them know about Maddy's injuries. Then he collapsed on the sofa. *One more day to get through.*

EVERYONE HELPED EXPLAIN THINGS TO GUPPY. TRYING TO GET through to his parrot wore Jimmy out. Not even a text seemed to explain the issue. After the third time climbing the stairs to try to comfort the parrot, Mrs. Potts gave up. Her visit was replaced by Jenkins, Betty, and Toombs. Duncan sent up a bowl of fruit, veggies, and nuts, but the bird was too upset and only picked at his food.

Near the appointed time, Jimmy carried Guppy out to the Honda and settled him in the traveling cage. "We're going to Doc Halliday's to see Maddy. She has to stay at the vet's until she's better."

"MADDY!"

"Yes, we're going to see Maddy. She's with Doc Halliday. She's hurt and can't come home yet." Jimmy hoped Guppy would accept that. He worried how they both would react to seeing his beloved cat so banged up.

Jimmy double-checked that the travel cage was secure, then he hopped into the driver's seat and they took off. Just a few minutes later, the Honda SUV pulled up to the parking area for the veterinarian's office. Jimmy unbuckled the seatbelt that secured Guppy's travel cage and carefully hauled it out of the back seat.

"Ready to see Maddy?"

"MADDY!"

"Okay, be a good boy. Maddy has a big boo-boo and she has to stay with Doc Halliday tonight, understand?"

"MADDY!"

"Okay. Quiet now."

Jimmy carried the cage to the front door and discovered it was locked. He tapped on the glass, shaded his eyes with his free hand, and peered through the door. He saw Doc Halliday walking down the hallway. The doc waved at Jimmy, arrived at the front door and unlocked it.

"Sorry, Jimmy. If I don't lock the door, I'd never get out of here until midnight." He chuckled. "Hi Guppy!" The vet looked Jimmy in the eye. "Maddy looks a mess, but she's on the mend."

They walked to the back where the vet treated the animals, then through another door, where caged dogs, cats, and a rabbit waited for treatment or were boarding while their owners were out of town.

Doc Halliday walked Jimmy and Guppy up to a cage that housed Maddy.

Jimmy held his feelings under control while he looked his beloved cat over. It was disturbing to see the end results of the senseless kidnapping. No one knew who the kidnapper was, or why he did what he did only to lose his life in the end.

Guppy looked this way and that way until he got his head around to understanding that his best friend was sleeping and looked all banged up.

"Maddy!" Guppy said, rather quiet.

"Guppy, Maddy was in an accident. She's hurt, but sleeping. She'll go home in a couple of days," Doc Halliday explained. He looked the parrot in the eyes, hoping the bird understood some of that.

"None of it makes sense, Doc Halliday. The kidnapper's dead. No one at the mansion's ever seen him before. Who would want to kidnap my cat?" Jimmy sniffled back tears.

Doc Halliday patted Jimmy's back. "The police will get to the bottom of this mystery. In the meantime, Maddy has a way to go before she's fully ready to go home."

Maddy's eyes opened and she let out a garbled meow when she saw Guppy and Jimmy.

"MADDY!" Guppy squawked.

Doc Halliday's hand went to his ear. "Whoa! That's loud! Does he talk like this all the time?"

Jimmy gruffed out a chuckle. "He has his moments." He bent to the cage and looked his cat over. There was a cleaned gash over her left eye and other cuts and scrapes. One paw was bandaged, and the opposite front leg was in a sling.

"She'll have to wear that Velpeau sling for a couple of weeks for her dislocated shoulder to heal properly. I'll send home a cone in case she tries to remove the sling."

Jimmy snapped a photo of Maddy, then another, with Guppy stretching his beak toward the cage. It was a sad moment for both the Amazon parrot and his human.

"Well, I guess we'd better go. Thanks for letting Guppy see Maddy. Hopefully, he'll calm down when we get back to the mansion." Jimmy took one last look at Maddy, then they walked back to the front of the office. The vet unlocked the door, and Jimmy left. Once they were settled in the SUV, Jimmy texted the photos to his list.

WHEN THEY ARRIVED HOME, JIMMY BROUGHT GUPPY BACK upstairs. The bird was unusually quiet. Jimmy petted his feathers. "Maddy will be home soon, Guppy. Don't worry."

The parrot entered his sleep cage and tucked his beak into his wing.

Jimmy rocked heel to toe for a moment. "Well, okay. Take a nap. I'm going to see Mrs. Potts." His phone dinged multiple text messages. He acknowledged them, then left his suite.

He found Mrs. Potts in her favorite reading chair. Jimmy tapped on the open door to announce his visit.

"Oh, Jimmy! Maddy is lucky to have survived that crash! Poor thing! How long will she have to wear that sling?"

He reiterated what the vet said. "Guppy's so upset. He's sleeping in his cage upstairs. I hope he'll be okay. This was very traumatic for him to see her at the vet's, and us not bringing her home."

Mrs. Potts shook her head. "Those poor animals. I'll go see him in a little while. He's not down for the night, is he?"

Jimmy shrugged. "He's never gone to bed this early before. It's still light outside, and he's usually on squirrel duty until twilight."

THE ALARM CLOCK SOUNDED AT SEVEN THE NEXT MORNING. Jimmy flopped an arm across the bed to the nightstand and silenced the annoyance. The heir pulled himself to a sitting position, his feet hitting the floor feeling around for his slippers. When a big toe found them, he slipped his feet into his house shoes and stood. Jimmy shuffled to the bedroom door and grabbed his bathrobe off the hook on the back of it.

He flipped on the light in the other room and pulled cat food cans and bird food bins out of the fridge that held fruits and veggies. He missed having his own kitchen. Aunt Betty had the refrigerator installed previously, but he missed a stove and oven. Then he remembered that Maddy wasn't here to eat breakfast, so he put her cans back in the fridge.

Jimmy went over to the fake tree and removed the sleeping cloth from Guppy's sleep cage. He blinked. Feathers littered the floor of the cage. Guppy had molted or pulled feathers out last night.

"Guppy! Are you okay, buddy? Look at all your feathers!" Jimmy was shocked to see feathers had spilled over to the floor around his tree. He had bald spots all over his body. "Breakfast and clean water coming right up." Jimmy grabbed the bowls and washed them out at the sink and refilled them. He returned the water bowl back to the tree.

Jimmy filled Guppy's bowls with food. He returned them to the fake tree and installed them into the round steel holders, then grabbed the smaller bird seed bin. He washed, dried and refilled it. "Here you go, Gup. Don't worry about Maddy. Doc Halliday is taking care of her."

A tap sounded on the door to his suite. He opened the door to his former landlady.

"Mrs. Potts! Guppy's molting like crazy!"

Oddly, the parrot didn't greet his former babysitter. Typically, when anyone knocked on the door, entered the suite, or engaged in conversation, Guppy was on it with a very loud greeting.

She rushed over to the fake tree and saw the mess of feathers in the cage and on the floor. "Oh, you poor boy." Mrs. Potts ran her hand down Guppy's head to the base of his back. He pecked at his food, not giving it any gusto, as he always did while enjoying his food. "Have you called Doc Halliday for an update yet?"

"No, I just woke up. Maddy may be there one more day while he monitors her liver." Jimmy shielded his eyes with a hand. "Why did this have to happen? Maddy is my world. I don't know what I would do without her."

"She'll pull through. Have faith." Mrs. Potts stood behind her conviction. Maddy was a strong cat. She'd fight for her life.

Jimmy's cellphone rang. He rushed to the sound of the ring, trying to find where he left it. He uncovered it from between sofa cushions. "Hello?"

"Jimmy? Doc Halliday here. Maddy's recovered nicely overnight. She's responsive, ate some food and drank some water, so she won't require an IV."

"Oh, I'm so glad to hear that. Guppy's really freaked out. He's molted overnight. There's feathers everywhere! When can Maddy come home?"

"Oh, poor bird. Don't worry, molting from stress is common. He'll grow his feathers back. Let's wait until tomorrow morning. If Maddy continues to heal, I'll release her then."

"Okay. One more day. Thanks, Doc Halliday." Jimmy returned to the fake tree. "Guppy, that was Doc Halliday. Maddy is doing better and she will come home tomorrow morning. Okay?"

Guppy squawked, spewing seeds from his beak. He seemed to perk up with hearing the news.

CHAPTER TWENTY-ONE

Jimmy flopped on the sofa. Mrs. Potts sat in a chair.

"It sounds like Maddy is healing to the vet's satisfaction," Bertha Potts said.

Jimmy let loose a loud sigh. "He said she's eating and drinking so he doesn't have to use an IV. I'm so glad. He also said molting is typical when a bird is stressed. His feathers will grow back."

"Our poor Gup!" Mrs. Potts cared deeply about the animals. It saddened her to think they were suffering. "I'm going to go over to the building site this morning. Want to tag along?"

"Sure! I can't wait to see the progress. I'll get dressed after I get some breakfast downstairs, then I'll come get you."

CHAPTER TWENTY-TWO

Jimmy drove Mrs. Potts over to the boarding house site. She squealed in delight when Jimmy parked opposite the new structures. The house and garage were completely framed. They got out of the car and walked to the front of the property.

"It won't be long now," Jimmy stated. "You should call Norris Trusty and ask if the appliances and everything else he had to order has come in. There's nothing worse than a holdup, waiting for something."

"I'm so excited to have a garage, Jimmy! Now our vehicles won't bake in the sun for most of the year!"

They walked around the property, keeping their distance from the work being performed.

"The next time we visit, they will most likely have the roof on. I looked it up once, and I think homebuilders called it *drying the home in*. They'll have the interior walls, insulation, and some of the plumbing installed. We'll have to look it up." Jimmy scratched his head, thinking about it.

They headed back to the SUV and returned to the mansion.

"I'm going to step up my shopping online. There's so many

things to replace!" Mrs. Potts was excited to furnish her new house, especially the kitchen.

"Have you looked at the video's we took last year for your homeowners insurance?" Jimmy asked.

Mrs. Potts' mental lightbulb went off. "Oh! I forgot all about that. We opened cabinets, closets and everything. Where can I find those on my laptop?"

"You'll be able to open the video and stop it so you can see what you need to buy." Jimmy was thankful he remembered the complete inventory the videos included. It would save his landlady a lot of time.

Brian's vehicle was in the driveway.

"Brian must have come home for lunch," Mrs. Potts said.

"Huh. He typically goes out with Danny and me and we meet up with Celebrity and Ramirez." Jimmy thought out loud. "I wonder why he's here?"

"Well, if we get out of the car and go inside, we'll find out," Mrs. Potts joked.

As they did just that, and approached the front door, it opened and Brian emerged, in a hurry.

"What's going on?" Jimmy asked.

"Had to change my shirt. Going to meet up with Lena and her mom. Can't talk now!" Brian waved as he rushed past them, jumped into his car and took off.

"Lunch with the mother and the girlfriend? That sounds interesting," Mrs. Potts exclaimed.

"He didn't say lunch, just that he was meeting them somewhere," Jimmy noted.

They went inside and Jimmy followed Mrs. Potts to her suite. He searched her laptop for the video files and found them in the insurance folder. "Here you go. There's three videos. I think it will help you to replace everything without overlooking something you use but don't remember."

His landlady rubbed her hands together in anticipation of a

good time. She slipped into her chair and set her pad of paper beside the keyboard so she could write down what she saw in drawers and cupboards in the videos.

Jimmy went to the conservatory to see if Guppy was there in his second favorite tree. When he didn't see his parrot, Jimmy took the stairs two at a time and entered his suite. Guppy was tucked into his sleep cage, which wasn't where he should be at this time of the day.

"Hey, Gup, you okay? Why aren't you guarding the house from those squirrels?"

His parrot didn't even squawk a greeting.

Jimmy ran his hands down Guppy's feathered head, neck, and back. "Listen, Guppy. Maddy was hurt in the car crash, but you saw her. She's at Doc Halliday's getting better. Tomorrow I'll pick her up and bring her home."

The Amazon parrot fluffed his wings, which were blotchy bald. He acknowledged. "Tomorrow!"

"That a boy. Everything will be okay. Your best friend will come home tomorrow. We will have to take good care of her." Jimmy felt Guppy was finally on board when he stepped out of his sleep cage and climbed on his limb and screeched out the window at the squirrels.

Every available set of eyes at the police station searched for the identity of the kidnapper, now dead, his attempt void. Stephanie, the dispatcher, and Butch, the front desk computer whiz, split up the work, so they didn't duplicate their efforts.

Celebrity and Ramirez, eyes focused on their monitors, checked online at prisons where their most recent criminals were located. All were accounted for.

The Chief had their offsite Twinkle expert sleuth checking

emails of said criminals to see if anyone had been in touch with someone to kidnap Maddy.

"Hey!" Butch called out. "Got a hit on the fingerprints from the dead guy, finally. Armand Beauvoir. Nicknamed "R". Resident of New Orleans. Minor offenses until two years ago when he seemed to step up his "business". Probably because of being unemployed. Most likely had a hard time finding a regular job because of his theft record."

Chief Price called out to Butch. "Send everyone, including Meaty, what you have. We have to find and connect the hidden dots."

No one was surprised that Butch discovered the information first. Was it just a year ago that the front desk slacker was so afraid of his computer he only wrote sticky notes? When the chief gave Butch the ultimatum to learn how to use the computer or tender his resignation, they never expected to end up with a mini-Meaty.

Around ten minutes later, Butch uttered, "Huh. This name sounds familiar, but I can't place it."

"What's the name?" Stephanie called out.

"Reuben Brown," Butch answered.

The chief was immediately out of his chair and into the outer room with his people. "Did you say Reuben Brown?"

"Yeah," Butch confirmed.

"Reuben Brown was working with Divinia Reynolds on the break-ins at Jimmy's place at the boarding house!" Chief Price couldn't get over the incident. He thought Reuben Brown was still serving a sentence. "When was he released from jail?"

Stephanie and Celebrity joined the chief. Ramirez swung his chair and stared at the huddle.

"Could Divinia be behind Maddy's kidnapping?" Celebrity asked. She couldn't see how that could happen, but prisoners had tablets with email and search capabilities.

CHAPTER TWENTY-TWO

"Stands to reason that witch would seek revenge," Ramirez suggested.

"Why would any of those people she hired be behind this? Didn't they learn the first time around with a prison sentence?" Stephanie couldn't see how anyone in their right mind would consider a repeat with a nutjob.

Chief Price shook his head. "You're dealing with people with low self-esteem who follow anyone that dangles the golden carrot. Good job, Butch. Send all that to Meaty, so he can tunnel through and get details."

MRS. POTTS ENLARGED THE VIDEO CLIP SECTIONS TO SPY through the drawers and doors in the kitchen. Smiling with glee, she recognized items she would have overlooked until needed. For the next two hours the cha-ching of her mental cash register sounded in her head as she used that bottomless card Jimmy had gifted her.

THE PHONE CALL CAME AT SEVEN-THIRTY IN THE MORNING. JIMMY rushed through his morning shower and shampoo, dressed, and fed Guppy. He couldn't remember where the cat carrier was, then remembered the fire at the boarding house had destroyed it and everything else.

Jimmy rushed down the stairs and out the front door. He drove over to the Wham-A-Rama and the pet aisle. He found a large wire cage he thought would be more comfortable than the smaller hand-carry carrier. Jimmy rounded up a basket, added the cage to it, and added the hand-carry carrier for when Maddy was all healed.

He searched for padded cushions for the cage and found two that were the correct size. Jimmy rushed to the front of the store to the checkout lanes, paid with his card, then hurried to his SUV. He added the cushions to the cage, then stuck it and the carrier in the back of the SUV.

Less than ten minutes later, he entered the vet clinic with the cage. The assistant guided him to an exam room, then took the cage to the back where animals were boarded or treated for their maladies.

A few minutes later, the assistant carried the cage to the exam room with Maddy inside, followed by Doc Halliday holding prescription bottles.

"Maddy is on the mend. I've given her the morning doses of her medicines already, so you won't have to give her the second doses until suppertime."

Jimmy bent to look at Maddy in the cage. Her eyes were open and she seemed a little groggy. "What type of medicine are they?"

"There's a pain pill, and another to prevent infections. I want to see her again in ten days," Doc Halliday said.

Jimmy shook the vet's hand. "Thanks for everything you did to save her. I don't know what I would have done if she didn't pull through. Guppy had been traumatized, but I think he'll be okay once I get Maddy home."

"Your parrot may continue to molt until his nerves are under control, but don't worry. Molting is common. His feathers will grow back." Doc Halliday said his goodbyes and left to see other patients.

Jimmy gently lifted the cage. The assistant opened the exam room door for him and followed him to the front of the office.

"I'll bring her out to the car and be right back," Jimmy told the front desk.

The assistant opened the front door of the clinic and Jimmy

carried the cage to his vehicle. He settled the cage on the ground.

"We'll be home in a few minutes, Maddy. Daddy's going to put you in the car, then I have to go back inside to pay Doc Halliday. You get some rest."

He settled the cage on the front seat so he could keep an eye on his beloved feline in the cage, then hurried back to the office. Jimmy slid the credit card across the counter. The transaction completed and he took the paperwork and left.

Jimmy drove carefully. He pulled into the circular driveway at the mansion and stopped at the front door. He knew Jenkins would see him on the monitor and would open the door.

He tried not to jostle the cage as he removed it from the passenger seat. Jimmy hit the door closed with a hip, then climbed the stairs to the front door. Jenkins swung the door open.

"There she is!" Jenkins bent to look inside the cage. "Welcome home, Maddy! Everyone missed you."

Jimmy turned sideways and entered the mansion. He carefully climbed the stairs, with Jenkins following. The butler scooted around them and opened the door to Jimmy's suite, then got out of the way. The heir placed the cage on the floor in the living room and opened the cage door.

"Guppy, look who's home!"

The parrot fluttered from the fake tree over to the cage and landed on top of it. Guppy squawked a welcoming. Maddy meowed faintly.

Jimmy let out a huge sigh. He flopped onto the sofa, completely drained of energy.

Jenkins patted him on the shoulder. "Everything will be okay now. Get some rest."

Jimmy slipped off his shoes, swung his legs up onto the sofa, and pulled the crochet blanket from the back of the couch on top of him. Once his head settled on the small pillow, he was out.

Nearly two hours later, Jimmy woke, disoriented. Then he remembered he brought Maddy home. He sprung to a sitting position and took note of the room. Maddy was still in the cage, but Guppy was in there with her. It was the sweetest thing he had ever seen. Guppy had spread his wings over Maddy, protecting her.

Jimmy quietly slipped his phone out of his pocket and snapped a photo from where he sat on the sofa, then crept over to the cage and knelt to capture another picture.

He determined his animals were recovering from stress because they didn't even budge awake when he snapped the closeup photo. Jimmy pulled up his list and sent the closeup photo to everyone.

Responses were immediate. Everyone was relieved that Maddy was back home again. They all reacted as surprised as he was to see Guppy in the cage with her. Jimmy had a moment, then sent the photo to Doc Halliday.

The vet responded with, *Well, look at that! You should submit that picture to a magazine or photo contest!*

Jimmy texted, *Good idea! Thanks.*

He got up, picked up her water and food dishes from what became the kitchen area in his suite, and cleaned them. Jimmy figured Guppy may decide to spend time in the cage with Maddy until she recovered, so he could not place the bowls inside the cage. He placed a hand towel on the floor by the cage, then set a fresh bowl of water and a small dish of wet food on the towel.

After thinking things through, Jimmy placed a folded queen sheet on the floor and set the litter box on top of it. He knew it would be a chore for Maddy to drag herself to the box, her food and water. They would make the best of it until she could get around better.

His stomach rumbled. Jimmy slipped his shoes on, then went downstairs to find out what Duncan had available for him to munch on.

MEATY WAS GOBSMACKED WHEN HE READ THE EMAILS FROM THE police department. The gall of Divinia Reynolds trying to pull another scam! At least her dumbo, Armand Beauvoir, failed at the job and got himself killed.

"Reuben Brown... when did you get released from prison?"

Fingers rapid-fired across the keyboard as Meaty checked into the matter. He went to the Texas Department of Criminal Justice (.gov) website and typed in Reuben Brown. "Four days ago? How? I thought he had a five-year sentence!" He read further into the file. They released Brown early for good behavior. Meaty translated that to mean they needed the cell for someone more seriously into crime.

He tapped his fingers on the edge of his desk, thinking through things as they occurred. Meaty typed Divinia Reynolds into the search bar of the website. She wasn't going anywhere for another three decades, no matter how sweet and helpful she came across.

Next up, he checked to see if she had a tablet and an email associated with the justice system. She sure did. He tunneled into that account and discovered a couple of interesting items. Divinia had created a folder system with various people's names and emails. Didn't she think they monitored those tablets? After a moment's thought, Meaty determined that those prisoners' emails were completely unmonitored.

Meaty let loose a loud groan.

He dug into each of the twelve folders, discovered sub-folders and damning evidence against the former librarian. Meaty gathered screen captures of emails, folders, and plans.

There were too many to send to the Chief, so he compartmentalized everything into a new folder on his machine, which took a while.

An hour later, Meaty waved to his uncle at the Foo and headed over to the Chief's office with his personal laptop.

CHAPTER TWENTY-THREE

Meaty entered the police station and stopped at Butch's desk. "We're going to need the conference room."

Butch sent a text to the Chief and the team, then escorted Meaty back to the room. When everyone was in place, the security expert set up his laptop to use the large screen on the wall.

"This is not going to be pretty, folks. It seems as if the inmates are running the prison."

Butch turned to leave the room when the chief stopped him. "Take a seat, Butch. You were the one who discovered a lot of the information."

The former deadbeat was surprised that he was invited to participate. He pulled out a chair and sank into it, his heart pounding.

Meaty jumped into it. "Reuben Brown was released from prison four days ago."

Ramirez jumped to his feet. "WHAT? How could that be?"

"That's plain ridiculous!" Chief Price said, using his loud cop voice.

Meaty continued with the information. "Divinia Reynolds

had a plan to fund the next thirty years of her prison vacay. That dimwit Armand Beauvoir was supposed to take Maddy to wherever he was living and send a demand notice to Jimmy."

Celebrity looked at the people around the table. "I wonder if she knows her guy crashed the car and got himself killed?"

"The good thing is, she doesn't know we have her plan," Butch threw out there.

Meaty uploaded several JPGs onto the big screen so everyone could see her folders, the people she had lined up, and emails. Meaty used a digital pointer that placed a red dot on what he was talking about on the screen so everyone could follow along.

"This is where Divinia contacted these people for her odd jobs. We'll need to surveil them. She conveniently provided their release dates from prison." The red dot moved. "Now, I found this interesting. She determined that if they couldn't snatch Maddy, they'd grab Guppy or Jimmy."

"Are the animals chipped? We need to ask Jimmy and get the chip information so we can track them just in case," Celebrity exclaimed.

Ramirez had a thought. "We should put a tracking device on Jimmy's shoes and car, just in case."

Chief Price nodded. "Good idea."

"Here are the demand notices. She must have cut words and letters out of magazines and newspapers. I wondered how she took a picture since she doesn't have a phone—at least I don't think she does. Then I realized she could take a photo with her tablet."

Meaty clicked on the sent emails he'd captured. "Divinia sent one of the notices to Reuben. I'm guessing she would do like a drip plan."

"What's a drip plan?" Butch asked.

"She didn't think Reuben was smart enough to understand the names of the notices and how they worked. I'm betting she planned to send the notices out one message at a time. When Reuben completed each assignment, he'd get another one," Chief Price explained.

"That's the price of cheap labor," Ramirez stated.

"How long do you think it will be before Divinia discovers Armand Beauvoir is dead?" Meaty asked the chief.

"Did you find an email or text from Beauvoir when he snatched Maddy? I don't think he had time before he crashed the car, but maybe he alerted her he was going to the mansion that day?" Celebrity asked.

"I'll have to see if I can find a cellphone for him, or a message from his email to her with any information before his demise." Meaty made himself a note on his phone.

"By any chance do you have photos of those people she planned to use for her revenge plan?" Butch asked. "We need to make sure we know who to look out for. Maybe have a town meeting at the Stardust Ballroom? Everyone knows everyone in a small town, and that could be to our advantage."

Everyone around the table nodded their heads.

"That's a good plan, Butch." Ramirez looked at his colleague with renewed respect.

Butch felt like his heart expanded in his chest. He was exhilarated his participation and input was valuable to this team.

"We need to get the word out by mouth, not the TIN. Divinia could easily access the online version of the newspaper." Meaty had another thought. "What about emailing everyone for an emergency meeting? Don't provide details, just that there's an emergency meeting at the ballroom? We have that emergency email list that Mrs. Potts put together. It was updated when the poison shut things down last year."

Chief Price nodded. "I think that would work. Let me call Harry Miller, the manager over there and find out if we can have the place for an hour within the next 24 hours. That will give us enough time to send the initial email immediately, then a follow-up email half an hour before the meeting."

"Should we provide snacks?" Butch asked. "People may be missing meals."

"Is an hour enough time?" Ramirez asked.

"All we need is for people to show up. Then we can have a slide show on the big TVs. Maybe even tell them to make a citizen's arrest if they see someone before we can get there?" Celebrity couldn't think of anything else, and she didn't think they needed food.

"Okay. Let me call Harry." Chief Price called the Stardust Ballroom on speakerphone. He explained the situation.

How's tomorrow morning at 10?

"That will do nicely. We can send the first email out in a little while, then send a reminder around 9:30. Thanks, Harry." He turned to Celebrity. "Will you compose the email? Send it to us so we can see if we need to tweak it. I'm going over to the TIN. I don't want Sylvan and Bill to feel excluded."

The meeting broke up and the attendees had their tasks to accomplish. The chief left the police station and drove over to the TIN. Milly Montoya greeted him.

"Are you arresting Deuce? None of his girlfriends have shown up lately." She snorted a very unladylike sound while covering her mouth.

"Watch it, Milly. I have handcuffs in your size," Chief Price joked as he jangled his handcuffs.

Milly stuck her hands out in front of her, then her phone rang.

"You're too easy," Chief Price whispered. He pointed to the offices in the back, then strode to Sylvan's door. He tapped on the door.

"Hey, Kenton! Come on in. What brings you my way?" Sylvan Stonerich stood. He and the chief shook hands.

"Can you call Bill in here?"

"Uh oh." Sylvan rolled his chair over to the wall he shared with Bill Trance, the managing editor. He banged on the wall three times. "He'll be right in."

Sure enough, Bill stuck his head in the door. His eyebrows rose when he saw the police chief. He entered Sylvan's office and closed the door after him. "What's up?"

Everyone sat.

"We have a situation." Chief Price explained about Maddy's kidnapping, the dead guy who was someone they had dealt with before, then he threw in the former librarian's name. "We have a plan, but you can't do a news story because prisoners have tablets, which means they have access to the internet. She could very well be reading the TIN online."

"Oh, Lord!" Sylvan exclaimed. "Why do we even have prisons?"

"Here's what we're going to do," the chief explained. "Harry's going to let us use the ballroom tomorrow morning at 10. Celebrity is creating an email that will be sent out to everyone in town immediately. If we're missing some emails, hopefully everyone knows those who don't have an online presence, and they'll share the news. Meaty's gathering all the photos of these scumbags and we'll have a slideshow tomorrow morning. "

Bill nodded. "It sounds like you've covered all the bases. We can do a great writeup when these people are arrested. What about Divinia? Is there proof of her orchestrating this scheme?"

The Chief scowled. "When this is behind us, I'll speak to the DA and see what he wants to do, or what he can do. Divinia and her little gang have to be dealt with. We can't be looking over our shoulders to protect Jimmy and his animals at every turn for the next thirty years."

"How is Maddy?" Sylvan asked.

The chief pulled up the photo of Guppy inside Maddy's cage. While it was sweet, Maddy had a fairly long recovery time ahead of her.

"Let me make a folder for the writeup. Can you send me that picture, and any others you have related to this kidnapping?" Sylvan's fingers clacked on his keyboard while he created a folder. "We'll have a staff meeting and make sure everyone here understands the situation."

The chief stood, followed by Bill and Sylvan. They shook hands, then the chief left.

BUTCH'S FRUSTRATION FROM THE NONSTOP PHONE CALLS relating to the email Celebrity sent to the townsfolk's erupted. "Listen up, Mrs. Bogenford. Just attend the meeting and you'll find out what the emergency is all about. Make sure you check in with your elderly neighbor so he knows to attend."

Stephanie caught the overflow of the calls. After answering her fifth call, she placed the phones on the night rotation and walked up front to let Butch know.

"They'll show up, or miss out," Stephanie declared.

"I don't understand what's wrong with people. Celebrity's email was perfectly clear," Butch stated.

Ramirez and the chief rode over to the mansion. Jenkins showed them inside, and they bounded up the stairs to the opened door. Ramirez knocked on the doorframe. "Jimmy?"

The heir trotted over to the door and invited them inside. Ramirez and Chief Price strode over to the cage in the living area. Guppy was still beside his best friend. Maddy wasn't noticeably better.

"Doc Halliday said it would take several weeks before she was fully mended," Jimmy explained. "Guppy hardly ever leaves her side."

"Meaty wants their chip numbers so he can set up a tracking program," Ramirez clarified.

"Jimmy, we're going to install a tracking device on your vehicle," the chief said. "Do you wear the same shoes every day?"

"More or less," Jimmy replied. "Why?"

"Meaty's going to put a tracking device on your shoes, just in case," Ramirez stated.

"Just in case of what? You think someone's going to attempt to kidnap me again?" Jimmy remembered the incident in San Antonio. He nodded his understanding. "Oh, good idea, now that I think about it."

Chief Price texted Meaty. "He'll come over on his lunch break. In the meantime, send him Maddy and Guppy's chip numbers."

STEPHANIE, BUTCH, RAMIREZ, AND CELEBRITY helped HARRY set up the folding chairs. The big clock on the wall showed 9:35. They knew early stragglers would show up to get the best seats.

Meaty and the chief were at the table under the big screen on the wall getting the PowerPoint set up.

The entire mansion staff came through the door. Chief Price raised an eyebrow wondering who was watching over the place.

Toombs raised a thumb and held up his phone. The chief nodded, thinking Toombs probably had the place wired, cameras at the ready, and all his security tricks in place. Toombs, Jimmy, and Jenkins escorted Betty to the front row with her entourage following. They settled into the chairs and waited.

At 9:57, the ballroom was nearly full. Meaty decided it was time to begin. He nudged the chief to get to the podium while he managed the laptop.

"Thank you all for coming. We have a dire situation that everyone needs to be aware of." Chief Price explained about Maddy's kidnapping. The overhead screen had Divinia's photo front and center. As the chief went on to expose the former head librarian's plan, Meaty clicked to the next slide, which showed all the players pictures with their names under each one: John Dinkwell, Reuben Brown, Ashford Cully, Tom Snider, and Conley Gratinford.

"We need all your eyes on these people! Everyone knows who belongs in this town. When you see a stranger, look at the piece of paper being handed out that shows these criminals."

The police department staff stood at the end of the rows of chairs and handed out the document that showed the known kidnappers' photos. People studied the headshots and names.

"If you recognize any of these people, call 9-1-1 immediately. If you are capable, perform a citizen's arrest. But, ONLY if you are capable. We don't need people being beaten up while trying to do this. If you're big, strong, or with a group, then you can attempt a citizen's arrest. If you don't know your own capabilities, do not attempt this. Wait for the police to show up."

Chief Price looked the group over. "Everyone understand?"

He went on to explain what happened with Maddy's kidnapping. A picture of deceased kidnapper, Armand Beauvoir, appeared next. His photo was not included with the printouts being handed out.

"This man showed up at the kitchen in Betty Katz-Diaz' mansion. No one knew who he was, and they all assumed he was a new employee. That won't happen again there, or anywhere else, because you all will ask questions, not take things for granted."

Meaty showed the pictures from the car wreck. Discovering Maddy when the wrecked vehicle was lifted and moved, and a picture of the body bag.

There were gasps from the audience.

GUPPY WADDLED OUT OF MADDY'S CAGE. "I'M GOING TO CHECK to see if we have any messages or texts."

Maddy dragged herself out of the cage to her water and food bowls. "Okay."

The Amazon parrot moved the mouse with a nudge of a foot. The iPad woke. He studied the screen. There were several texts. He pressed his beak on the green messages icon in the system tray.

"Everyone wishes you a fast recovery, Maddy."

Maddy crawled over to her comfy pillow on the floor near the laptop, which was only a couple of feet away. It was an arduous task that left her out of breath. She studied the screen. "What's that last text?"

Guppy pecked the text to open the message from Meaty. "There's a meeting right now at that ballroom. Everyone was invited."

"Ask Meaty what's going on." Maddy looked over to the cage. She did not have the energy to crawl back over there so she snuggled down on her pillow, her energy spent.

Guppy clicked in the Reply area and got busy pecking letters and the space bar. "They're at the meeting now, so we most likely won't find out until a little later."

Maddy conked out and missed what Guppy said. He waddled over to the pillow and stood vigil over his wounded friend.

CHAPTER TWENTY-FOUR

After the meeting broke up, Jimmy, Mrs. Potts, Aunt Betty, Brian, Danny, Celebrity, and Meaty stopped by the new boarding house site. Mrs. Potts was thrilled to see the shingles on the roof. They wandered around the exterior and met the foreman who handed out hard hats so they could take a look inside.

Duct work for the heating, ventilating and air conditioning was in place, along with electrical wiring, switches, outlets and breaker boxes. The foreman pointed out the low voltage and specialty wiring for TV's and internet.

"Once all this is finished, the city will send an inspector. Then we'll install the insulation and drywall."

"I'm so excited!" Mrs. Potts exclaimed. "The work seems to be going quickly. When do you think it will be move-in ready?"

"Maybe another forty-five days," the foreman said.

MEATY SAT AT HIS LAPTOP UPSTAIRS IN THE SECURITY OFFICE AT the Foo. *Office* really wasn't the right word, but the space was adequate for what he needed to do, and what he required: peace, quiet, and privacy to focus.

Maddy and Guppy's chip numbers were now in a program Meaty created to track their whereabouts. The chips couldn't be removed by anyone other than a vet or a clinic. A scanner was needed to locate them inside the body, typically just under the scruff or neck area.

Meaty didn't think any potential kidnappers would even consider tracking chips, so it was low on his list of concerns. *Let's face it, we're not dealing with super intelligent people here. Divinia's dipping into the bottom of the barrel for her workforce.*

He got up and walked over to his containers of helpful devices and such. Meaty stopped at the third container, flipped the latches open and took a look at the contents. He needed trackers for Jimmy's shoes and clothing. He examined some button trackers for suit jackets. Then he fingered through some tiny square trackers that had tiny prongs. Those could attach to the breast of the heel which was under the arch of the sole. The breast was the forward-facing part of the heel.

Meaty snagged a small zip bag and filled it with button and heel trackers. He grabbed a different tracker he planned installing inside Jimmy's trunk of the SUV. There already was a tracking device installed on the underside of the car, but that could be easily found and removed. The device for the trunk would become invisible in the fabric.

Once armed with everything he needed, Meaty shut his laptop down, and placed it inside the travel case along with the small bag of tracking devices. He went downstairs to find his uncle.

JIMMY WATCHED MEATY WHO SAT ON THE FLOOR OF HIS CLOSET

fiddling with his shoes, including the pair Jimmy was about to put on when the security guy arrived.

"What about my tennis shoes?" Jimmy asked.

"How often do you wear them?" Meaty asked.

"Now that I think about it, not often. I'm typically in dress shoes," Jimmy admitted.

"We'll deal with those later. I've got some button trackers for your suits. Take that jacket off so I can install a button tracker."

Jimmy slipped the jacket off and handed it over to Meaty.

"A lot of good menswear have a spare button inside the bottom of the jacket. That's where I'll put this button." Meaty stood, went to the table and spread the jacket out on the surface and pulled a button tracker out of his bag of tricks. He compared it to the buttons on the front of the jacket, and it was a near perfect choice.

Meaty slipped the prongs into the fabric, checked that they did not come through to the front of the jacket, then pressed the prongs to close. He brought out a small pair of needle-nose pliers and made sure the prongs were closed and wouldn't stick Jimmy.

He installed the button trackers on Jimmy's two other favorite jackets. "Make sure you only wear these three jackets until I can install trackers on the rest of these, and your shoes."

Meaty opened his laptop and clicked on the spreadsheet that contained all the devices and their numbers. He filled in the details (jacket, shoes, vehicle).

"Would it be okay if I scanned the kids? I want to make sure their tracking numbers match what I have in the system."

"Go ahead. It shouldn't bother them," Jimmy said. He watched Meaty take the scanner out of his case. Meaty approached Guppy first, held the scanner out to the back of the parrot's neck, and waited for the beep. It sounded. Meaty checked the number against what he had; it was a match. Next up, he scanned Maddy's neck. Her chip number matched what was in the spreadsheet.

"All set. You guys are as secure as I can make you. Let's hope we round up these bozos and put them away for a very long time. I doubt if they'll learn any lessons from dealing with Divinia, but we can always hope." Meaty shook his head. Some criminals didn't have the intelligence of a banana to figure things out.

VINCE BABELTON PUSHED A SHOPPING CART AT THE FOO. HE perused the cat food shelves for Expresso's favorite kibble, and loaded two large bags into the cart. Then he eyeballed the Fancy Feast cans of grilled fare. He learned a while back that it was easier to take the cardboard containers and fill them with the small cans. Feeding his humungous Main Coon was expensive, but Expresso was his cat-child and Vince would spare no expense to keep him healthy and happy.

He wheeled over to the next aisle, made his choices, then headed over to the coolers. Vince added two flats of cage-free brown eggs, orange juice with high pulp, yogurt, and milk to the cart. Produce was next. He grabbed two bags of Mandarin oranges, a large bunch of bananas, a pint of blueberries, a container of sliced portabella mushrooms, a bag of precut and washed salad. He already had potatoes and onions at home so he skipped those and headed to the meat department.

Vince searched and finally found the salmon pinwheels. He and Expresso loved them. Three packages containing two each went into the cart. Next up, he looked over the choices for steaks. Rib eyes were nineteen dollars a pound! Vince gritted his teeth while looking through the packages. He found one perfectly marbled and gawked at the sticker price of thirty-one dollars and twenty-eight cents.

After the sticker shock wore off, he tossed the package into the cart. He continued through the pork section, grabbed his favorite thick chops and a package of ribs, then rolled the cart toward the chicken selection. As he was looking over the offerings of legs, thighs and breasts, he muttered about the exorbitant prices. A man beside him snorted agreement.

"I can't believe these prices!" The man dug through packages of legs and found the lowest price for a large package. He tossed them into his cart.

Vince eyeballed the guy and his brain switched from shopping to alerts, alarmed. "Reuben?"

The man stiffened. "Do I know you?"

Vince hollered out, "CITIZENS ARREST! REUBEN BROWN, I'M PLACING YOU UNDER A CITIZEN'S ARREST!" He latched onto one of Reuben's arms. The felon grabbed a package of thighs and whacked Vince in the face, stunning him which made him release Reuben from his grip.

Alerted shoppers jumped into action. Two men and a woman wrestled Reuben to the floor.

"Call the cops!" one of them yelled out.

Cell phones were heard making the call.

Upstairs, Meaty glanced at the store monitors and saw what was going on. He grabbed a pair of handcuffs, raced down the stairs and through the store to the meat department. Meaty wrestled Reuben's hands behind his back while the man was held down, and cuffed him.

"Good job, everyone!" Meaty congratulated them. Their plan was successfully in place and people stepped up and took action.

Sirens were heard, approaching the Foo. Ramirez and Chief Price hurried over to the cuffed man. Ramirez hauled Reuben to his feet. "Didn't you learn the first time around?" He grabbed the man's arm and ushered him through the store to the waiting police car outside.

"Good work, Vince." Chief Price took a look at the man. Vince's face was swelling and turning red where the package of chicken clobbered him. His left eye was going to sport a shiner, all in the name of protecting Twinkle's most valuable and vulnerable resident: Jimmy Katz and his animals.

"One down, four to go," Ramirez noted.

"Happy to clear the streets of dangerous criminals," Vince said. "I'd better get this food checked out and home while I can drive with one eye." He pushed the shopping cart to the front of the store and loaded everything onto the conveyor.

Brink Hellman, the Foo manager, rushed over to the cashier. "Give Mr. Babelton a twenty percent discount for his heroism!" Brink beamed at the man with the bashed face. "Mr. Babelton, why don't you allow Meaty to drive you and your groceries home? When you can see better, we can pick you up so you can retrieve your vehicle."

By this time, Vince's left eye was completely closed and his head was pounding. "Maybe I'd better take you up on that offer. Thanks so much."

Brink called Meaty to the register, and let him know he volunteered him to drive Vince home. Both of the Foo men tackled the bagging using Vince's bags.

"Do you have any coupons?" the cashier asked.

"Not today," Vince mumbled. He was going downhill fast. He managed to pay for his weekly fare and was happy for the discount.

When everything was bagged and in the cart, Vince let Meaty roll the cart out to the parking lot. Meaty's vehicle was in the employee parking area. "Wait right here and I'll bring my car around." He took off running to his car and drove up to where Vince and the cart waited. Meaty helped Vince into the passenger seat then loaded all the food into the trunk area.

Vince unlocked his front door. He opened the door to

Expresso running to greet him and the stranger. The cat leapt against Vince's legs, like a dog. Being a very large Main Coon, the cat almost toppled his human.

"Whoa! That's a cat?" Meaty had never seen such a large cat before.

"Expresso! Daddy's got a big boo-boo. Take it easy, will you?" Vince staggered as his cat leaned into his legs. "I'll just put the things in the fridge and freezer. Everything else can wait until I take a nap."

Meaty went back to the car to retrieve more bags. "This is everything. Want me to help put these things up?"

"That would be great. Just throw everything into the fridge for now. I'll repackage things for the freezer later. I really appreciate your help." Vince held onto the counter to stabilize himself.

"Vince, want me to take you to the clinic to make sure you're okay?" Meaty worried that the hit to the face caused more damage than what was clearly noticeable.

"Nah. I'll be okay once I lay down."

THREE DAYS PASSED WITHOUT ANY SIGHTINGS OF DIVINIA'S people. Chief Price and Meaty figured if she didn't hear from Reuben within a certain timeframe, she'd send someone else. Stephanie sent an email to the townspeople reminding them to be alert, and they should expect to see someone new, so keep the photo of the criminals handy.

In the meantime, Celebrity, Ramirez, and the other law officers kept track of kids who caused trouble, drunks, shoplifters, and the whole lot of minor offenders. Butch and Stephanie updated charts, downloaded new versions of their programs, and kept the police station current.

Bill Hill, the owner of the Wellness Center, had a 2-fer-one sale. It brought people out to take advantage of the sale. His three top sellers were his own formulas: Wellness In A Bottle, Get It Up, and Thump, Thump, Thump. He had also educated people about the benefits of Colloidal Silver, which was another top seller. Bill's new assistant, Hooper Delbaron, carried boxes of stock to refill emptying shelves. The twenty-year-old had a knack for sales and easily learned the benefits of the products.

Bill was busy checking people out at the cash register. He scanned four bottles for the current customer, got the total and looked up to tell the customer the price, and to ask how he wanted to pay. Bill's memory clicked in. This guy was John Dinkwell from the photo spread!

Without thinking, Bill yelled out the identity of the man. "JOHN DINKWELL, I'M PLACING YOU UNDER CITIZENS ARREST!"

Dinkwell grabbed a bottle of pills and threw it toward Bill's face, which he luckily ducked in time and only got grazed on the side of his head. Two people in line behind Dinkwell jumped into action. They weren't going to let this criminal get away. The Mountain, who stood at 6' 8" blocked the door. John Dinkwell was apprehended.

Hooper ran to the office and grabbed the roll of duct tape. "Get him in that chair. I'll tape him down!"

They all worked as a team, hauling the man to the chair and holding him there while Hooper taped the man's wrists tightly through the chairback, and taped each leg to a chair leg.

"He's not going anywhere." Bill was on the phone with Stephanie, the 9-1-1 operator. "Steph, we've got one of the kidnappers here. John Dinkwell!" The call ended. "The cops will be here in a jiffy."

The tacklers picked their bottles off the floor.

"Good teamwork," Bill announced. He thumped Hooper on the back. "Quick thinking, Hooper!"

They heard the sirens approaching fast. Ramirez beat the Chief and Celebrity, his vehicle screeched to a halt. He was out of his car and at the door to the Wellness Center when the two other cop cars arrived.

CHAPTER TWENTY-FIVE

Ramirez was inside the Wellness Center. John Dinkwell was duct-taped to a chair and The Mountain stood beside him. No one could get past Sordus Blankenburg, AKA The Mountain, and be one hundred percent whole again. He often forgot his own strength and wrecked many doors just opening or closing them with a swift push. The Mountain was like Twinkle's own superhero.

Ramirez fist bumped Sordus. "Good work, everyone. Two down."

Chief Price and Celebrity entered the store.

The Chief stood in front of John Dinkwell. "I take it you've never worked with Divinia Reynolds before? Here's a huge hint for you... she's in prison. Her plans never work out. Guess where you're going?"

Celebrity helped Ramirez un-tape the man. Ramirez handcuffed Dinkwell and they took him out to his police car and settled him in the back.

"When's this going to stop?" Celebrity shook her head, rage just under the surface.

Ramirez thumped her back, which he meant as a tap. "That

spiteful woman has her own agenda. The Chief needs to talk to the DA and see what can be done."

"I wonder how she finds these guys?" Celebrity speculated a website for "odd jobs" where minor criminals congregated.

They returned to the Wellness Center where the Chief asked people to stop by the station to give their statements.

The Mountain, Bill Hill, and everyone else said they would. People shook hands, but avoided shaking hands with The Mountain because he sometimes squeezed too hard and broke a few bones. He rarely offered his hand anymore, and no one was offended.

The police left the shop. "Get that man into a cell. I'm going to stop by the courthouse and talk with the DA." Chief Kenton Price had had enough.

DIVINIA REYNOLDS SAT ON HER COT IN HER WHITE PULLOVER shirt and white elastic-waist pants. Flip-flops lay forgotten half under the cot. She balanced her tablet on her lap and checked her email for the nth time. No word from either of the two losers she set onto her kidnapping scheme. The former head librarian pulled up her list of people. She opened the document and used the strike-through feature to eliminate the two names.

She swiped a hand across her face. *Can't these bozos do anything right?* Divinia couldn't see that she was the head bozo, as her original scheme had landed her in prison. She felt confident that her plan would succeed when the right person accepted the job.

Little did she know that superspy Arthur Hellman, AKA, Meaty, watched her movements on her prison tablet with a simple program he created just for her. Anytime she opened the tablet, the spy program activated and recorded all her movements. Searches, emails, any typing whatsoever, and all trackpad activity.

Divinia looked at the time on the tablet up in the left-hand corner. Hours inched by alarmingly slow. A day felt like a week. She didn't know how she could survive her sentence. Ten years would feel like decades.

Reuben had been reliable the first time around. She wondered what became of him. It most likely involved a woman. John Dinkwell was not someone she knew very much about, but her dialogue with him appeared to be authentic. She thought Dinkwell could get the job done.

Suddenly, her tablet shut down without warning. It had been fully charged so she didn't know what happened. She tried rebooting it. It did not come alive again. Divinia was not a technological genius, so she yelled across to her neighbor.

"Hey, my tablet just quit. Is yours still working?"

"Yeah, maybe the battery needs to be replaced."

"It's fully charged."

"Doesn't make any difference. Could be a faulty battery. Tell the guard. It's going to take a while to get your tablet back though."

Divinia cursed under her breath. How was she going to keep track of her plan? What if someone was waiting for instructions?

MEATY CHUCKLED. HE WAS SCREWING WITH DIVINIA REYNOLDS' head. With a few strokes, he had shut down her tablet. Now, he woke the tablet so she could frantically try to communicate with her people.

Footsteps coming up the stairs in the Foo to his domain had him swinging his eyes over to see who came to visit. Ramirez appeared first, followed by Chief Price.

Meaty stood. "Hey, what's up?"

The Chief sat in a guest chair, and Ramirez pulled another chair over and plunked down in it. Meaty returned to his chair.

"There's nothing we can do about Divinia's ongoing business from prison," Chief Price all but snarled. "They could take away her tablet privileges for sixty to ninety days, but that's about it. Can't retry her even with proof. Just doesn't seem like the legal system works anymore."

"Why do we even have law enforcement when nobody enforces it?" Ramirez' disgust appeared visible on his face.

Meaty then explained how he heckled Divinia Reynolds through her tablet.

Ramirez snorted. "I'll bet she about freaked out. Can you do something with her camera to see her?"

"That's a good idea. I'll work on that and will let you know." Meaty's face lit with the fun he expected. "There's three other people who signed up to her plot that we haven't come across yet. Ashford Cully, Tom Snider, and Conley Gratinford. We should send out an email with those names and faces so everyone can keep on their toes."

"Twinkle folks take things seriously. Look at how they took down Dinkwell and Brown!" Chief Price appeared proud of his friends and neighbors. "I'll ask Stephanie and Butch to put together an email about these three. If Divinia wants to sign up others, we'll be ready."

"Good deal." Meaty was proud of his part in the plan.

Mrs. Potts drove to Dime Water. She looked at her GPS coordinates and found Allstar Appliances. She went inside and looked around. A sales clerk approached her.

"How may I help you?" the young man asked.

"I'm rebuilding my home after a house fire, and I'd like to see high-end kitchen appliances."

The salesman led the landlady over to the stoves. She saw those flat surface stovetops, which she didn't want.

"Where are your gas stovetops?"

"Oh, not many people want those anymore, but we do carry some." He steered her through a maze of appliances to where the samples stood.

"People don't seem to realize that the huge benefit to gas stovetops is that if your power was out from a hurricane or some other disaster, you can still cook any meal as long as you have matches or a lighter." Mrs. Potts noticed the man raise his brows. "I take it you never gave that a thought?"

"Actually, I didn't. That's a good selling point. Obviously, you can't take a match to a flattop stovetop."

Mrs. Potts looked over the gas stovetops and gas stoves. She remembered on the house plans, Cal Masters had drawn the stovetop over a cabinet, and two separate ovens on a wall. She pulled a tape measure out of her purse and a pen and small notebook. She measured and jotted notes beside the names of each product.

"How about refrigerators, freezers, and dishwashers?" She had made up her mind to have a full-sized refrigerator and a stand-alone freezer. Cal had placed the refrigerator in the kitchen area, and the freezer was in the butler's pantry. Again, Mrs. Potts explored the options and took the measurements. She made sure the dishwasher had an adjustable third shelf which was handy for custard cups and other small items.

"Norris Trusty is my builder, and I'm pretty sure he orders appliances from your store," Bertha explained.

"Yes, he does. How far along is your build?" the salesman asked. He handed her brochures of the appliances she looked at.

"I think it's about that time for appliances to be worked in before they are ordered, so I need to make sure the right ones show up. Thanks so much for your help."

Mrs. Potts sat in her car and referred to her notes, then the brochures. She folded over the ones she was not interested in so she would not get confused. Then she headed back to Twinkle, and Calvin Masters office.

She tapped on his open office door.

"Hey, Mrs. Potts!" Cal greeted her with a huge smile. "Come in. Take a seat."

"Cal, I just went to the appliances store in Dime Water. I hope I didn't wait too long to look things over." She figured if she had missed the end date, she might be stuck with something she really didn't want. She pulled the brochures out of her purse along with her notebook.

"Let's see what you've got and compare the sizes to what's on the plans." Cal held out his hand for the brochures and opened the dishwasher pamphlet.

A woman entered his office, came around Cal's desk and placed some documents on his desk. She glanced at the full-color brochure Cal was holding.

"Oh! Three shelves?"

"They're adjustable!" Mrs. Potts exclaimed, excited.

"Mrs. Potts, this is Dotty, my assistant."

"If you replace your old dishwasher, don't get the one that has silverware holders for the top shelf. To me, it's a total waste of good space. You can always get a metal toothbrush holder and stick silverware in that on the middle shelf." Mrs. Potts had thought this out thoroughly as she looked at the different models.

Dotty was on board. "That's a good point. I could really use that top shelf for small things I typically wash by hand."

Mrs. Potts beamed. "There's never room for custard cups on the top shelf of my dishwasher, and I can't put them on the bottom shelf. Whoever came up with this third shelf should be elevated on a pedestal."

Dotty pondered the third shelf. "To be clear, when you said the shelves were adjustable, they can be raised and lowered? Do you think it's easy?"

"The salesclerk showed me on this dishwasher. There's two levers, one on each side on the top rack. You just flip the levers and move the rack to where you want it." Mrs. Potts beamed excited.

"Well ladies, I'm happy to hear about this third shelf, because I never gave it a thought. I can see how useful this appliance would be in a busy kitchen." Cal looked over the dimensions, pulled out the boarding house plans, and noted two changes.

Dotty left Cal's office after exchanging contact info with Mrs. Potts.

The stovetop was half an inch wider than the intended space, and the dishwasher required an additional inch as well. "I'll go over to Norris' place and show him the changes. Don't worry, there's enough time. If he already ordered appliances, he can change them to your choices."

Mrs. Potts blushed. "I'm so sorry it took me so long to think about this."

"Not to worry. You've experienced a shock and things are bound to become muddled. It's good that you went to Dime Water to see what was available."

The landlady stood, shook his hand, and left. She drove back to the mansion and sought Betty. She found her in the conservatory talking to the plants.

"Betty, I drove over to that appliance store in Dime Water. I don't know why I didn't go over there sooner, but I've been in sort of a haze since the fire."

Betty guided Mrs. Potts to a small, comfortable sitting room. She fiddled with her phone sending a text. A few minutes later, one of the kitchen people brought iced tea and a plate of brownies.

"Did you have fun looking over appliances?" Betty asked.

"I'm so glad I went. I've always wanted one of those dishwashers with the third shelf. I'll be able to use that for things I typically wash by hand." Bertha Potts could hardly contain her excitement.

"I wonder if we have one of those? I know we have multiple dishwashers, but I don't know anything about them," Betty admitted.

"You should ask Duncan," Mrs. Potts suggested. "I also looked over the gas stovetops. The young man who waited on me didn't even think about the importance of having a gas stove. I explained about power outages and that no matter how long the power was out, you could still cook a meal as long as you had matches or a lighter. I've even baked a cake on the stovetop!"

Betty nodded with thought. "That's a pretty important piece of information. I'll bet gas stove sales skyrocket in Dime Water."

They shared a snicker.

"Cal Masters will get with Norris Trusty about the size difference for the stovetop and the dishwasher. I don't think anything will be a problem, and if Norris already ordered appliances, they'll have to be changed if he ordered something different." Bertha Potts thought about the separate refrigerator and freezer. She saw the different brands and configurations and decided it didn't make any difference. Having the separate appliances gave her more storage room for the meals she prepared and the canning jars which held frozen sauces, home-baked beans and other things she cooked.

"Let's go see what appliances Duncan uses." Betty stood and led the way to the kitchen.

The kitchen staff were all aflutter. The big boss rarely

entered the kitchen, and she brought someone with her. Duncan approached Betty.

"Mrs. Diaz, what can I help you and your friend with?"

"Duncan, this is Mrs. Potts. She went to the appliance store in Dime Water and I wondered what type of dishwashers we have."

Duncan wondered what was so important about the dishwashers, but he guided the women over to the first dishwasher. "This is the main unit we use."

Mrs. Potts opened the brochure. "Do your dishwashers have this top shelf?"

Duncan looked over Mrs. Potts shoulder at the pictures on the page. "Third shelf? It's adjustable?"

He opened the door of the dishwasher and discovered only two typical shelves. He checked out the second dishwasher only to discover the same configuration.

Mrs. Potts couldn't hold herself back. "I just ordered this one for my new house. The shelves can be adjusted up and down. You don't want the top shelf to hold silverware slots. It's a waste of good space. I'll be using that shelf for those small things I have to wash by hand. Saves time."

Duncan raised an eyebrow when he glanced over at Betty.

"Go ahead and have them replaced," Betty said. She turned to Bertha. "Do you need the brochure? Duncan needs to make sure he orders the right thing."

Mrs. Potts dug through her purse and pulled out the business card the salesclerk handed to her. She handed it over to Duncan. "Call this man and tell him you want the same type of top shelf he showed me. I was telling Dotty over at Cal Masters office that the silverware configuration top shelf was such a waste of valuable space. All you really need is something like a metal toothbrush holder to hold more silverware. You can probably get those at Wham-A-Rama."

"Thanks, Mrs. Potts! You made my day." Duncan gleamed. He gathered his people and they huddled around the brochure.

CHAPTER TWENTY-SIX

Celebrity and Jimmy sat at Francesca's Café finishing up lunch.

"Looks like the boarding house will be finished soon. Why don't we go to your storage unit and see what's there? You need to determine what you want in your new space, and if any of your mom's kitchenware is in those boxes. You found that loaf pan, so maybe her dishes and silverware are there."

Jimmy thought about it. "Yeah, good idea. I need to figure out what I want to replace and what of my parents things I want to bring over to the new place."

They finished lunch, left a tip on the table and paid at the register. Celebrity drove in the unmarked car and pulled up to the storage property. "What's the gate code?"

Jimmy got out his wallet and pulled a card out of his wallet. "42834."

Celebrity rolled down her window and pressed the buttons on the keypad. The gate groaned open and she drove them through and parked in front of Jimmy's unit. He unlocked the padlock, rolled up the door and they stepped inside. Jimmy plugged the lamp cord into the extension cord, then that into the socket near the door. He clicked the light and the place lit up.

"Where should we start?" Celebrity looked around at all the boxes, some of which were opened.

"Just dig in. We can start new boxes. What to keep, and what to donate." Jimmy walked over to the nearest open box and poked around. "Oh, here's some custard cups and desert dishes." He pulled those out of the box and went deeper. Jimmy found soup cups and salad plates, a matching set of four. He piled everything back in the box and carried it over to the wall near the door. He found the marker and box cutter. He wrote a K on all sides of the box. "This is stuff to keep. Mark the box with a K. For donations, write a D."

Celebrity was pulling wrapped items out of a box. She carefully unwrapped an item and found a vase. She set it aside with keep in mind. Four more vases were uncovered. "Do you think you'll need four vases?"

"Are they different sizes, or all the same size?"

"They're all practically the same size. Maybe keep two and donate two?"

"Sounds good."

Celebrity set two aside, then dug back into the box. "Here's smaller ones. We should keep these."

Jimmy moved on to an open box he had never explored. He lifted off crumpled paper to expose some of his mother's cooking pots. "Found my mom's pots and pans, or at least some of them. These are the good kind. Seven layers of steel, not aluminum. They still look brand new even though she bought them for her hope chest."

"Hope chest? I haven't heard that term in a long time. I wonder if girls still collect things for when they will go out on their own, or hope to get married?" Celebrity never had a hope chest. She bought her own things when she got her first apartment. Of course, her mother contributed to some of her possessions, but for the most part, Celebrity bought things as she needed them.

By the time they finished for the day, they found the everyday dishes and Jimmy's grandmother's fine china. Seven boxes were marked with K, and three were in the D stack.

"Let's ride by the boarding house and see how far along they are now." Jimmy called Mrs. Potts for her to meet them there.

They stood at the exterior of the property. The builder had cleared away the debris and swept the place for nails. A walkway from the parking area in front of the garage to the front door of the house was curing.

The foreman handed out hardhats to the visitors. He explained they were in the *wallout and enamel* phase of the build. This was when the interior trim and the interior doors were installed, along with kitchen and bathroom cabinets.

"If you return in a few days, we'll have the plumbing and electrical fixtures installed, along with light fixtures, HVAC vents and grills. Then an inspector will come out and take a look."

"When will the appliances be installed?" Mrs. Potts asked.

"We need to install the kitchen backsplash, and the bathroom tiles, tubs and showers. After the flooring is installed, the last thing to be installed are your expensive kitchen appliances." The foreman was very helpful.

"Looks like we'll be ready to move in within a week or two," said Jimmy.

"After everything is in place, the project manager and your warranty service rep will thoroughly inspect the place. If they find any problems, those have to be fixed, and maybe inspected again before the warranty is approved and placed in your name."

Mrs. Potts beamed. She was so excited she couldn't even speak. She finally found her voice. "I guess I'd better get busy ordering furniture and things. I have some items already, but there's so much more I don't have."

Celebrity patted Mrs. Potts on the back. "Wait until you do the final walk-through before you order furniture. You need to see how things will be placed and what sizes to buy."

"Oh, I almost jumped from the boat into the water, didn't I?" Mrs. Potts calmed herself. "You're right. Jimmy told me that months ago. It's easy to bypass common sense when you're excited. I can't wait to sit at my kitchen table again!"

MADDY APPEARED MORE ALERT. SHE ATTEMPTED TO GROOM herself on her pillow, still unstable from her injuries. Guppy monitored the dangerous squirrels from his fake tree. He made sure no squirrels approached the windows to gain access to the house.

Jimmy entered the suite. He was happy to see Maddy sitting upright, but knew her paw and the opposite shoulder still in the sling would take a while to heal. Grooming was difficult, as he watched her lick her damaged paw to wash her face.

"Honey, how about you let me wipe your face with a washcloth?" He went into the bathroom and ran the hot water to warm it up, then grabbed a clean washcloth. He wrung it out as dry as possible, then returned to the living area.

"Close your eyes and Daddy will wash your face." He gently wiped her face, then ran the washcloth down her back and tail, then wiped her chest and front legs. "Does that feel better?"

"Meow."

"Your welcome. Rest up. Doc Halliday said you need to rest for a couple of weeks to heal your injuries."

Maddy awkwardly turned in a circle on the pillow and flopped down. The sling made it difficult to cuddle down, but she did the best as she could.

Jimmy eyeballed the cage. "Guess it's time to dismantle the cage." He removed the bedding, the temporary potty box, and dumped the unused litter in the regular potty box. Jimmy removed the food bowl that was clamped to the cage, and the water bottle that was similar to a hamster cage water bottle. Then he collapsed the cage into a flat stack, picked it up and hauled it to the bedroom closet.

"Guppy, you're in charge when Daddy isn't here. Keep an eye on things and protect Maddy."

"AWK! Killer bird!"

Jimmy ran his hand down his parrot's feathers. "I'll bet you learned a lot about fighting and protection from that sea captain."

"Captain Patch!" Guppy squawked out.

Jimmy stopped what he was doing to stare at his bird. "I didn't know his name was Captain Patch. Look how long we've been together and you've never talked about your time on the ship."

The Amazon parrot shifted from one leg to the other, remembering his past. It made him uncomfortable thinking of all the years he endured with the wicked captain, and all the bad things he had witnessed.

Jimmy wondered how he could learn about those years Guppy was on the ship. He made a mental note to contact the pet shop owner where he bought his parrot. To Jimmy, the term *bought* was insufferable. He *adopted* his animals, and they were a major part of his family. They were not disposable. In his mind and heart, once you adopted an animal, you were their caretaker for life.

The heir sighed, trying to keep it quiet, but he had things swirling around in his head that he didn't want to think about. He'd talk with Celebrity about some of his concerns. She was like him regarding animals. Jimmy knew it would never have worked out between them if she didn't have a big heart for Maddy and Guppy.

"I'm going over to the dojo. Moses is going to teach me some new moves."

"Protection!" Guppy belted out.

"Yes, protection!"

AFTER MOSES THREW JIMMY AROUND THE MATS ON THE FLOOR for an hour, the heir stumbled over to his car and drove over to the Biggem diner. He limped inside, waved to The Mountain, then joined Celebrity, Ramirez, Brian and Danny.

Danny eyed him. "Did you fall down the stairs or something?"

"Or something," Jimmy grunted out. "Moses..."

Danny, Ramirez and Brian chortled loudly.

"It's not funny learning how to protect yourself," Jimmy scowled. Even his face felt sore. Most likely from all the face plants on the mats with Moses landing on top of him.

Oatie, Danny's girlfriend and their personal wait-person, wandered over to the table with the tea pitcher. "Hey, Jimmy. What can I get you today?" She topped off tea glasses and filled his.

"Better bring him chicken noodle soup. He can't chew," Ramirez smirked.

Jimmy glared at the detective. "Very funny." He eyeballed Oatie and didn't see pity or anything bad, just impatience for him to order. "I'll have my regular with fruit."

"Gotcha," Oatie said, heading back to the order counter.

"I think all this business with Maddy getting hurt has stirred memories in Guppy." He turned to Brian, his childhood friend who knew when Jimmy adopted the parrot and remembered all the bad language and bad behavior in those early days. "He called the sea captain, Captain Patch."

Brian gawked at his friend. "Seriously? Guppy never mentioned his name in all these years. Did he say anything else?"

"No, he clammed up and wouldn't answer my questions. I'm going to contact the pet shop where I found him and see if they have any written records they'll send me."

"He must have been traumatized by that captain," Celebrity said. "He's never said anything relating to his time at sea, or what happened on the ship."

"When I first moved to Twinkle, Mrs. Potts took a firm hand in getting Guppy's bad language under control. She had many conversations with him about being nice and not saying bad words."

"I briefly remember the shop owner mentioning that Guppy was beaten when he tried to fly anywhere on the ship, even in the captain's cabin." He turned to Brian. "Remember how long it took him to realize he could fly around my apartment and he wouldn't get beaten?"

"Some people should never be responsible for anything or anyone other than themselves," said Ramirez while chewing. "Those are the types that I have a hard time not heating up. They hurt women, children and animals."

Danny was busy making notes in his little notepad. "That would make a great article. I won't mention Guppy, but there's been complaints in the past about animal cruelty, and it should be addressed again."

"Do you want to drive over to the Big City and visit the shop?" Celebrity asked.

Jimmy shook his head. "After the fiasco of San Antonio? No thanks. A phone call should do it. They can email me all the records they have."

Oatie returned with Jimmy's plate and he dug in.

Three men lumbered inside the diner, spotted an empty table and headed that way. Sordus Blankenburg's eyes took in the men. The Mountain jumped to his feet, table crashing on its side as he hollered. "TAKE THOSE THREE CRIMINALS DOWN!"

The Mountain plowed into Ashford Cully, Tom Snider, and Conley Gratinford, Divinia's last three kidnappers that everyone was on the lookout for. Ramirez and Celebrity were on their feet and at the huddle of limp bodies with handcuffs at the ready. Danny and Brian's phones clicked photos of the three nitwits, The Mountain, and the detectives.

After police handcuffed the three and took them to the police cars, everyone returned to their lunches. Sordus received pats on the back for his quick thinking.

MEATY RUBBED HIS HANDS TOGETHER OVER THE KEYBOARD OF HIS laptop. He had one last opportunity to heckle the former Twinkle head librarian before all hell broke loose for the woman.

The District Attorney presented his case to the prison officials. Divinia Reynolds would be placed in solitary confinement for ninety days and lose the use of her tablet for six months.

Meaty pulled up the woman's prison email. He attached a photo of her three dingbats being clobbered to the floor by The Mountain. Meaty typed his message: *Doesn't look like you're living on the French Riviera where successful criminals hide away in luxury. Take that as a hint that you're not smart enough to succeed at any scam.*

Meaty blind carbon copied the Chief, then hit the Send button without another thought. Divinia would have just enough time to read his message before guards approached her cell and confiscated her tablet. They would bring her before the warden for a good dressing down and then haul her off to solitary confinement.

He had a thought and sent an email to Sylvan at the TIN with a note. *FYI. Keeping you in the loop. Better not print my message to Divinia, but I'll leave that to your discretion.* He included the information about the DAs online meeting with the warden, and the results of said meeting. That could be printed.

The next morning all readers of the Twinkle Independent News, fondly called the TIN, read the headline:

Former Twinkle Librarian's Criminal Activity Foiled Again

Meaty was pretty sure everyone who had a subscription to the TIN was reading the article written by Danny Stonerich and Brian McKinley while drinking their coffee and eating breakfast. A photo spread on page three showed The Mountain walloping the trio of criminals with a body slam, the sorry police photos of the three bozos, the last photo of Divinia Reynolds the TIN had on file, and a picture of the DA (reelections were near).

Brian had a quote from the warden about the double entrende of the tablets. How beneficial the tablets were for many of the inmates seeking online courses to gain a trade or a college degree to better their lives. And how others used them, like Divinia, for their own schemes.

Danny scored an interview with the DA about the holes in the system and how difficult it was to plug them up.

Meaty set aside his newspaper then scanned the monitors to make sure no one was shoplifting at the Foo.

CHAPTER TWENTY-SEVEN

J immy sat on the sofa with Maddy on his lap on top of her pillow. Celebrity sat beside them while Guppy tried to groom her hair. Celebrity swatted him repeatedly to no avail. The parrot would not find any bugs in her hair. "Hopefully, with those three minions of Divinia's under lock and key, and her out of commission in solitary confinement, we'll have some peace and quiet." Jimmy was ready to end the insanity. He didn't know what it would take to put a stop to the crazy former librarian's actions. She had no one to blame but herself for all her troubles.

Celebrity patted his arm. "There's no telling what's going through her head. I thought it was all sorted with Betty telling Divinia about the codicil to her will that would expand the library. That info came too late, but why she continues this business of hers is beyond comprehension."

Maddy wobbled to her feet and meowed.

"Want to get down?" Jimmy asked. He didn't wait for an answer. He lifted Maddy and gently brought her to the kitchen area where the food and water dishes were located.

She was getting around better, but still couldn't jump onto or off the sofa. Her shoulder had healed, but the front paw was still in a cast. Doc Halliday said he would X-Ray in another week to see how the delicate bones were doing. He didn't think she would have a permanent limp, but it was all up to her mental adaptability.

Jimmy's phone chimed a reminder. "Oops. Have to get to my meeting with the DDS. It's scary... I'm actually beginning to understand this stuff!"

Celebrity chuckled. "Ha. You'd better learn it because one day you'll be in charge and you don't want anyone taking advantage of your newness to it all."

He and Celebrity stood. Jimmy placed Maddy's pillow on the floor in the spot that was convenient to the TV and laptop.

Celebrity patted Guppy. "Sorry, Gup. Have to get back to work."

"COP!" Guppy let loose.

Jimmy stroked his parrot. "You be a good boy and watch over Maddy while Daddy's away."

"PROTECTOR!" Guppy squawked out.

"Yes, you be the protector." Jimmy and Celebrity left his suite and headed down the stairs. Jenkins was in his cubby monitoring the front of the house from the hidden cameras.

"Everything okay?" Celebrity asked, in cop mode.

"Knock on wood," Jenkins replied. He switched the viewing to the side of the house, then the back which covered the target practice area. "The new camera system helps tremendously. Meaty set up the system so that it recorded then downloaded every twenty-four hours so nothing is lost."

"That's good for when you're not here."

"I thought he over-installed the number of cameras, but every nook and cranny is captured now. No one is getting away with anything. Plus, the new badging system." Jenkins held out his lapel where his new badge was attached.

"Aunt Betty needs the security. It's a shame that after all these years of being safe in this town, a couple of rotten people changed everything. You can never tell when some old wound festers that's been building year after year." Jimmy shook his head. He remembered when Celebrity had been clobbered by Caleb Armbruster, the town drunk, then Reggie, Caleb's father went off the rails.

"Let's not get all maudlin," Celebrity warned. "Things are in place now to keep everyone in the mansion safe. Come on, Jimmy. You're going to be late for the DDS."

PETE DAIGLE, JUDSON DIAZ, GODFREY (STONEY) AND JUNIOR Stonerich, otherwise known at the DDS law office, sat in open mouth surprise as Jimmy Katz rattled off something that mystified him just a few weeks ago. Somewhere along the way, things must have sunk into his head after months and months of drilling by the DDS team.

After they sufficiently recovered from this latest surprise, the meeting ran quicker than ever before. Their star pupil was fast becoming knowledgeable on the different phases of the Katz-Diaz empire. It would likely be years before Jimmy could spew off facts and figures like his Aunt Betty, but he was now well on his way to digesting the immense conglomerate divisions, and all that belonged to them.

For the first time, Jimmy walked out of the DDS offices after a meeting and didn't feel as if his brain had leaked out of his ears. It had been two weeks since his last visit to the homesite, so he stopped by on his way around town. Mr. Clipton, the project manager was in a discussion with someone in front of the new boarding house. He waved Jimmy over.

"The inspections have passed with flying colors. You and

Mrs. Potts can do a walkthrough and point out anything we may have overlooked."

"Oh! Fantastic! Mrs. Potts is going to go ballistic!" Jimmy wore a huge smile. He hopped back in his SUV, sent his landlady a text to get ready, and took off to the mansion.

Mrs. Potts was on the bottom stair when Jimmy pulled up in front of the mansion. He never had a chance to get out and open the door for her. She hopped into the SUV. "Oh, I can't wait to see what everything looks like! Now, I'll be able to go look at furniture and order the big things."

They arrived at the brand-new boarding house and garage and scrambled out of the car. Mr. Clipton met them at the front door. "I'll walk through with you and make a note of anything you want changed."

They entered through the front door to a wide foyer. The staircase was off to the side, which was a good choice for Feng Shui. Mrs. Potts made a beeline to the kitchen and gasped in wonderment.

"Oh, my! It's better than I ever would have expected, even after seeing the plans!" She ran her hand across the smooth, gray concrete countertops. "Can you believe this is concrete, Jimmy?"

"Wow! I've heard about them, but never saw any concrete countertops. This is beautiful, Mrs. Potts!"

Mrs. Potts ran her hand over the new refrigerator, the new gas cooktop, across the handle of the sparkling dishwasher, and studied where the bar stools would go, and the kitchen table she would order.

They opened drawers and cabinets. Mrs. Potts' heart fluttered when she pulled a bottom shelf out of a cabinet. "No more crawling on the floor digging for something! Oh, Jimmy, this is going to cut down on my time spent prepping each meal. Everything is practically at my fingertips."

The laundry facilities were in the huge butler's pantry and contained a folding counter, a hanging rack, and a utility sink. No more folding clothes on the kitchen table! Mrs. Potts was beyond excited.

After ninety minutes walking through the house and opening every conceivable closet, cabinet, and drawer, they visually inspected every surface, while Mrs. Potts mentally saw where furniture would be placed. They headed through the kitchen to the garage. Four stalls that had been designed wider and longer than average to accommodate today's vehicles, and each with their own rolling door, looked great. There was extra space along the sides and back of the garage for tools, racks, or whatever an owner wanted to keep in the garage.

Neither Jimmy or Mrs. Potts found anything that should be changed, to the delight of Mr. Clipton, the project manager. He handed over two sets of keys, one to Mrs. Potts and one to Jimmy, then he walked to his truck and left the site.

"The grass will be installed in a few days," said Mrs. Potts. "I've been thinking... why not have a heated pool installed? Would you and Brian use it? A pool would be great exercise for me. I'd have to make the decision within a day or two and get with Norris Trusty before the lawn is installed. Don't want to waste any grass."

"A pool would be great! I know Brian used the pool at his apartment complex in the Big City. I bet Celebrity would like the idea." Jimmy wondered if their friends would come to pool parties.

"I'm going to head to Starlight Furniture in Dime Water tomorrow and order furniture now that I know the layout of the place. Do you want to come with me? We can see if Brian can get away for a couple of hours to join us." Mrs. Potts was wound up with excitement.

"I'm not telling the kids we're moving until everything is

delivered. Maddy still needs a few weeks of recovery, and I don't want Guppy overexcited." Jimmy couldn't wait to get back to a normal schedule. He knew his animals would be thrilled to have access to the gazebo again. "That reminds me, I'll have to order an extra fake tree for Guppy. I think he'd like to spend time outside at the pool when we're out there."

Mrs. Potts reached for her phone. "I'll call Norris Trusty so he can cancel some of that grass."

THE STARLIGHT FURNITURE SALES REP THAT TAGGED ALONG WITH Mrs. Potts, Jimmy, and Brian knew he would have the largest sale for the entire month, never mind the week. He would also win the pool and get two-hundred-fifty bucks right off the bat. As he followed the shoppers, he checked the stock of all items that were chosen, and put them on hold so no one else could mess up his orders.

The salesman whispered loudly into his phone while talking with the warehouse when he was told about a damaged headboard and two other missing items that showed they were in stock but couldn't be located.

Those three items were not immediately available for delivery, but would be delivered directly from the manufacturer within two-three weeks. Mrs. Potts assured him she could live without the extra bedside table, the spare room headboard, and chest of drawers.

The clerk determined it would take two trucks and extra crew to deliver the full house of furniture. Next, he got on the phone to the shipping department and they worked out the schedule for Thursday. There was nothing better than a customer paying for thousands of dollars' worth of furniture with a high-end credit card. The salesman mentally thought about what he could do with his pool money and his commissions.

SINCE THEY WERE ALREADY IN DIME WATER, THEY HEADED OVER to the Target store where everyone split up with their own shopping carts. Mrs. Potts headed straight for the kitchen section and filled her cart with many of the items she hadn't bought online yet. She also added a couple of boxes that contained table and floor lamps to the cart.

As she wandered up and down aisles she came across clothes hangers. Mrs. Potts hadn't even thought about them since many of the clothing items were still in shopping bags back at the mansion. She grabbed several packages that contained a dozen or more hangers each, then added even more to the cart because she didn't think the guys would think about hangers. The spare bedroom and the coat closet would require hangers as well.

At that moment, she realized the need for a clothes basket and a hamper. There was very little room left in the shopping cart, so she removed the hangers from the cart and added them to the clothes basket, then placed the basket into the shopping cart with the hamper balanced on top, precariously.

Mrs. Potts was ready for a nap by the time they headed back to Twinkle. She would have three days before the furniture was delivered, but she could get the kitchen set up with what she had purchased today and with what she had in the storage unit. She realized she could also bring the new clothes over to the house and wash them. Now equipped with clothes hangers, she could hang them as they came out of the dryer, then haul them to her new bedroom.

Bertha Potts realized she was too excited to take a nap. Once they arrived at the mansion, she retrieved the bags of clothing from her suite, and hauled them out to the car. Then, with brand new keys in hand, she drove over to the new boarding house. She realized she didn't have a garage opener so she parked in front of the house and unlocked the door for the very first time. She took a minute to stand inside the new house all by herself, and sobbed in relief. After she dabbed her eyes with a wilted tissue, she began unloading her car.

In the kitchen she discovered the four remote garage openers with sticky notes under each. The built-in garage openers were on the wall by the kitchen door which led to the garage. She discovered which opener was for the garage slot closest to the kitchen door and returned to her vehicle and moved it into the garage.

It was so much easier carrying things directly into the kitchen instead of weaving through the house. The laundry basket was brought to the butler's pantry where the washer and dryer sat. She carried a scissors to open packages of hangers when she realized she had no trash cans for any of the rooms.

Mrs. Potts opened the dishwasher. She figured she might as well load it with the new kitchen items rather than put them away in cabinets and drawers. An immediate trip to the Wham-A-Rama was called for to purchase kitchen and bathroom cleaners, laundry soap and vinegar, which she used as a replacement for bleach in the washing machine. There were so many things to replace her head spun.

After she deposited hangers in all the bedrooms and the coat closet, she wadded up the packaging and left it on the kitchen floor where the recycling container would be placed once she returned home from the Wham. Mrs. Potts finished hauling things out of the car. She made a mental note to pick up more scissors. There should be a pair in the kitchen, the laundry room, and in the bathrooms. At this point she pulled her notepad and pen out of her purse and made a list.

Mrs. Pott' car passed Jimmy's vehicle. She waved, then saw he was slowing, so she slowed her car and lowered her driver's window while he backed up his vehicle so their drivers' windows were opposite each other. "I'm going to the Wham to pick up cleaning materials and other things I overlooked. Be back soon, then I'm going to finish loading the dishwasher and do a load of clothes."

"How about I go to the storage unit and bring over all the kitchen and other items that are there?"

"Yes," Mrs. Potts nodded. "Then you can close it out."

They each went their separate ways.

Over an hour and a half later, Mrs. Potts pulled her vehicle into her garage slot and began emptying her vehicle. The back seat was filled with trash and recycling cans along with cases of different size canning jars. The trunk was filled with everything else, including nonperishable canned items and refrigerated items. Just as she finished hauling the last bag into the kitchen, the kitchen door opened and Jimmy carried in the first of many packages from the now closed storage unit.

They went about opening packages and delivering them to either the butler's pantry, the dishwasher, or the washing machine.

"I can't wait until the furniture is delivered!" Mrs. Potts placed ice cream in the freezer, then cheese, eggs, milk and juice in their places in the refrigerator. She would make another trip to the Foo when the bar stools, kitchen table and chairs arrived so they could sit down for the first meal in the new house.

"I'll have to look at those pictures again to see what else I should order." She found custard cups at Target which were now in that top third rack in the dishwasher.

The front door opened and they heard bags rustling and headed that way. They found Brian with store bags hanging from his cramped fingers.

"How much more?" Jimmy asked.

"Couple of trips," Brian said. "This was fun." He headed to his new suite and unloaded his items. "Oh, hangers! Thanks, Mrs. Potts. I never thought about hangers!"

"This time I was one step ahead of you." She returned to the kitchen and started the dishwasher. It was so quiet she bent her ear nearer the machine to make sure it was working. Then she opened packages in the laundry area and sorted things for different loads.

CHAPTER TWENTY-EIGHT

They determined all three of them should be at the new house when the furniture trucks arrived. It was important for items to be delivered to where they belonged, to not waste time moving them from place to place. Brian and Jimmy labeled doors to direct movers.

Mrs. Potts gathered the movers. She pointed to Brian and Jimmy and explained about the door signs. She also explained they would direct them to the ground floor or the upstairs and they should follow the directions one of them would give them.

The trucks emptied and the workforce assembled furniture. Brian, Jimmy and Mrs. Potts directed the movers to get the assembled furniture in place in each room. The lead mover told them the three items on backorder would arrive within the next two to three weeks. The accepted the generous tip from Jimmy, then the trucks lumbered down the street and returned to the warehouse.

Mrs. Potts, followed by Jimmy and Brian, explored the entire boarding house to make sure everything had been delivered and was where they expected it to sit.

"There's clean sheets and blankets in the linen closet. Did

you buy your quilt or bedspread? If you have everything, start making your beds. I think it would be best if we had food delivered for supper. I'm too tired to attempt to cook right now."

The brand-new doorbell rang for the very first time. All three of them headed to the front door. Mrs. Potts opened the door to Betty and Toombs who had their hands filled with foil covered platters and bowls.

"We've come bearing your first meal in the new boarding house, and new serving bowls and platters," Betty exclaimed.

They heard a loud squawk from the car.

"Oh, you've brought my animals! Thank you so much! They're going to be excited to explore the new place."

"Guppy's tree is in the trunk along with Maddy's supplies and food for both," Toombs explained.

"We all want the grand tour," Betty said. "You'll have to carry Maddy though, she isn't strong enough to wander the whole house or traverse the stairs yet."

Toombs walked over to one of the ovens in the wall of the kitchen and set it to warm. He placed his items in the oven, then retrieved what Betty was holding and placed her items in the oven as well.

"Let's go get your pets and their supplies," Toombs suggested.

Jimmy and Brian followed Toombs out to the car. Jimmy carefully lifted Maddy's pillow while Brian offered his arm to Guppy.

"AWK! New House!" Guppy shrilled.

"Yes," Brian agreed. "This is our new house!"

Maddy meowed softly from her pillow in Jimmy's arms.

"Let's give everyone a tour!" Jimmy suggested.

The landlady led the way through the downstairs. "I still have so many items to order, but the majority of what's needed is here. We had taken pictures for my homeowner's policy last year with all the cabinets and drawers open, and I'm slowly going through the pictures to order items."

"Oh, that's a very good idea. I'll have to ask Duncan if he's done that in his area of the house. Jenkins will know if we have a visual inventory of the rest of the house." Betty was texting Jenkins.

They climbed the stairs and the animals liked their new bedroom.

"Let's get the fake tree and the toolbox," Toombs suggested. They traipsed downstairs.

"Brian, bring Guppy over to a chair and he can wait there until the tree is assembled," Mrs. Potts suggested.

Guppy looked around from his perch on a kitchen chair. "DANGER! STOVE!"

"Yes! The stove is dangerous. Do not go near the stove, Guppy!" Mrs. Potts implored the bird.

"Good boy, Gup," Jimmy congratulated his parrot for understanding the danger.

Betty emptied a bag of produce into the refrigerator drawer, then placed cat food cans in the pantry. "Where do you want Maddy's dishes?"

"Over here in the pantry. There's this special place all carved out for her food and water. Her potty box can go over there." Mrs. Potts pointed to where she and Jimmy had agreed on for the downstairs litter box.

The men hauled the fake tree and the toolbox up the stairs to Jimmy's suite.

"I put this toolbox together for you for immediate needs," Toombs said. "You have screwdrivers, hammers, pliers, needle-nose pliers, a level, a couple of different wrenches, some screws and nails in different sizes—common items to get you through something needing fixing."

"Oh, thank you so much! Tomorrow I'll head over to the

Wham and get a stepladder and a few other things I've just thought of." Jimmy poked through the toolbox.

Toombs and Brian assembled the tree they had disassembled from Jimmy's suite at the mansion to fit into the trunk. It only took five minutes to attach the sturdy branches to the tree trunk.

"I'd better run out and buy a newspaper!" Jimmy exclaimed.

"I brought some." Toombs jogged down the stairs and out to the car. He grabbed a handful of various newspapers Betty had saved and jogged up the stairs.

"Thanks for remembering the newspapers. I'd better get my subscription going, and this reminds me I need to buy another bin to hold them." Jimmy's mental list for the Wham-A-Rama was growing by the minute.

After Betty and Toombs left and an early dinner ended, Mrs. Potts retreated to the living room. She settled into the new leather La-Z-Boy recliner which had built-in massage, heat, and lumbar support. The chair lived up to its reputation as she relaxed with a heated massage. All she wanted to do was get to know the new house. She squelched down deep sadness for losing the original home and all her possessions. Mrs. Potts realized she needed to let all of that go so she could enjoy the brand-new place.

After her nap, with her purse in hand, she drove over to the Foo to stock the refrigerator and freezer. Tomorrow she would continue going through the video's and photos of drawers and cabinets. There was plenty of time to order items she needed immediately, along with those things that were only used periodically. It was fun, but slightly exhausting.

Upstairs, Guppy sang out the windows on squirrel watch, loudly squawking at the activity in the trees. Mrs. Potts wondered if he would miss the conservatory with all Betty's plants and trees, but the parrot seemed to settle into his old habits.

Maddy had food, water, and potty boxes upstairs and downstairs. It would be a few weeks before she could traverse the stairs on her own, so when Jimmy was away, Mrs. Potts climbed the stairs several times a day to make sure the cat was okay, or carried the cushioned cat downstairs so she could be where the activity was taking place.

The landlady had a thought and texted Jimmy. *Why don't you buy Maddy a heating pad for her cushion, or if they have one, a heated cushion?*

She received an immediate reply. *Good idea. I'll head over to the Wham and see if they have something like that. If not, I'll go online to Chewy.com.*

Everything was falling into place. Mrs. Potts had become obsessive in checking that the stove burners were shut off. Guppy announced the danger whenever he flew into the kitchen, or was brought there. It was getting a little old to hear, but on the flip side, they wanted him to remember the danger of going near the stove.

AFTER THREE WEEKS LIVING IN THE NEW HOUSE, THE BACK YARD was excavated, the pool installed, and some landscaping put into place. Guppy's new fake tree was set up, which would have to be brought inside when any heavy weather struck.

Maddy attempted to climb the stairs to their new suite. It was a little difficult, but she made it upstairs on her own. The trick was going downstairs without tumbling. Her shoulder was healed, and her paw was still slightly tender, but she decided that if she didn't use it the paw would remain weak.

Settling in front of the tablet in the living room in their

suite, Maddy gripped her yellow pencil and whacked the on/off button. The tablet came to life.

Guppy fluttered to the floor. "Want help?"

"Not yet. If I get tired, you can take over."

"K."

It had been weeks since they had checked messages or emails, or explored YouTube. The email icon showed 43 unread emails and the green Messages showed twice as many.

"Why don't we begin with the messages?" Maddy suggested.

"Yes. Those should be quick." Guppy liked texting.

After reading three or four messages that wished Maddy well, her jaw was sore. Guppy took the lead and pecked the appropriate keys to read the next message, then the next. They decided to go through all the messages, then reply to all messages from each person with only one text. They were not going to waste time replying to 120 messages from a short list of people.

Guppy studied the home screen trying to remember how to copy and paste using the link supplied to them. He eventually got it right after fumbling through three attempts. He and Maddy came up with a standard reply Guppy could paste into each message.

We're back on our tablet and going through all messages. Please be patient.

Then Guppy tackled the emails. First things first was to delete all spam ads and emails asking them to click links for all manner of *special* things. They learned all about these bad things from watching their Russian YouTuber. When Guppy deleted all the trash emails, only four remained. Boris Ivanov sent one email announcing a new video about blocking apps, keeping devices up to date with every announced update, and using the best available security systems.

Guppy and Maddy had installed Malware Bytes to the tablet before Maddy's injury that Boris recommended. The Russian was all about keeping thieves out and content safe. Now that they knew how important it was to keep all devices and programs up to date, Guppy clicked over to Boris' YouTube channel to learn about blocking apps.

"It's so good to use our tablet again!" Maddy exclaimed as her pal used his beak to click on the Russian's latest video.

The end.

BOOK 5 - COMING IN 2026

There's never a dull moment in Twinkle, Texas.

The new boarding house was hopping with an Open House party after a month of proprietor Bertha Potts, tenants Brian McKinley, and Jimmy Katz settling in. Celebrity, Jimmy's fiancé, Lena, Brian's girlfriend, and Oatie, Danny's girlfriend conspire to find Ramirez a girlfriend.

Jimmy's aunt Betty, the matriarch of Twinkle and Starlight County, along with Toombs, her security person, and Jenkins, the butler, brought goodies Chef Duncan had whipped up.

The TIN staff were all present. Deuce Bainbridge ducked alongside the refrigerator when he spotted one of his exes who didn't *go away quietly*. Danny spotted him and told him when the coast was clear.

Chief Price, Ramirez, Stephanie, and Butch were present, but monitoring their phones for any calls while chatting with Meaty, Twinkle's own government security contractor. Meaty could hunt down information and squirrel out thieves in a blink.

Mrs. Potts' neighbors were in full party mode. Vince was

chatting with Katrina Ewaldone, who had recently moved to the neighborhood. Those who overheard the conversation of the mean-spirited woman did not lurk. Vince's pleading eyes caught Jimmy's attention. He and Celebrity rescued their friend. Katrina wandered around from group to group. No one wanted to engage with her and they would soon find out why.

Maddy had fully recovered from her injuries and could finally traverse the stairs. She and her parrot friend, Guppy, watched the party from upstairs so they didn't accidentally get trampled.

Guppy was happy with his squirrel monitoring fake tree upstairs, and regular trips to the gazebo. The pool was a new concept for Maddy and Guppy. When they first saw it, Maddy had swatted the water. It was lukewarm from the hot sunshine. She and Guppy Googled *pool*, then narrowed it down to *swimming pool* and learned all about them.

When a body showed up on the doorstep of the police department, Butch thought it was a vagrant passed out. The front desk greeter freaked out when he realized he stepped over a dead person.

ABOUT THE AUTHOR

 DG Ireland aka D.E. Greenfield and Dawn Greenfield Ireland are all the same person. She's an award-winning author of 20 novels, including 5 series (cozy mystery, sci fi/fantasy, billionaire shapeshifters, and dystopian), and a stand-alone sci-fi romantic adventure.

Most of her 7 nonfiction books have won awards, and she has adapted a few of her screenplays into book format. You will also discover over 50 themed notebooks.

Two of her screenplays were optioned, and she worked on a screenwriter-for-hire project. Dawn has a certificate from the Professional Program in Screenwriting from UCLA (2002), and ScreenwritingU.

Dawn writes full time. She lives among dreams and fantasies with two cats and moving boxes. Her head is filled with stories. She doesn't suffer from writer's block.

Her business, Artistic Origins, has been around since 1995. Besides writing, she coaches writers, edits, formats and publishes clients' books.

Her former day job as an award-winning technical writer played a major role in her fiction writing. She is detailed-oriented, the organizational queen of the known universe, and never misses a deadline.

She would love to hear from you, but don't spam her.

facebook.com/dawn.ireland.18
x.com/dawnireland
instagram.com/dawngreenfieldIreland
goodreads.com/dawnireland
linkedin.com/in/degreenfield